WHAT'S UNIQUE ABOUT YOUR BOOK IS THAT YOU GAVE THIS SOLDIER LIFE.
—ABC TV

SMILEY HAS LABORED TO BRING DANIEL'S STORY TO LIFE AND IT BREATHES WITH ECHOES OF VOICES LONG SILENT. IT CAPTURES THE EMOTION . . . . A REMARKABLE INTIMATE LOOK INTO LIFE BEFORE AND DURING THE CIVIL WAR.
—MANASSAS JOURNAL

I FELT I WAS WALKING BY DANIEL'S SIDE THROUGH EVERY BATTLE. YOU MADE HIS PAIN AND HIS SORROWS COME TO LIFE.
—SANDY MEADOWS

BASED ON FACTS CAREFULLY RESEARCHED; IT IS THE KIND OF BOOK THAT GRABS THE READERS INTEREST AND KEEPS IT UNTIL THE BOOK IS COMPLETE.
—APPOMATTOX TIMES

YOU HAVE CAPTURED THE TRUE MEANING OF THE CIVIL WAR AS NO OTHER AUTHOR I HAVE READ HAS DONE.
—DEAN HARRIS

A FASCINATING STORY, EXTENSIVELY RESEARCHED . . . RAISING EXCITEMENT ALL ACROSS THE COUNTRY . . . EXCELLENT TIPS ON GENEALOGY.
—CABLE TALK WITH BARRY LEE

WONDERFUL STORY, HIGHLY READABLE, WELL WRITTEN, VERY TOUCHING. TEACHES VALUES AND HISTORY. . . . . . .
I ENCOURAGE ALL TO READ IT.
—W.A.M.V. RADIO

THANKS TO METICULOUS RESEARCH, A CONFEDERATE SOLDIER LIVES AGAIN IN THE PAGES OF THIS HISTORICAL NOVEL.
—BEDFORD BULLETIN

A GREAT DEAL OF AUTHENTICITY FROM A LONG AND DETAILED INVESTIGATION.
—MARIETTA JOURNAL

I HAVE READ MANY BOOKS IN MY LIFE BUT NONE HAS BROUGHT ME CLOSER TO THE HARDSHIPS OF WAR AND THE ENDURANCE OF THE HUMAN SPIRIT. A REAL KINDRED STORY THAT BRINGS YOU SO CLOSE TO THE CHARACTERS THAT YOU FEEL AS THOUGH YOU KNOW THEM.
—THE VININGS GAZETTE

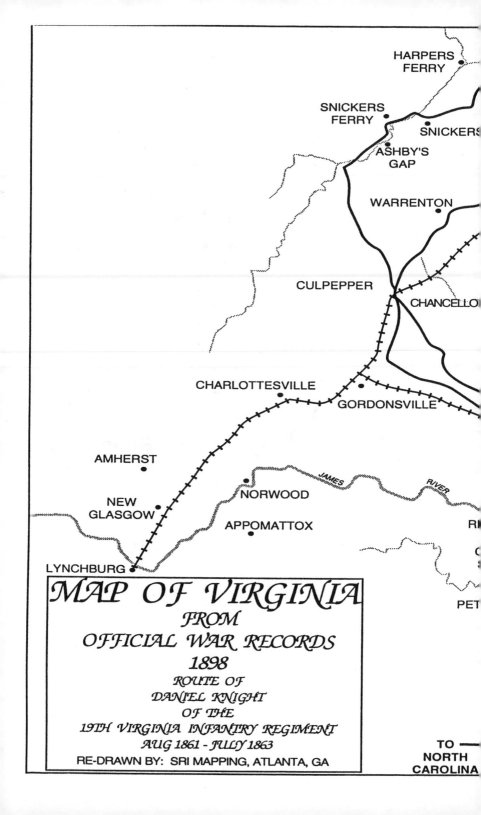

MAP OF VIRGINIA
FROM
OFFICIAL WAR RECORDS
1898
ROUTE OF
DANIEL KNIGHT
OF THE
19TH VIRGINIA INFANTRY REGIMENT
AUG 1861 - JULY 1863

RE-DRAWN BY: SRI MAPPING, ATLANTA, GA

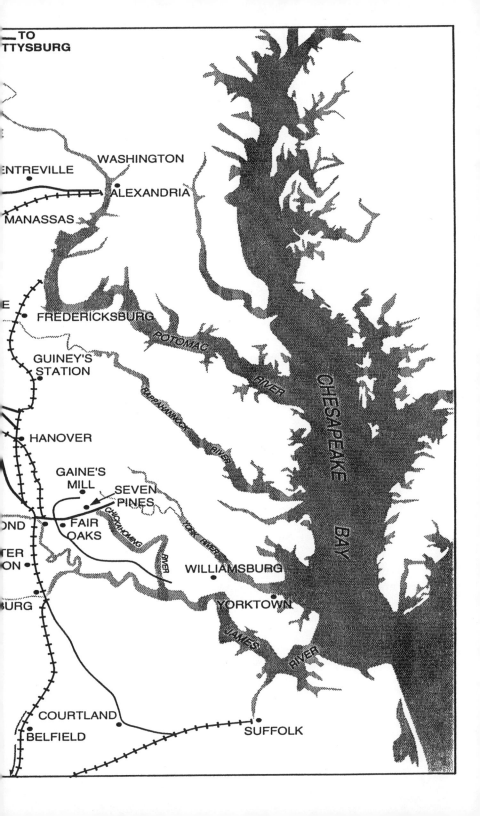

THE STONE WALL

Printed in the United States of America

KENNESAW PUBLISHING COMPANY
Carrollton, Georgia

KENPUB@worldnet.att.net

First printing June, 1998
Fifth printing November, 1999
Sixth printing July, 2000

ISBN 0-9664424-0-7 (paper)
ISBN 0-9664424-1-5 (cloth)

THE STONE WALL

THE STORY OF
A CONFEDERATE SOLDIER

BY BRAD SMILEY

To Scott

Best Wishes

Brad Smiley

12-00

TIPS ON
RESERCHING GENEALOGY

BY BARB SMILEY

DEDICATED

TO MY WIFE,

BARB,

who spent enormous hours gathering data and
compiling information.
Her love and encouragement inspired me to
complete this book,

and
to our grandchildren

Samantha, Lindsey, Christy, Candice, Matthew,
Tyler, and Drew

CONTENTS

PART I

ACKNOWLEDGMENTS
FOREWORD
THE GREAT CAUSE
I BECAME A SOLDIER
WINTER ENCAMPMENT
COURAGE UNDER FIRE
HOLD YOUR GROUND (Seven Pines)
THE BATTLE OF GAINES' MILL
THE SECOND MANASSAS
A TIME TO HEAL
MY SWEET SARAH
DEATH OF A HERO
GETTYSBURG
A SOLDIER RETURNS
AFTERWORD

PART II

GLOSSARY
SOURCES OF INFORMATION
19TH VIRGINIA INFANTRY

PART III

GENEALOGY RESEARCH

ACKNOWLEDGMENTS

Kenneth and Jean Schaar

Like their parents, they have lived in New Glasgow all their lives. They were very helpful in pointing out the location of the old country store, railroad depot, and churches, as well as other places long since gone.

Leslie Fogus

Born in 1908, he is the third generation of Fogues to live in New Glasgow. He provided stories handed down through the family.

Otto Evans

Has resided in Amherst County the last 55 years, right down the road from where Daniel and his brothers and sisters were raised.

Henry Smiley

From Lynchburg, Virginia. At 83, Henry provided me with stories handed down through generations regarding the Knights and the Smileys. He was also instrumental in helping me locate old cemeteries and family plots.

Knight and Dorie Smiley

Provided documents and facts regarding the Knight family.

Lydia Martin

A beautiful, vivacious lady who has lived in the area all of her life. She provided facts on the Knights, Hills, and Smileys. She is truly an inspiration to all who know her.

Eloise "Vicky" Gregory

To her friends, she is known as Vicky. She introduced me to true southern hospitality, Virginia style.

Maynard Carter

From Norwood, Virginia, he lived within a five-mile radius of Norwood all his life. At an age greater than 70, he hiked up mountains, pointing out old cemeteries and family plots long since grown over. Frankly, I couldn't keep up with him.

Paul Rumley

At 86, Paul, my father-in-law, described the way tobacco was grown in the days before tractors and trucks were used. He walked many a mile behind a mule, in the tobacco fields of Tennessee.

Donna Jordan

Who gave me confidence and inspired me to continue writing.

DeWitt Sosebee

I am grateful to DeWitt for reviewing my manuscript and offering invaluable advice.

Foreword

❧❧

*T*he voices of those who lived and fought during the Civil War have long been silenced. No longer can they speak for themselves, but they continue to be heard through stories handed down from generation to generation, in letters preserved in museums, and in family Bibles found buried in the attics of homes and old trunks.

Countless books have been written about the War Between the States, mostly about the great battles or the generals who commanded them, many by historians to document events, times, and places. But this is the story of a boy named Daniel Colwell Knight, who was born in 1843.

Four years ago, with my wife's help, the journey, in search of my southern roots, began.

Our trip started in Daniel's hometown of New Glasgow that is located in the Piedmont Plateau of Virginia, just west of the James River.

Although long-since abandoned and in

complete disarray, the family's two-story house still stands. Large locust trees grow in the front, and the remains of apple trees and grape arbors flourish to the side. The remnant of a lone rose bush under the window is a reminder of the past.

I carefully entered this once lively home. In the parlor I discovered the only piece of furniture in the house, a piano, its luster long since gone, stripped by time, weather, and neglect. Had I found Daniel's mother's piano? From a notation in the family Bible I was aware everything of value was sold to help feed and clothe the army. However, Daniel's father, Billy, refused to sell the piano he had given his wife, Susan, on their twenty-fifth wedding anniversary.

At first, I wanted to take the piano with me, but I soon realized the cherished musical instrument was where it belonged. Someday, the house will come crashing down and, rightfully, the piano will be buried with it.

I climbed the stairs to where the bedroom Daniel once shared with his younger brother Stephen was located. From the window I could see the rolling land once used for growing tobacco, and the Blue Ridge mountains to the West, exactly as he must have seen them, some 135 years ago. For a long time I stood there meditating. What fascinating thoughts develop when the imagination breathes on the dust of yesteryear. In my mind I envisioned the years gone by, and how the roses must have been in bloom that warm, summer day, in August of 1861 when Daniel departed from his home to join Company H of the 19th Virginia Infantry Regiment.

I walked away from the house with a better understanding of Daniel than ever before. It was then I knew I must tell his story, a story of a time we can never change, of a time we can never, no, never forget. THE STONE WALL is a true story based on real people, events, and places. In many cases, names were changed and liberties taken regarding conversations Daniel had with others.

As one whose veins run deep with Southern heritage, and on behalf of the voiceless dead, I have tried to bring to life Daniel's story, his hopes, and his dreams for the future.

I hope you enjoy reading THE STONE WALL as much as I enjoyed writing it.

And so it began . . . . !

THE PIANO

DANIEL'S HOME AFTER YEARS OF NEGLECT
ONE OF TWO CHIMNEYS MADE OF FIELDSTONE
NOTICE THE BRICK-STACKED TOP

ORIGINAL LOGS WERE COVERED BY WEATHER-BOARD AND LATER WITH ASBESTOS

AUTHOR, BRAD SMILEY, CLIMBS THE STEEP
STAIRS TO DANIEL'S ROOM

SMOKE SHROUDED MOUNTAINS AS SEEN FROM DANIEL'S WINDOW

The Great Cause

❦

A shell burst directly in front of me, killing several. It left me sprawled on my back. I didn't feel any pain, only numbness over my body. The smell of powder filled my nostrils.

The Yanks surrounded us and ordered our surrender. My brother Ossen refused. Other boys in gray were advancing. Fearing for their lives, the Yanks retreated behind the stone wall. Ossen shouted out to wounded soldiers heading back to our lines.

"Help! Carry this soldier back with you."

"Looks like he's dead to me."

"No, no, he's not dead, he's only wounded. Please help me, he's my brother, Daniel Knight."

Two men rushed forward.

"Daniel, these fellows will take care of you," Ossen said.

Without saying a word they slid their arms around my neck and dragged me, through the smoke, fire, and roar of battle, back down the hill.

"Wait! Stop! I can't go on," I cried out. Let me rest

for awhile in the shade of that apple tree."

A copious outflow of blood raced down my face and into my eyes, blinding me. I felt a strange and peaceful calm sweep over me, as I lay on the ground entirely helpless. I wiped the blood from my burning eyes.

The sounds of the battle grew dim; memories flooded back . . . . Papa was calling, "Y'all hurry up now, the trains coming."

❧

A loud blast from a piercing whistle commanded everyone's attention, including mine. In the distance, puffs of black smoke rose in rapid succession, signaling the approaching train. As it drew nearer in a cloud of dust, its iron wheels locked down on the iron tracks, producing a screeching sound. With a final blast of hissing steam, the iron horse came to a grinding halt.

"New Glasgow," shouted the stationmaster to the arriving passengers. A hush fell over the crowd that had flocked to the depot for news of their loved ones. I could see the worried looks etched in people's faces as wounded soldiers began exiting the train slowly, some on their own, while others had to be helped. Makeshift bandages stained with blood shocked everyone into realizing the horrors of war. Emotions ran high; mothers, wives, and daughters tearfully pushed forward in search of their loved ones.

A number of wagons blocked the road as drivers desperately tried to unload supplies. Other wagons waiting to transport wounded soldiers to hospitals added to the confusion. Tempers flared, and I over-heard one man shout, "Get your wagon away from the platform! I have supplies I need to load on the train." A driver yelled back in an angry voice, "I'm waiting for wounded soldiers. Where do I go?"

Just two years earlier, our town had been a sleepy little community, and the people were content, happy, and kind to each other. I suppose war changes everything.

When the railroad was completed, linking New Glasgow to Richmond, no one could have known that in less than fifteen months, the Orange and Alexandria Railroad would be transporting Confederate soldiers to the battlefield of Manassas and returning with Amherst county's wounded.

Hospitals in Richmond were filled to capacity and overflowing. The mayor of Amherst wired Richmond saying, "The injured young men were our own, and our surrounding communities will take care of them." In reply to his request, the town converted schools, factories, churches, and private homes into workable hospitals. In Lynchburg, a plea for volunteers went out requesting nurses to care for the sick and the wounded. Southern women, possessing a steadfast devotion to their beloved South accepted the challenge. Soon the wounded began receiving the care they desperately needed.

I watched the changes happening every day and wondered what came about that caused the North and South to engage in a war between the states.

Most agreed that many circumstances contributed to the decision.

Congress, which was northern by a large majority, had adopted in 1838 the "States Rights Act," confirming that the Federal Government had no right to interfere with slavery in states where it existed. In 1850, the legislation re-affirmed the citizens had the right to decide the question of slavery for themselves. Slavery was certainly an issue, but many Union generals and their subordinates fought not for abolition of slavery or for civil rights of blacks, but for the preservation of the Union. The South as a whole, and certainly Virginia, fought for recognition of its independence. Neither side would accept a compromise. When President Lincoln called for federal troops to invade Virginia and force the South to rejoin the Union, everyone considered Lincoln's decision the final insult. His actions evoked strong resentment throughout the South, and Virginia decided to secede from the union. "To Arms! To Arms," was heard everywhere.

At the Amherst County courthouse, an eager, anxious crowd assembled to hear the latest news.

In April, of 1861 the governor was authorized to call into service volunteers to resist and repel the threatening invaders, and to protect the citizens of Virginia.

Amid great shouts we raised the Confederate flag on our campus and rallied to defend ourselves against aggression. Some couples rushed to get married before the men left to fight. On doors of many businesses was a notice: Closed. Enlisted in the army. Photograph galleries were crowded with soldiers having their picture taken for their family and sweethearts. Former President John Taylor wrote that the South shall not be crushed until the life of the last man is trampled.

The "Great Cause," as we often referred to it, signified our southern independence, and our motto became "Victory or Death." Amherst and the surrounding counties of Albemarle and Nelson joined together and formed the 19th and the 28th Virginia Regiments, which consisted of ten companies each, roughly a total of 2,000 men. Each county donated to the newly formed regiments what little equipment and supplies it had stored for its local militia guard.

My brothers, Ossen and Sam, were among the first to volunteer.

Ossen was the older of the two. He was forty-one and a graduate of Lynchburg Academy, where he studied agriculture. He owned his own farm in Amherst County, where he lived with his wife Emma Ann. Like most of the farmers in Virginia, they grew tobacco. They had planned to move to Coleman Falls in Bedford County on a section of land they purchased from Emma's father, Jesse Jeter, but decided to wait until after the war. Nearly six feet tall with a wiry frame, Ossen had a closely cropped sandy beard and mustache. He had a gentle quality about him and a smile for everyone. After the death of Papa's first wife, Papa and Mama were married. From the first day, Ossen called Mama "Snookie," rather than Mama or Susan.

Sam, at thirty-five, was Mama's son from a previous marriage to Thomas Hill. A muscular, steel-eyed man, Sam had broad shoulders and a weathered complexion, probably from being out in the sun laying tracks for the Alexander and Orange Railroad. He worked from early morning to sundown to gain experience and pay his own way through college. Bright in manner and conversation, he had graduated second in his class from the Academy in Lynchburg. His life-long dream was to direct the affairs for a major railroad. "Daniel," he told me, "I want to be there when we drive that gold spike into the ground linking the East to the West Coast. It'll be a historical event."

It seems like only yesterday, although it was four months ago, that Papa and I stood one stormy evening at the depot in Charlottesville with crowds of people waving their handkerchiefs and shouting "God speed." Ossen and Sam boarded a train that departed North to a place called Harper's Ferry. Mama was worried that the boys might not get enough to eat. "Don't worry," said Sam. "With a fishing line, a rifle, and some shot, we can live in the woods forever. We'll do just fine, Mama."

Shortly thereafter, Captain Radford came to our house recruiting men for the cavalry. He had gathered horses from the surrounding counties and formed the 2nd Virginia Cavalry, under the command of General Jeb Stuart. I tried to convince Papa to let me join, but he said seventeen was too young; besides, I was needed at home. My two other brothers, Paul and Marcellus, promptly volunteered.

Paul, a handsome and sensitive man of twenty-four, had keen dark eyes and fine features. He stood erect, like Papa. Before the war, Paul purchased a section of land in Talcott, West Virginia, where he planned to farm and to breed a high-quality line of show horses. He had recently become engaged to

Jane Butts. They decided to postpone their marriage until he returned.

Marcellus, at twenty-two, had attended the University of Virginia. He had all the requirements to become a good politician. A diligent student of law and a gifted speaker with a sense of humor, he intended to pursue a career in politics, but the war took precedence over his decision to complete school. Clean-shaven, statuesque, with a firm handshake, he was assertive in his manner and speech. He joked about the war and his indestructibility and was sure the war would end quickly. Marcellus said he would be home within four months. "A war was unnecessary. Slavery's ridiculous," he told anyone who would listen. "It's just a matter of time before the Negroes are given their freedom, and that can be done without any bloodshed."

The following day, being troubled, I went out to the barn. My horse, Prince, whinnied in acknowledgement. I rubbed his neck and scratched behind his ears. He responded by laying his head on my shoulder, as if he understood I was deeply disturbed. Papa used to tell me to keep in mind that horses, like humans, are individuals, and must be treated as such. He always said good and loving care usually leads to a healthy horse. Prince, a Saddlebred, stood sixteen hands high. He was sorrel in color with white stockings on his back legs, a star on his forehead and a snip on his nose. His forelock always stuck out, giving him an innocent, youthful look. I poured out my frustrations to Prince. Four of my brothers had joined the army in support of Virginia, and there I was, believing so strongly in our cause, remaining at home.

Later I discussed the issues with Professor Palmer, when he visited our home. I watched as he stood, hands clasped behind his back, eyes staring upward, apparently in deep thought. He paused for what seemed like a long time, before advising me to listen to my father, but follow my own heart. "War is a terrible price to pay," he said, "but since it has happened, then go and fight it on their ground; don't wait for it to come to your back yard."

I decided to ride over to see what my best friend George Mays was doing. George was something of a character, with his carrot-color hair and green eyes. Everybody loved him. We had lived next door to each other all our lives and were the best of friends. Built like a buffalo, with broad shoulders and a muscular neck, George wasn't afraid of anything. He lived life to its fullest. He was the captain on our school's baseball team, and also our catcher. I recall George becoming angry when he believed a batter was out at home, instead of safe. Well, George picked up the bat and whacked the runner over the head. "He's out now," he hollered.

George was chopping firewood as I rode up the path to his house. He stopped and looked up. Mopping his face with his handkerchief he shouted, "Hey, Daniel, glad you came over. Wanna go hunting today?"

"Okay, but I got something on my mind that I need to talk to you about. Let's go. I'll tell you about it later."

"Ah ha, is it about Betty?"

"No, it's not about Betty. Anyway I think she likes Leon more than she likes me."

We gave our horses long reins. Prince loved to run, and anyone could tell it, eyes wide, nostrils flaring as he proceeded at a full gallop. His powerful legs propelled him over fallen trees and small creek beds as we continued in a straight line toward the forest. We raced across the gentle rolling fields covered in wild flowers. The brilliant splashes of color, the green buds on the trees, and the sap flowing warm reminded me that spring had arrived.

A flock of geese traveled overhead in a V formation, honking loudly. The birds settled in the water about a hundred paces in front of us. Finding a good place in the shade of an oak tree, we quickly unsaddled our horses and left them to graze on the tall grass. By the time we neared the marsh, the geese had taken flight. We proceeded to the edge of the swamp, where we hunted for the better part of the afternoon.

At sunset, red squirrels come out to gather seeds for winter. We waited under a large pine tree, but didn't have to wait long before killing three squirrels.

We departed for home, pausing only long enough to watch as a hawk soared overhead, then plunged feet first into the river, locking its sharp talons on a bass. He flapped his long wings as he flew away to return to his nest, carrying his catch with him.

"What's troubling you Daniel?"

"Oh, it's not important, I suppose. It's just that I aim to join the army, but Papa thinks I'm too young. What do you think?"

"Frankly, I don't believe your papa thinks you're too young. He's already had four of his sons go off to war, and he doesn't wanna give anymore. I wanna join myself. It's probably the only chance I'll ever get to see all those faraway places and the big cities."

"Then let's do it."

We mounted our horses and raced back through the woods and thicket, across a ford, to George's house.

Mrs. Mays became upset when George told her of his plans. He, after all, was their only son. "Please consider everything. Nothing but mischief can come from leaving home and traveling so far away. Besides it would serve no purpose. You may even get yourself killed."

"Ma, all this is so unnecessary. I was hoping my decision would not be displeasing to either you or Pa. This is my duty."

"Your duty is to stay and help your father bring in the crops."

" That's something I've thought a lot about Ma; somebody's got to take a stance against those Yankees. I've made up my mind!"

" Hush your talk, here comes your Pa."

George's Pa reached for a dipper of water as he entered the kitchen. " Been replacing fence rails all day," he said wiping his face on his shirtsleeve.

"George and Daniel are planing on joining up," said Mrs. Mays.

Mr. Mays shook his head wearily as he brushed the dust from his pants.

"I've made up my mind Pa, Daniel and I plan to join up."

George's father sat down heavily before answering. "Your ma is upset. You know you have our full support on any decision you reach. We're both just worried about you."

It was already dark outside, and I knew Papa would be coming in from the barn after brushing down and feeding the mules, expecting dinner to be on the table. I excused myself and set out for home.

That evening, I talked to my sister, Althea. We were close, and I often confided in her. Everyone said there was no denying our being brother and sister. Except for Althea's chestnut hair versus my blond hair, we had the same blue eyes, smile, and mannerisms.

"Althea, promise me you won't mention this to Mama or Papa for now."

"If you ask me not to, you know I won't. I was in town today, and I overheard Sergeant Jordan say they had reached their quota for this month, and it could be awhile before they called for additional volunteers. Anyway, I understand you're not of the proper age, you must be eighteen to join."

"Aw shucks the war will be over, before I get a chance to serve."

✧᠉

The summer crept by. It was as if the hot, humid air ceased to move. The Yanks were threatening Richmond, and in August, Governor Letcher called for additional volunteers to be pressed into service.

Sis was right. At that time, only men eighteen and older with a matching upper and lower tooth, for the purpose of tearing open a bullet pack, were accepted. I was almost eighteen, but I had seen others being turned away, so George and I took slips of paper and wrote "18" on them. We placed them in our shoes, and when the recruiting sergeant asked my name and age, I quickly replied, "My name is Daniel Colwell Knight, and I'm standing over eighteen." He let us both sign the enlistment papers. It was August 22, 1861.

That Wednesday evening, I told my family I had enlisted. Mama was deeply concerned for my safety.

"I don't understand clearly, why everybody want's to join up."

"To show 'em we're ready. When the Yanks see that they'll quit and go home."

"I knew sooner or later it would happen. Such a crisis in our country, I guess every family is going to have to sacrifice in some way but isn't it enough your four older brothers joined?"

"No Ma, I need to do my part."

"If you must go, then go, but fight as a Christian with a worthy cause. I want you to promise you'll not be swayed by the temptations of camp life and that you will write me a letter whenever you can."

"Yes ma'am, I will. Now don't you go feeling bad Ma. This fuss isn't going to amount to anything. It's only gonna last a few more months."

"I suppose so. It appears your mind is made up; you're bound to go, I know that."

"Yes ' Ma. I'm bound to go."

"How soon?"

"To-morrow."

Papa put down his newspaper. Peering through his steel-rimmed spectacles, from his chair he spoke. "Well Son, you're old enough to make your own decisions. Besides, whatever I say would appear old-fashioned to you. Old men are fond of giving advice. If your mind is made up, then go, but don't get shot in the back running from the enemy."

I would always remember Papa's words. I could never bring disgrace to my family or Virginia.

"Mama and I have been expecting this for some time now; we ordered you a little something from the catalogue last month."

I carefully untied the string that bound the gift to discover they had bought me a small pocket-sized New Testament. I gave each of them a hug. "I'll always carry it with me."

"Can you read it okay?"

"Yes, Papa, I can read it just fine."

"Sure is small print. Guess you have to be young and have good eyes. Read a chapter every morning and evening, when you can."

That night I spent a considerable amount of time cleaning my musket and waterproofing my brogans with the grease from a tallow candle. The army had requested each man bring his own weapon.

I talked at length to my brother. "Stephen, you may only be ten, but you're now Papa's right-hand man. You must take care of Mama and your sisters. I'll be home as soon as I can."

On a balmy August morning, after I had taken breakfast, which consisted of cornmeal mush and sweet milk, I slipped into a new butternut-colored uniform Mama had made for me using a brownish dye she had extracted from walnuts. I had laid out a few necessary articles, and Althea packed them into a canvas bag she had made. I slung the bag over my shoulder, and together we walked down to the gate, where Papa, Mama, and Stephen waited with the wagon. My other sisters, Susan, and Victoria, had already left to help the hospital receive the wounded. The two of them rolled bandages and picked linen into lint all week, making ready for the soldiers' arrival. Althea refused to be denied her good-byes.

Papa drove us to the armory where Sergent Jordan was waiting. "Now listen up men," he said. "We're gonna march right down main street to the railroad depot. Every man keep in step. No talking, and don't spit were the ladies can see you."

Businesses closed early and the citizens turned out to cheer us on. From every porch and balcony handkerchiefs waived. We must have been a sight, stumbling and straggling forward. Most had never marched before. Some started out with their left foot first; others, their right. A feeling of excitement filled the air. From the crowd I heard someone shout out, "Hurrah for Southern rights." I glanced to my left and saw my family standing in the crowd, cheering and waving. Althea was crying. I tried to remain straight-faced. To give in would have brought on a volume of tears. Somehow, although stumbling along the way, we made it to the railroad depot. There we learned our first lesson in the military, "Hurry up and wait." We waited and waited in the hot August sun.

The engineer was in a hurry to depart, once

supplies had been loaded.

The train whistle let out a loud blast. The crowd cheered us on, shouting its approval.

I turned to hug Mama. "Good-by Daniel," she said. "Please be careful." I reached out one last time to touch the hands of my loved ones before boarding. I looked out the window. My family waved. Stephen ran toward me, carrying a package. "Mama wanted you to have this. I'm gonna miss you, Daniel."

The train whistle blew two long blasts; we slowly moved forward. I looked back until the station was out of sight.

I turned to face forward and tried to comprehend what would happen next. After a few minutes, I unwrapped Mama's package. She had baked my favorite: molasses cookies. I leaned back against the seat and closed my eyes, deep in thought as the train picked up speed, moving onward toward Richmond.

The rocking back and forth made me sleepy as the wheels continued their clickety-clack, clickety-clack.

I thought of our home, a large house built from logs Papa hewed himself. It was old, but it was my home, and I loved it, or at least the memories it provided me. I had hoped I would never have to leave. I was born in that house and had lived there all my life. The sun and the rain had long before worn away its luster. I sometimes wondered if it had any luster to begin with. It was well constructed, two stories tall and had an air of elegance about it that I find hard to explain. Stephen's and my bedroom, and my sisters' bedroom were upstairs. From my window, I could see large tobacco leaves in the surrounding fields swaying gently in the breeze. A brown path, bare of grass, led from the road to our home and showed the ruts of the many carriages and wagons that had approached us over the years. Some evenings, I would lie in bed looking out my window watching as the rays of sunset tipped the leaves of the trees with fire. I'd think to myself of the time when I would be responsible for the care of that land. In the distance, the mountains rose majestically up to the sky. Those peaks were essential to the beauty of the whole area. To the north, our property was bound by the Buffalo River; a gentle shimmering blue stream so peaceful I could sit for hours at a time fishing or just watching the water drift slowly over the rocks as it wound it's way through the hillside.

This was my first time away from home, and I was already beginning to miss it. Funny how you take for granted the things you have, until you lose them.

∾⟨⟩∾

A loud blast from the train whistle awakened me. I turned to George. "Where are we?" I asked.

"Boy, were you sleeping. We're about to arrive in Charlottesville."

As he spoke, I heard the grinding sound of metal wheels locking down as the train came to a halt.

Citizens, lined the tracks, waved, cheered and shouted such things as, "Push 'em back out of Virginia boys; we're behind you one hundred percent. Hurrah for Jeff Davis." Welcomes greeted us everywhere.

People reached up to the windows and handed us all kinds of fresh fruit, home made pies and other foods.

We stopped only long enough for additional troops to board.

A tired and ragged-looking soldier with one leg missing boarded and sat next to Milton. He removed his jacket and wadded it to form a pillow. After a long pause, Milton's growing curiosity got the best of him, and he asked, "Did you lose your leg at Manassas?"

"No."

"Well, where did you lose it?"

"At Richmond."

"How did it happen?"

"Look, I'll tell you, on condition you promise not to ask me another question. I'm tired and want to catch some sleep.

"Very well; just tell me how you lost it."

"It was bitten off."

"I declare; what on airt . . . ."

"No sir, not another question, not one." He sternly pointed his finger at Milton, then turned his head to the side, and was soon fast asleep.

The whistle blasted, the train drifted back a few feet, then with a quick jerk, lunged forward.

Once we got under way, a tall, lanky boy who had just boarded jumped up and ran his bow over his fiddle, sawing away with quick short strokes. It quickly broke the ice.

Drawing his bow with a sound like a sigh, he said, "I'm gonna stick to it till the bottom falls out, b' jigs. Don't play nothin' but plain tunes boys. If my kind don't suit you, pass on. I ain't got no use for them

Hungarian fancy tunes."

Someone managed to get a large jug of pure corn liquor aboard, which was passed around. When it came my way, I took a large swig.

The music and singing grew loud. One song ended and another began. When he played "Dixie," we all joined in, except for the more serious fellows who had spread a blanket on the floor and were shooting craps. "Read `em and weep," they shouted. I soon learned the shooters' emphasis was on the "weep." Others played draw poker in the back of the car.

Good Virginia tobacco was readily available and someone handed me a cigar, my very first. I puffed away, turning green, but still puffing, feeling no pain. A soldier holding a jug over his shoulder looked in my direction and said, "Boy, after we push those Yanks all the way back to Washington, I'm going to take you with me to Mother Russell's Bake Oven in D.C."

"What's that?" I said.

"Why, it's the most famous brothel in the nation, and that's worth fighting for."

Before long, the fiddler struck up "Old Suzanna." I got a lump in my throat. Maybe Mama was sending me a message. My head spun. I was having a 'whirly' spell. That was the last thing I remember until we reached Richmond.

"Move it, soldier," Sergeant Jordan shouted into my ear. My head was about to split open. He didn't need to yell, but I did get his message. With a sigh, I slowly dragged myself to my feet. By leaning on George or George leaning on me, we managed to exit the train.

VIRGINIA CENTRAL TRAIN - ORANGE AND ALEXANDRIA RAILROAD

I Became a Soldier

⊷⊷

*O*n a gray, drizzly evening, we arrived at our camp just outside Richmond, near the Chickahominy River. Dusk was deepening; soon it would be dark. The camp, such as it was, lay on a ridge above the swamp. The stark ruggedness of the place was a shock and took quite an adjustment for me. Trees had been felled for firewood. Old newspapers, clothing, broken boxes, lay scattered about. Hundreds of tents, stretching out for miles, were illuminated by lanterns that produced silhouettes of soldiers moving about, playing cards, reading or cooking their evening meal; others sat smoking their pipes, gazing somberly at their hissing fire, while still others hurried about attempting to secure enough pine cones and dry wood to start a fire in the misty rain that continued to fall.

That evening we were issued a small amount of hardtack and coffee. Few tents were available, and George grumbled as we gathered wet pine needles to form our beds. "I've never seen the likes of this before.

Wonder how long they're gonna keep us here. I know how to shoot a rifle; it's a fight I'm raring for. Besides, I consider Yankees sanctimonious, and chicken-livered, and would be mighty pleased to show 'em my feelings."

" Don't be so impatient George. We got a few things to learn about soldiering, first."

"Yeah, but by then the war will be over. I think it's only gonna take one more battle to prove we ain't taking this here invasion stuff lightly."

During the next few days, we were drilled in the manual of military exercises. We had been raw recruits; gradually we were becoming disciplined soldiers. Each day, bugles sounded at dawn. We assembled for roll call. Afterwards, we were dismissed for thirty minutes to wash, shave, or sleep, before a second bugle call summoned us to breakfast. After yet another bugle announcing sick call, we began our day fighting mosquitoes and flies as we marched. At first we held to the winding narrow roads, but the mud was slippery and brought hardships that caused us to alter our march by choosing a roundabout way through the swamps and waist-high swollen creeks.

"I don't see what good it does to make us wear out our legs for nothing," George grumbled, as we trudged along.

Some officers were in training themselves. The day before, Lieutenant Moye, while marching his men, forgot the command to halt. As we approached a fence, he shouted in a frantic voice, "Men, will you please stop for now. Let's all rest for fifteen minutes, and when you fall back in, please assemble on the other side of the fence."

Each afternoon we brushed off our uniforms, cleaned our rifles, and marched in a parade, sloshing along the mud-filled grounds. Before dismissal, we stood at parade rest in the rain and listened to patriotic speeches, reminding us that our purpose for being here was to resist and repel any and all invasions. Then, unless you drew picket duty, you had free time before lamps were out and taps played at 10:30.

One evening, I went looking for George; the boys were starting up a poker game. I found him alone honing his knife on a wagon wheel. The knife had a handle made out of an elk bone; its eight-inch blade was curved like a saber. He always carried his knife under his belt, like a sword, in case he run out of bullets, he said.

"What ails you?" I asked.

After a gloomy pause George blurted out, "Something I need to get off my chest is this standing guard every evening. It's the most senseless thing we do. There's not a Yankee within fifty miles of here. Officers must lie awake nights, thinking up things for us to do."

As George was speaking, we heard rifle fire from our picket line. Thinking we had come under attack, we rushed to arm ourselves. Even those who were sick and confined to bed joined in. Captain Smith deployed skirmishers forward into the wooded countryside in pursuit of the enemy. We found no one, but spent the better part of the night holding our position. Apparently our pickets mistook a wild animal for a Yankee soldier. Finally the Captain announced it was a false alarm, and we all returned to our campsite. I guess you could say we longed for the opportunity of fighting with the enemy.

Accidents with weapons were common. Some men had brought blunderbusses from home that exploded when the antiquated pieces were fired. With the careless use of firearms and overindulgence in drinking, local citizens became nervous and complained, but little could be done, because soldiers were there only long enough to receive basic training, then transferred out to combat regiments. Eventually we were issued Enfield rifles, "shooting irons," that had been purchased aboard for us.

Wood detail was a major task. The Yanks had burned everything, including the fences along the road. If you drew wood detail, you could be gone for days, looking, chopping, and loading wood to bring back to camp. Water detail was almost as hard. Both soldiers and animals had muddied the water in the river next to our camp so badly it was not fit to drink. On wagons, we took barrels upstream and filled them for drinking or cooking water.

Camp was beginning to take its toll on me. It was nothing like home life. Only those who have actually experienced it can appreciate the transition from home to the life of a soldier.

Most evenings, if the rain was not too severe, the regimental band played for us. I found myself thinking about my home as I listened to the music. Before I left home, every evening after dinner, our family gathered in the parlor and Mama played the piano that Papa had given her for their twenty-fifth wedding anniversary. She especially liked "Rock Of Ages" and "Amazing Grace." After Mama finished playing, Papa read a passage from the Scriptures.

With each passing year, he had to get closer to the lamp and hold the book at arm's length to read. When he was through, he stood and led us in a closing hymn. His favorite was "Nearer My God To Thee." I can see him now in my memory, standing rigid, singing with sincerity in his baritone voice while swaying back and forth.

Food was a major concern. Our supply consisted of beans, flour, corn, and a small amount of, more often than not, spoiled pork. If we were lucky enough to receive fresh beef, it was saturated in salt or was so infested with worms that if you looked close enough, you could see the little critters lift it up and try to walk away with it. Occasionally when we were issued some lard, we fried both the beef and the worms together. It was enough to make a mule defect.

Our main staple was hardtack made from flour and water that had to be crumbled into coffee, otherwise we risked losing a tooth. It was shipped to us in crates that were stamped, B. C., denoting, Brigade Commissary. George was convinced the letters actually stood for the date they were baked. The food threatened me with an untimely death, and sometimes I thought I would rather face a Yankee bullet than eat another bite of hardtack. I longed for some of Mama's collard greens with bacon drippings, sweet potato pie, and baked bread.

Many days we received no rations at all and survived by living off the fat of the land. Fruits and game contributed to our survival. During marches into neighboring counties, we came across cornfields and beehives that yielded their supplies and supplemented our diets. When I wrote home, I always asked

Mama to send me anything she could spare, but packages rarely caught up to us, and when they did, the food was spoiled. We learned to leave behind the well-cooked meals served at tables and comfortable beds in dry homes and traded them for blankets under the sky. We learned to live with less. Maybe the toughness of our existence taught us to become survivors.

Over the next few days, fevers became rampant and colds quickly turned into pneumonia as the deluge of rain continued. We soon realized the most destructive enemy we had was not the enemy itself, but the invisible organism that filled our camp with sickness. I developed a cough and reported to sick call. The doctor prescribed a mixture of vinegar and salt. I had to take a teaspoonful of it several times a day. It tasted awful, but it worked. Other illnesses, such as chicken pox, measles, and diarrhea, had many soldiers reporting to sick call. I suppose when you assemble that many bodies together, illnesses tend to spread. Sergeant Jordon told us that by the time we completed our basic training, we would be looking forward to battle as a relief from the dreary and despairing camp.

Finally, we began to receive some basic equipment. We were issued a hat, one shirt, a pair of pants, a pair of drawers, one blanket, a gun cloth, an oil cloth to wrap our blanket in or use as a ground cloth, a haversack, and a strong tin cup. Tents were still scarce and issued only to every other soldier until the commissariat run out. George and I shared, and because of the shortage, we decided to ask his cousin, Harry Anderson, to join us. The tent was just wide enough to hold the three of us when we lay in spoon alignment on the ground. By sharing our blankets, we managed to sleep warmly; at least the man in the middle was quite comfortable. After lying about an hour or so on the rocky ground, our bones would begin to ache, and the first man to wake up would punch the others, so we could all turn together, without losing our blankets. We soon got the system down to a science. Whichever man wanted to turn over would shout out, "Right face" or "Left face," and we would all roll in the same direction at the same time. Although our tent provided some protection from the rain, everything, including our blankets, stayed saturated from the soaked surroundings.

One day, a gaunt, lean, stranger rode into our camp. He looked like a man with a message, like a prophet. He had long and uneven black hair, rather harsh, and a homely face. He stood briefly before speaking, as if to give every man a chance to pass judgement on him. He spoke in slow, measured words, his voice as abrupt as his manner. He informed us he had been assigned to be the minister of the 28th Regiment.

A young soldier yelled out, "Boys, here comes Father Abraham!"

The minister whipped off his fur cap. The shine of near-baldness in contrast to coal-black whiskers startled us as he calmly responded, "You are mistaken, sir." I am Saul, the son of Kish, in search of my father's asses, and I think I have found them!"

"Of course you have," replied George, as the men burst into laughter.

"Bravo!" Roared the Reverend Wilbanks.

The next day, we prepared for another all-day march. The officer in charge, Captain Hill, was small in statute, standing maybe five feet tall with his boots on. The bugle call was followed by someone saying, "And a little child shall lead them--on a damn big horse."

We could feel the chill of the early morning air as we marched through the Virginia mountains. The hills and valleys produced a panoramic view of bright yellow buttercups and other wild flowers as the grayness melted the darkness and the sun peeked over the horizon.

The first hour or so, we were quiet. After a while someone whistled a tune, someone else began singing a song, and soon the entire column set about singing, laughing, talking, and joking.

George asked me, "How do you keep on marching day after day without ever complaining?"

I smiled and answered, "I rely on my strength from God,"

"Well, I wish he would do something about my sore feet."

"Have you ever asked him?"

"Not lately, but I'm gonna tonight."

That evening, as we sat around our camp fire, rumors spread.

"Were goin t' move out in the mornin," said George.

"What makes you so sure?" I replied.

"A fellow over at headquarters, told me so."

The next morning, we did march, but not out of the Richmond area, and not to engage the enemy. Corporal Payne, returning from picket duty, was assured the Yanks were planning an attack at the first light of dawn. Again, it didn't happen.

When we weren't marching, our drill master taught us how to use our rifles properly. Most Virginians had handled firearms since boyhood, and prided themselves on their marksmanship. Every man felt himself superior to three Yanks. At least the firearms class gave us a break from marching.

Bayonet practice taught us how to defend ourselves, dig a trench, and open a can of rations. Occasionally a soldier used his bayonet as a skewer to roast a small animal over his fire.

Friday evenings, the regimental band would play for us. I remember one particular Friday. About an hour after the band began to play, the band master ordered the band to stop in the middle of "Home Sweet Home." I could tell he was all fired up about something. He walked across the parade ground straight into Colonel Strange's tent, where we overheard a conniption fit like I had never witnessed before. He apparently had a bit too much brandy to drink. For calling the colonel a louse, he was arrested and taken to the guard house. The following day, he was released, and by Saturday evening, all was normal. I later learned he was upset over his band leader pay of twelve dollars a month, which he felt was insufficient to care for his family back home.

⟨⟩

We were becoming a team. In battle, we understood we would have to rely on each other. Our life might depend on it. However, bringing men together from such different backgrounds was difficult. I think some were raised in the wilderness. Many never had any schooling and could neither read nor write. Some couldn't speak without using profanity. In fact, if profanity was outlawed, some might not have been able to carry on a conversation at all. Others were lawyers with extensive educational backgrounds. In some cases, a gentleman in high standing back home was a private in the army, reporting to an officer who worked for him before the war. Needless to say, all that shift in status created a few problems that took time to work out.

I was surprised at how rowdy some of the men were. There was one fellow called "Hog." I suppose he got the name because he liked to wallow in the mud. Hog decided, after a drink of whiskey that he'd fight the whole boodle of Yankees himself. He cussed and carried on to the point that everyone tried to stay clear of him, especially when he was drinking. Personally, I think he was as crazy as a loon.

All the cussing in camp made me remember a particular morning years before, which was the only time I had ever heard my father use a cuss word. Stephen and I were playing with some bricks left over from a walkway Papa was having built. Papa said we could play with the bricks, but had to re-stack them against the barn when we were finished. I don't believe I completely understood the significance of that request, and when Mama called us to dinner, we left the bricks where they were. After dinner and our evening devotion, I had completely forgotten about the bricks and went straight to bed. In the middle of the night, I heard an awful banging and bumping sound, as if someone fell into the side of the barn. "Damn it all to hell," Papa's voice said. Evidently, on his run to the outhouse, he had tripped over the bricks. I knew the woodshed would not be long in coming, the next morning. By dawn, he had calmed down, limping, but fully composed and collected. His expression was stern as he told me that was never to happen again. That was the last of it. I understood, and Papa never mentioned the incident again.

∽ら⌒

Every Saturday in camp, we received a ration of whiskey, and our spirits were elevated. It was made of bark juice, tar water, turpentine, brown sugar, lamp oil, and alcohol. I decided to partake in only one small drink. I noticed, after drinking, one fellow quickly became so inebriated he walked straight into a tree and required stitches on his forehead.

Poker players set up makeshift tables and sat on crates. Others spread blankets on the ground for shooting dice. George decided he would play poker awhile.

"Be careful," I said, "you may end up losing what money you have."

"I may, Daniel, but if you read the Scriptures they say, whenever two or more soldiers are gathered together, there will be a deck of cards."

"I believe that's stretching it a bit, George."

About the same time we received word that a

group of ladies from Saint Paul's Church was on their way over with baskets of cakes and cookies they had made for us. I'm not sure if it was the food or the women themselves, but cursing, gambling, drunk, dirty soldiers jumped into the creek to bathe and emerged gentlemen, before the ladies arrived. Reverend Starnes, always seeing the positive in everything, raised his arms and proclaimed a miracle had occurred. It began to rain, and I sought refuge under a tree as my memories continued to flood back.

I remembered my sixteenth birthday. The grandfather clock struck six times with its resounding chimes of "Bong, Bong," as if it were telling me it was time to get up. There was a chill in the air, and I wasn't quite ready to get out of bed. Still half asleep, I realized old Bossy would be heading to the barn, ready to be milked.

Dawn peeked over the mountains. I looked out my window and saw the shining leaves on the trees tilted forward, letting drops of water roll from one leaf to another.

A bright red-and-black woodpecker with white-striped wings flew from tree to tree, tapping on each one with his precise rat-a-tat-tat. In the distance, I could see the majestic mountains. At times they were shrouded with a smoke-like fog. I often dreamed of someday crossing those mountains to see what was on the other side.

"Daniel," Althea called out. "Will you come down here?"

I could smell the scent of a fresh-baked cake drifting up to my room. I hit the floor running and descended the steps to the kitchen. My brothers,

Ossen, Paul, Marcellus, and Sam were already there. They were all older and had moved out to places of their own. I wondered if someday I would move to a place of my own. I didn't want to think about it. Instead, I thought about all I had to be thankful for. I was truly blessed. I was especially surprised to see Sam that morning because he was in charge of the men laying track for the railroad. Normally, he had to be at work by daybreak.

"Surprise!" everyone said. I went along with them. Mama was holding my favorite, a chocolate cake. On the table was a small package nicely wrapped. Ossen said, "Well, open it, little brother." I was all thumbs, but as soon as I saw what it was, I could hardly contain myself. "Look everyone!" I said excitedly. It was what I had always wanted, a Case pocketknife, and the best one I had ever seen. "Thank you, everybody," I said. "I can't wait to use it."

Mama, in her protective way, told me to be careful, because it was very sharp. I was checking it out by whittling on a piece of wood when Papa walked over to the fireplace and retrieved Cackling Sally, the musket rifle his father had given him when he was a boy.

"Want to shoot her?"

"Yes, sir," I replied.

Once outside my brothers stood watching, their arms folded, wishing to be the one to show me how to use the old, double-barreled gun. Ossen paced back and forth with his hands on his hips.

Papa explained, "It's not like any other musket you've ever fired. This one is heavy, and it'll kick you like a mule, if you don't hold it tight against your shoulder. You must stand with your legs apart and lean forward slightly, place your weight on your front leg. Aim high, allowing for the ball to drop slightly. Take a deep breath, let it halfway out, hold it, and slowly squeeze the trigger."

I had dreamed of someday firing Cackling Sally. I wondered how old she was. She hung over the fireplace as long as I could remember, glimmering with a faint shine. I knew that someday Papa would let me fire her. I was ready. I had fired a musket rifle before, but never one as magnificent as Cackling Sally, which was a 10-gauge double-barrel, designed to handle heavy charges of black powder. It contained a number of silver inlays, which Papa polished every so often. Grandfather had purchased it new on a trip to Europe. When he died, he left a note to Papa telling him about the gun and the gunsmith who had made it.

I loaded Cackling Sally with powder and two mini balls. I removed the ramrod and packed the barrels tightly. As I raised the shotgun to my shoulder, Ossen, who could no longer contain himself, cried out, "For God's sakes, don't pull both triggers at the same time, or you'll land somewhere down the road."

"BAARROOOM," she roared, like a cannon. Everyone stared in amazement. "His first shot, and he hit the side of the barn!" Paul yelled.

"There's no question of that," replied Sam.

Papa didn't think that was funny at all. He told me later that I was lucky the horses were out. I had one more shot left. A rabbit ran by. I fired, but I missed. I had fulfilled my dream. I had fired Papa's gun.

Sam had to leave for the railroad depot, so

the party broke up. Ossen returned to the house to place Cackling Sally back over the fireplace. Paul and Marcellus wanted to show Papa Paul's new horse. My younger brother Stephen asked me to play a game of marbles, but I still had to milk Bossy, and I wanted some time alone to examine my new knife.

∽∾

Army life was beginning to wear me down. I was plumb tuckered out. Everything was regimented. Every day we did the same thing, over and over again. I could tell I was beginning to be transformed from a farm boy into a fighting, disciplined soldier. As Oliver Wendell Homes Jr. wrote, "I started in this army as a boy; I am now a man."

Even though we were told that our principal reason for being there was to engage in conflict with the enemy, we had yet to see a Yank. All I had been fighting since arrival was heat, mud, dust, and diarrhea.

George rushed up to me waving a slip of paper. "Daniel, Daniel," he shouted. "I got us both a twenty-four-hour pass. Come on, let's get cleaned up, and go to town. Hurry up; we're meeting some goober grabbers at the Haystack."

"Uuuh, I like those boys from Georgia, but I'm not going to a brothel."

"Aw shucks, Daniel, I don't have any money. I just want to see the place and be able to say I've been there."

"I reckon I would like to see Richmond. I heard

there were a lot of beautiful women there."

"Heck, I haven't seen a girl in so long I wouldn't know what to do with her if I were to meet one."

"I think you would learn before you left her, George."

We decided to bathe before going to town. I was seized with a chill as I took a plunge in a pool of water by the side of a hill. I didn't linger long, mountain streams always ran cold. I was soon ready to go.

Richmond had become a city of refuge; an air of unrest hovered everywhere. The city was abuzz with activity. Factories tediously turned out war materials, including pistols, rifles, cannons, and powder. Street vendors hawked a wide variety of goods and services. Wagons poured in from every direction with the wounded and supplies. At the depot, we saw wounded men being unloaded from the livestock cars that earlier had been used to transport horses to our lines. There was no way to wash out the manure before loading men with open wounds into the cars. Miserable, dispirited soldiers gazed about. The stench overwhelmed everyone. Swarms of flies whirled about the injured men's wounds and overhead. I couldn't watch any longer.

"There's a tavern over there Daniel. Let's check it out."

It was a small place located in the basement of a building and appropriately named "The Hole In The Wall." Loud music and singing attracted our attention. Inside the door, there was an empty coffin, which George inspected with great curiosity. A sign read, "This Is For You, Abe Lincoln." A gentleman offered to buy us a drink, and as I was talking to him, George decided to crawl into the casket, I suppose to try it on for size or possibly to check its comfort level. About that time, a captain with his girlfriend arrived, and as she glanced at George lying there with his eyes closed, George sat up and said, "Boo." The girl shrieked and took off running down the street, screaming all the way. Two burly bartenders grabbed George by the collar. I tried to intervene before George became angry, and decided to beat the tar out of those two fellows. We were both tossed out into the street.

George said, contemptuously, "The music is too loud. Let's go across the street."

We walked across the street. It was dusk and I paused for a moment to watch the lamplighter hook his ladder on the post and climb up to light the gas lamp for the evening. We entered the establishment known as "The Bottoms Up Saloon." Inside was a long bar where pernicious looking characters crowded about, elbow to elbow at the bar. A number of frock-coated gamblers and civilians in booted trousers and vest sat at tables playing poker. Empty bottles filled the room with a musty odor that caused the building to reek. Two girls scantily dressed moved with hip-swaying invitations and a steady rhythm as they drew whisky and beer from tapped kegs.

The piano player noticed us entering and banged out a few chords of "Dixie." A short man with a boisterous voice that could have staggered an army sergeant at thirty paces called out, "Let me buy you boys a drink. What's your pleasure?"

"Whisky," said George.

The man grabbed a full bottle from the bar and

swaggered toward us. By then, my eyes were adjusting to the smoky haze, so I clearly saw the man had a hawk nose, stocky build, and a full beard. He turned and shouted out for everyone to hear, "Three cheers for our boys in gray. Hip, hip, hurray. Drink up, my friends. I think a toast is in order."

George lifted his glass in an appreciative salute to his new-found friends and proceeded to drain it in one long, breathless gulp.

"Have another," the stranger said. Sensing my Christian upbringing was being tested, I graciously declined. But George, feeling the pleasant anesthetic of the whisky, readily accepted .

Around midnight, we bid our farewells. The drizzly weather was still about us as we stepped outside. A cool refreshing numbness flowed through my body. I pulled down the brim of my hat, turned my collar up, and thrust my hands deep into my pockets in an attempt to stay dry.

About a mile outside of town, George noticed a suspicious-looking group of men coming down the road toward us. A cloud covered the moon, making it pitch black and hard to see, but lamplight from nearby houses illuminated the streets well enough to cast a shadow on them as they approached.

"Daniel," George whispered, "I believe that's a federal patrol on a reconnaissance mission. If they spot us, they'll kill us."

"I think you're right." I knew to make a run for it would be to invite a bullet in our backs. "Let's slowly walk to that church. It should be unlocked, and we can hid in there."

Carefully, we sneaked across the dirt road and

slipped into the church. We discovered a small opening to the attic and climbed inside.

We were so scared, we didn't dare move even a finger. I must have drifted off to sleep. I awoke to the sound of voices and realized people were arriving. Peeking through the cracks in the ceiling, I soon discovered we were in a black folk's church, and they were having a wedding, which was to be followed by their Saturday night revival.

The wedding ceremony began with the preacher asking the man, "Do you want this woman?"

"Yasur," he replied.

He then asked the girl, "Do you want this man?"

"I sho-nuf do."

The deacon fetched a broom, and while the preacher held one end, the deacon held the other, the couple jumped the broom. It sealed their vows, and the preacher said, "That's your wife."

Time came for the evening revival. For what felt like two hours, the preacher continued to stir everyone with a powerful hell-fire-and-damnation sermon. The louder he raised his voice, the more rapidly the old mammies fanned themselves.

"If you done any wrong, de devil gonna come down and get you."

"Amen."

"He gonna come down hollering and shake hi' tail. He gonna paw de yearth and make it quiver."

"Amen."

I had lain as still as I could for such a long time my legs were beginning to cramp. I had to move. As I did, the ceiling gave way, and down I came with a crash, ending upright between the pulpit and the preacher. Fifty years of dust and dirt covered me from my head to my toes.

"Who dat?" asked the preacher.

"Tis I, the devil," said George as he stuck his head out from the hole in the ceiling, grinning, like a possum.

Well, the darkies thought for sure he was the devil and had come to get them. They carried on like they were all possessed, jumping out the windows and door, whooping and a hollering. It took less than a minute to clear out the church. George could hardly contain himself as he dropped down to the floor. We exited through the back door, safely disappearing into the woods.

"Well, Daniel, you did it to me again. I went to town to visit the Haystack, and what did I do? I'll tell you what I did. I spent four hours in church; that's what I did."

"Yes, you did, but won't it be a great story you can tell someday to your grandchildren?"

By the time we got to camp, I was totally exhausted. I can hardly remember crawling into our tent. I soon sank into a fitful sleep of exhaustion with my clothes on.

Winter Encampment

❧❀

*T*he population of Richmond grew daily. Civilians arrived by trains and wagons in an attempt to gain sanctuary from the advancing Yanks. A state of panic developed among the people as the Yankees continued their aggressive march across Virginia, looting, vandalizing, and burning farms along the way. I had heard the union soldiers' orders were simple: live off the land as you go forward.

I was present when one woman, who had just arrived here with her children, told a group about a raiding party that entered her home looking for food, weapons, and money.

She said, "I was defenseless, because my husband was away in the army. Those men smashed all our trunks and broke everything in the house. They scattered our clothing around in the yard, looking for pistols and silver they thought we might have hidden in the clothing. They took all the bedding with them, including our towels. At the barn, other soldiers gathered empty feed sacks and filled them with our flour, corn, and oats.

They spread what corn was left around the yard and let their horses eat it. Afterwards, they completely destroyed the crops, burning what they couldn't carry off. I had just finished cooling a pot of preserves, and the soldiers ran their hands through the jam, licking their fingers, then reaching back into the pot for more. When I complained, they poured molasses all over the floor. Others were looking for whiskey, but while they were downstairs, I poured what little I had into the chamber pots. They didn't touch those. After emptying our smokehouse of hams, they burned it to the ground. They were about to torch our barn, but I pleaded with the officer in charge, and he ordered his men to stop. The officer then turned to our long-time household servant, Jim Barns, and told him he and his family were free to go. I was proud of Jim. He told the Yanks he had promised Master Thomas he would stay and look after us, and he planned to do just that. The officer in charge was not surprised. He said he had heard that before, from other slaves. He just turned and walked away. That evening, I became so frightened I was afraid to undress and go to sleep. Finally, the soldiers did leave, but they left me, the children and Jim without anything to eat. They took all our horses and didn't even leave me one to ride to go look for help or food. The children and I stood on the porch as the Yankees were leaving. As they passed by, we sang 'The Bonnie Blue Flag' followed by 'Dixie.' The next morning, I had no choice but to leave our home. With the help of Jim, who borrowed a horse from the Snell's plantation across the river, I made it to the railroad station, where I was able to get tickets on a train heading south to Richmond. Jim chose to remain and look after our home.

"People without tickets tried to push their way onto the train. They knew it was possibly the last train out. No seats were available, so the children and I had to stand all the way. A kind older woman offered to hold my youngest daughter in her lap. I was on the verge of collapsing from the pushing and the heat, when someone I didn't even know gave me a drink of water. By the grace of God, I made it here."

"What kind of people are these Yankees who invaded our land and were now making war on our woman and children?" I asked Captain Pitchford

He replied, "It's against orders for soldiers to strip houses and attack the woman, but some do it, anyway."

Richmond was so overcrowded that places to stay, especially for a family with children, were hard to come by. I offered to give her a letter of introduction to my father, if she went on to Amherst. My parents could offer her and her family a place to stay, or at least they could be of help to her in finding suitable accommodations, perhaps through the church. She gratefully declined, but thanked me for my caring and concern for her and her children's well-being. She told me she had relatives in Lynchburg and would contact them when she could.

That evening George said, "Daniel, there's a rumor we're marching away from here tomorrow."

"Do you suppose it's a joke?"

"I may not know much, but I do know the colonel had his orderly pack his bags today."

Later that same evening, we were placed on a

high alert and ordered to prepare for an early morning march. Rumors quickly circulated that at last we would be marching out, to repel the Yankees.

Early in the morning, our bugler sounded reveille. Where silence had reigned, the camp sprang into vigorous life. I grabbed a potato that had baked in its jacket all night beneath the hot ashes of our fire. The aroma of fresh-brewed coffee filled the morning air. We were told to strike camp, load the supply wagons, and prepare to march in one hour.

Breakfast over, George and I hurriedly struck our tent and rolled our blankets. The bugle summoned us to form ranks. I slung my knapsack over my shoulder and prepared to move out.

I looked back and saw our artillery, wagons, and ambulances taking their places in the line.

The command was given; "Shoulder armssss," followed by, "Foooorrrwaaarrrd maaarrch."

With muffled drums and banners flying high, we shuffled along the rugged mountain road through the most picturesque parts of Virginia I had ever seen.

Leaves had turned gold or russet brown on aspen and birch trees, scarlet on the red maples. The marshes and bottomlands were filled with song and game birds feasting on the bright red berries of the holly bushes. Wildflowers in a multitude of colors covered the woodlands and meadows. Fall was in the air.

From Richmond, the regiment crossed over the James River and passed a large cornfield on a narrow road before gaining open country.

During the next ten days, we traveled through extremely difficult and fatiguing terrain. Each time we crossed one mountain, I could see another in the distance that looked higher than the one we had just crossed. Heavy rains and spitting snow turned the roads into calf-deep quagmire. The snow rapidly accumulated over a landscape that had, the day before been green. I could hear the crunching, crispy sounds of fresh-fallen snow beneath my feet. Hunched against the whipping winds, we continued on.

That evening, the temperatures hovered near zero. Bone-chilling winds forced us to find shelter. Our company located an old church, where we were able to spread out on the floor before a comfortable fire. The captain said we had walked about nine miles over the mountains that day and although we were short on provisions, we were indeed lucky to have found dry shelter for the night.

For our evening meal, we ate a small amount of fried corn meal mush and parched corn intended to be used as horse fodder. I suppose we were fortunate to have anything at all to eat.

The fire flickered dimly; I poked at the coals, attempting to create a higher blaze. I picked up my coffee cup to hold in my hands, warming my frozen fingers against its sides. Pulling up a crate, I sat with my eyes fixed on the burning logs. Tobacco was running low, but Harry had a little kinnikinnic to smoke. Before departing Richmond, he had made up a fresh supply, which he kindly shared with us. "What is Kinnikinnic?" I asked, as I filled my pipe.

"It's a mixture of tobacco, sumac leaves, willow bark, and sage leaf ground up with buffalo bones," he replied.

I must write and tell Papa about this, I thought.

The next morning, under overcast skies, we started down the eastern slope of the mountain. Bitter winds caused the temperatures to fall rapidly. During the night, the road had frozen solid, and every pinnacle of mud had become an ice point that lacerated my feet. My shoes had completely worn out. There were red spots on the frozen road from the bleeding feet of others also without shoes. That afternoon, we reached the base of the mountain, where we had to ford a deep stream. The water was freezing cold, but felt good on my swollen feet.

I was sure we would all perish from the intense cold, when I spotted the town of Centreville. Across the way was Camp Mitchell dotted by hundreds of campfires stretching along the banks of the river. Fluttering smoke lazily drifted upward against the sky. In the evening moonlight, I could see the shadowy forms of soldiers bent over frying pans preparing their evening meal.

Several lightened their loads by discarding their knapsacks. Our pace quickened.

We had marched some sixteen hours that day in the mud, ice, and muck. Hungry, wet, and cold, we were fortunate Camp Mitchell had a small amount of rations for us. They were mainly turnips, onions, cabbage, and greens with a piece of salt pork. This, plus a little sassafras tea-doin's made from the dried leaves of blackberry bushes, filled our bellies for the evening.

I understood our strategy in going there. Centreville was located about twenty-five miles west of Washington. We were told our purpose was to alarm Washington into thinking we may be planning an attack, in hopes the President would order General McClellan out of Virginia and back to defend the Capital, rather than attack Richmond. That night we learned the strategy had worked.

For the next few days, with pick and shovel, we strengthened our position, digging trenches and throwing up breastworks around the area. Our fortifications of fences, timber, mud, stones, and sharpened trees provided a barricade to repel enemy charges.

I could see George growing impatient. "What's the problem?" I asked.

George, chewing a double wad of tobacco with vigor, spit, then leaned forward, his face serious. "Now look here, Daniel," he said. "You can't reasonably expect to come this far from home just to dig ditches. Fighting is okay with me, but digging and freezing . . .to hell with that. We ain't gonna solve anything by piling up the earth. We need to quit digging and go to fighting. As I see it, the objective of war is to crush the enemy's will to fight. That's the way you win a war. I'm itching for a fight, but it appears we don't know where to scratch. If the Yankees knew as much as I do about this place, they wouldn't be so all fired up anxious to come here. There ain't nothing but mud and water here. I reckon God was busy elsewhere, when this camp was made."

I nodded and listened.

"Something else I'd like to get off my chest. I know it's against the law to forage for food, and I'll accept that young lieutenant hollering at me yesterday, but I'll be damned if I'm going to let that farmer's chicken run out in the road and bite me without defending myself. Oh, and Daniel, I captured that scrawny chicken and tied it to a tent stake. I plan to fatten it up with some corn, before we eat it."

I paused for a moment, thinking about what George had said. He had a point I couldn't argue with, but our officers thought otherwise. We continued to dig our entrenchments, even on Sunday, although worship was not omitted. Many attended early morning services; others attended evening services.

As the fall of 1861 yielded to winter, each company was divided into messes of six to eight men. George and I teamed up with four others from back home.

There was Dave Butterfield, a small thin man, whom we called Bullet. He was faster than greased lightning and could outrun a bullet, most of the time. He was straightforward and bold, with an intelligent look about him. Bullet also was one of the best chess players I had ever met. He could carry on several games at the same time and win all of them.

Charles Horsefall was known as Charlie Horse. He limped all the way back to the rear, during a forced march at boot camp. Charlie had striking features. He was of medium build with curly blond hair and bright blue eyes. He had a constant smile and was quiet. He had entered the ministry before the war, but after much prayer and soul searching, he resigned from the church and joined the army as a private. Charlie would say, "I have no desire to be shooting people. I just want to protect my family and property. Besides, right now soldiers are more in demand than preachers. But with a wife and a child I worry about dying.

Who's gonna take care of them if I do?"

"It's only natural to worry. "This is a chancy life, but remember you got a lot of good folks back home praying for you."

"Yea, and that's what keeps me going."

We called Tom Truman Buzzard; he would eat anything. He had dark eyes, long dark hair, and a flowing beard. Rheumatism caused him to wear red flannel drawers constantly, in hopes of staying warm and reducing the pain. Usually he was good-natured, but in the mornings, as he straightened his aching limbs, every now and then, he let out a few choice swear words, that could be heard all over the camp. I suppose his pain was too severe for him to remain silent, but in spite of aches and pains, he always did his share of work without complaint.

Bob Ansel we called Hungry. He was a character. He was long and slim and looked like a hungry coon dog that had been fed on creek water. He stood about five-foot-nine inches tall and wore a huge handlebar mustache that gave him a military look.

Our mess was formed, and we pledged to stay together for the duration of this war.

The entire brigade was issued wall tents that could sleep eight. Tents were everywhere, separated only by regiments with flags waving in the breeze to mark each regiment's location.

We suffered from winds that constantly swept through our tents on ghostly moon-lit winter nights. Some of the men excavated three or four feet under their tents to escape the winds and sleep snug and warm.

I soon learned there were disadvantages to

digging out your floor.

One night I was heading out for guard duty, when I stopped by such a tent to call out a soldier who was joining me. Seeing the men grouped together in their "dug-out," quite secure from the wintry weather; I wished I could return to such a snug refuge after duty. That evening, it rained constantly, and when he returned to his tent, there was at least a foot of water in it and everything was afloat.

The miseries of winter continued. Each mess group had the choice of erecting a shelter or remaining in tents. Chilling rains and cutting sleet convinced me we needed to build a more protective shelter.

That evening in our tent, I told George all the reasons to build a shelter. I went into much detail, until I heard a soft snore.

The next day, we went into the woods and hacked down trees and gathered enough logs to build our shelter. The hard work was made worse because we had no horses and had to drag the logs and rough green pines out of the woods by hand. We staggered under the weight of the huge timbers.

Once we got them to the camp we cut them into proper length, notched and fitted them one on another. Our shelter began to take form. We split short logs into shingles for our roof. Bullet built our chimney out of rocks that Buzzard had dug from the river bank. George and I dug a pit deep enough to reach clay. We poured water into it and mixed the clay and water until we had a soupy mixture. Hungry and Charlie used it to seal every crack and crevice in the hut. For chairs, we secured empty wooden boxes from the quartermaster. Our table consisted of a board laid

CONFEDERATE WINTER QUARTERS, CENTREVILLE, VIRGINIA, 1862

across two logs. Others soon followed our lead, and by the New Year, row after row of log cabins covered the countryside, replacing most of the tents.

Together we collected wood and stockpiled it for use during the winter. We wanted to make sure we had a sufficient amount on hand.

The long winter months dragged on with the monotony of camp life. There was little to do except an occasional detail or turn at guard duty. We drilled on all but the very worst days. When it rained, we played cards, drank some whiskey, and tried to occupy our thoughts, so we wouldn't become homesick. We didn't have any money, but that didn't stop us. We played for grains of corn and potatoes.

Every now and then, someone received a much-prized newspaper from home, which was passed around or read aloud for everyone to hear, especially if it was about our unit, although sometimes the truth was stretched a bit.

Mail call was always the most important event in camp. Letters sometimes took weeks catching up to us but when they did, I would sit in a corner of our cabin for privacy and read each letter word for word over and over again. I felt sorry for those who didn't receive any mail. They tried to pretend it didn't matter, but I could tell it did. Sometimes we tried to convince ourselves that our letters got lost. Surely they would arrive by the next mail call.

One day I noticed Charlie clutching a letter and staring into space. I asked if everything was all right. He turned and looked up at me with a grim face. Tears were in his eyes as he said to me,

"My wife just informed me our daughter, Ella, died last week of smallpox. She was our only child."

I put my arm around his shoulder, and together we cried and prayed. George went to find the chaplain.

That evening, I was assigned to picket duty. It was sleeting, and I had to stomp my feet to keep from freezing. When you were out there at night, all alone, while others slept, you have lots of time to think about home and all the reasons of why you were there in the first place. Charlie's daughter dying and the disagreeable weather weighed heavily on my mind and added misery to my thoughts. I was shivering and drenched to the bones when I heard a tree branch snap. I shouted out, "Who goes there?" I didn't receive an answer, so again I shouted, "Give me the password, or I'll shoot."

A voice in the dark shouted back, "It's Colonel Strange."

"The password."

The intruder stood still in bewilderment, but quickly regained his composure. "I told you, I'm Colonel Strange, your commanding officer. I forgot the damn password, you idiot. I was checking to see if you were alert. Quit pointing that rifle at me."

"Sir, you're under arrest, and I will shoot, if you take one more step in this direction." We were about twenty paces from each other. I raised my musket and pulled down on him, easing back on the hammer. He realized the seriousness of my demands and lifted his hands high in the air. I marched him to our guardhouse. Even though I knew by then who he was, he could not give me the password, and I was aware I could have been locked up myself, if I hadn't challenged him. The sergeant of the guard went right along with me and locked him in our jail. He had to stay there only a few minutes, until the officer of the guard arrived to identify him and order his release. I'm sure Colonel Strange continued to test the pickets' readiness after that, but I bet he never forgot the password again.

Word spread quickly, all the way up to brigade headquarters, that a private had arrested the regiment's Colonel. Next week we held elections. Maybe it was coincidence, but the men voted to promote me to corporal. I got my stripes, and I was as proud as a pack of fleas on a hound dog.

Cold weather, combined with rain and sleet, began to take its toll. Diarrhea, typhus fever, malaria, and pneumonia sent more men to sick call than the number killed on a battlefield. An epidemic of influenza had our regiment doctors concocting a mixture of peach brandy and sulfur for coughs. I was thankful we had at least taken extra time to build a warm shelter.

January was bitter cold; the ground was covered with a deep snow. The trees hung heavy with icicles, causing limbs to bend and touch the ground. The weather was cold, but the scenery was beautiful. We all reverted to little boys. Eager for entertainment we made sleds out of boards, crate lids, and anything else that would slide down a hill. The less venturous laughed as they watched grown, hungry men tumbling head over heels into snow banks.

I almost had a mishap myself. I was sledding down a slope, straight toward our shelter, when I realized I had no way to stop. I leaped into the wet snow right before my board crashed into the side of our home. I made it without a scratch, but Hungry, who was right behind me, didn't see the cabin in time and crashed headlong into the wall. Thank God only his pride suffered.

During the night, the snow became packed. The next morning, we decided to play bandy. In the North they referred to the game as hockey and played it on ice. In the South, it was chiefly played on land. We gathered a few heavy dogwood sticks, whose root formed a curve, and with the hard knot of a wild grapevine for a ball, a battle took place. Once, and only once, in the midst of a heated game, I ran up behind an opponent as he commenced his back swing to strike the ball. I was struck above the eyebrow, giving me my first wound of the war. Reverend Starnes took out the needle case he carried for sewing on buttons and mending tents and sewed up my wound. A small scar remained for the rest of my life.

Snowball fighting quickly turned into our biggest sport of the season. Even our officers, who tried to resist the temptation, eventually gave in and became willing participants in the action. One morning, Colonel Strange took part in a snowball exchange. He soon became aware that the higher the rank, the more you were attacked and wisely chose not to play again.

The sport of snowballing grew. Soon each company was challenging another to battle, but the sport didn't stop there. Before we knew it, the 19th Regiment had set a date for an all-out attack against the 18th Regiment.

Officers met through the night in command headquarters to map out plans in detail. An ingenious plan was set in motion by the 19th. One company of about 50 men would make a direct frontal charge to pelt the enemy with a continuous shelling of fresh-made snowballs. The enemy, seeing only fifty men, would be drawn out with a counterattack, at which time we would fall back. The trap would then be set. The remaining members of the 19th would be hiding behind the hills and in the woods. As soon as the 18th arrived in pursuit of our retreating forces, we would leap from hiding and overpower them, close the retreat gap and pelt them from both sides, thus winning the battle.

We made hard-packed snowballs that evening. At daybreak, we lined up. With our officers' sabres drawn, the word "charge" rang out loud and clear, followed by our "Rebel yell," as we attacked with an armload of snowballs. Soon we were wrestling, trying to shove each other into the snow. Who knows who won? By evening, there wasn't a dry piece of clothing on anyone.

On Saturdays we held boxing matches; everyone looked forward to them. George was usually a favorite to win, and I, as his manager, held all bets. Before he entered the ring, he placed as much chewing tobacco as possible between his gums and cheeks to protect his teeth and keep them from being knocked out. The practice of using chewing tobacco caused the ring to get slippery. Each time George was hit in the mouth, his dippings flew everywhere.

"George, you need to keep your mouth shut," I hollered.

Turning in my direction he replied, "Makes no difference to me, when I spit he spits. You can tell a lot of stuff about a person from looking at his spit." A thunderous left hook caught George upside his head. "All right, you slab-sided dirty fighter, I plan to jump down your throat and beat the chittlins right out of you."

Despite our playfulness, Christmas was hard on everyone. Being away from home for the first time, I experienced a great deal of loneliness thinking of my family and friends. I re-read old letters I had received earlier. Thoughts of home became stronger than ever.

I recalled Christmases past. Papa would make a batch of well-spiked eggnog. We were all allowed to have at least one sip during the holidays.

To make camp as joyous as possible, I suggested George help me produce a batch of genuine eggnog to serve our friends. George readily accepted my idea and went in search of sugar, milk, and eggs, while Buzzard located the whiskey. Sugar and eggs were exceedingly scarce. George was able to locate a small amount of milk, which I thinned down with water, to stretch it further. Whiskey made up the biggest portion of our eggnog. We all stood eagerly waiting, our cups in our hands, as Buzzard, with discreet care, cooked and presented the full foaming pot of nectar to us. We could barely stomach the stuff. It didn't taste like eggnog at all. Nevertheless we drank it.

Just about everyone received a package from home. Mama sent me some meat, two quarts of flour, some salt, and a fruitcake. Mama's fruitcakes were always the best. She baked them in November. After she was finished, she sprinkled them with brandy, wrapped them in cheesecloth, and stored them in boxes under the bed until Christmas.

Although I felt honored to receive a whole fruitcake of my own, we pooled our goodies and shared equally, that Christmas Eve in Centreville. Afterwards, we told stories of Christmases past, as the sounds of music drifted throughout the camp. Charlie was first to share his Christmas story with us.

"Two days before Christmas, we would go out as a family to find the perfect tree. When we found it, we would mark it. On Christmas Eve morning, my dad and I went back to fetch it while mother, grandmother, and my sisters cooked and wrapped any last-minute gifts. That afternoon, friends would drop in for a slice of mother's date-nut bread and father's eggnog. The children made garlands from popcorn and cranberries. Our fingers always got stained. That evening, we decorated the tree, and Dad lifted the youngest child to hang an angel on the top."

I placed a log on the fire, paused for a moment, then spoke. "The thing I liked most about Christmas was the gathering of my brothers and sisters and their families. Everyone eventually ended up at our house, where a mug of eggnog, the smell of apples roasting, and fresh bread baking made us hungry for a turkey dinner, complete with mince-meat pie and fruitcake."

I remembered how we would bundle up on Christmas Eve, pulling stocking caps on our heads to keep warm before we went out to choose a tree. I continued with my story. "Papa cut it down as Althea and I teamed up against the others in a snowball fight. We were careful not to break a single limb as we carried our tree home."

"Afterwards we went to church to hear the Christmas story and sing carols. Once we arrived home, tired from a long day filled with excitement, I went straight to bed, hoping it would snow during the night."

"Christmas morning, before eating a big breakfast, we all gathered around the hearth in the parlor to exchange gifts. A new shawl for Mama, a handkerchief for Sis, a pair of gloves for Papa. No one was forgotten."

"Mama truly enjoyed the holidays."

"How about you, Hungry," someone asked.

"Christmas memories are hard for me," he said as he stroked his mustache. "Daddy died when I was young, and we never did much. I was the eldest son, so it seemed like I was always busy trying to make a living to support the family. I suppose the most important thing was we stayed together as a family."

❦

In the long, tedious winter months spent in camp, music was our favorite recreation. The woods rang out with hundreds of strong voices, swelling the strains of old hymns, recalling precious memories of home, Christmas and church of earlier years.

Christmas in camp could never be the same as Christmas at home, but somehow, we made it through the holidays, cold, wet, and depressed.

One day, George came in carrying an armload of firewood. "Daniel," he said, "have you noticed our woodpile shrinking faster than it should?"

"As a matter of fact I have, but I thought it was just my imagination."

"I think some scoundrel is making off with our wood. Take that pocketknife of yours and hollow out a hole in the end of this here log for me."

"Why," I asked.

"Just do it. You'll soon see why."

I dug out a hole about three inches deep and George filled it with gunpowder, then sealed it with mud. We carefully placed the log on the top of our pile and waited. The following night, shortly after ten o'clock, we heard an explosion that shook the camp. Everyone grabbed their rifles, thinking we were under attack. We learned a fireplace in one of the cabins down the road had blown up, tearing out the cabin wall. No one figured out how that happened, and we were not about to say, but we never had any more problems with wood being taken.

Once again, we didn't receive our pay on time, so we couldn't afford to purchase the basic staples we needed. No matter how hungry we got, we could not bring ourselves to take from the local farmers by force. Although at times we were starving, kind folks had given all they could at the risk of keeping enough to feed their own families. But seeing us hungry, they never refused to share with us a little of what they had. One day, George shot a rabbit, which he boiled in a pot with some water and a couple of potatoes. That night, the six of us had a meal.

The snow was beginning to melt; I was growing weary of sitting around. General Pickett had assumed command of the brigade and I knew it was just a matter of time before we would be marching.

On a crisp Monday morning in mid-March, the orders came down to prepare to abandon our cabins. The camp was all abuzz as though awakened from a long hibernation. I quickly finished a letter to Althea.

Sis, I must hurry and close for now, as the drum is beating. I will soon be marching again. I know not where. You are better informed in all happenings and events than I am, as I am kept so closely in camp. All war news is very scarce to me. Give my love to Mama, Papa, and the family. Tell all I will write to them as soon as I can. I remain your brother until death, Daniel.

I sealed the envelope and shoved the pencil and paper along with my other meager belongings into my knapsack before helping load the supply wagons. Rumors ran rampant. I wondered where we were heading.

"We're going to Richmond," said George. "We're sure enough moving out this time."

" I reckon so George."

We soon received confirmation that we would be marching within the hour, but the destination, at least for the moment, was kept a secret.

I returned to my cabin one last time. I had grown quite attached to our place and had mixed emotions about leaving, but it was time to go. Time to say farewell to our home and fireplace, the pile of wood we had cut and stacked, and the pile of straw I had placed between two logs that provided me with a bed to sleep on. I neatly rolled my blanket, folded it over my knapsack, and eased the straps, binding it to my back. George stuck the handle of our frying pan into the barrel of his musket, to carry it. The hour had come.

We were called to arms. I shouldered my rifle and placed my oil ground cloth over my head for protection. Colonel Strange drew his saber, pointed south while shouting the command, "Forward." Cracking whips bit the backs of mules. A mass of wagons and men sauntered southward through the mud in the ever falling rains.

Charlie reached for his corncob pipe and sack of tobacco. He offered some to others in our mess group. George brought forth his flint and an Indian arrowhead to strike a fire. Soon the sweet, pungent smoke drifted upwards.

I took one final look at the shelter we had built and knew that was probably the last time I would ever see it.

My thoughts turned to what lay ahead. The last I had heard, the Yankees were camped somewhere near Yorktown and the James River, and we were heading in that direction. I thought to myself, marching south would be a relief from the dreary and despairing routine of winter quarters. Perhaps soon I would be in an actual battle. I pondered the possibility that I would be expected to kill a fellow human being. I was confident I could live up to the demands placed upon me. I had been slowly transformed into a fighting soldier.

Courage Under Fire

⪻⪼

*I*n the early morning chill, at the first streak of dawn, we lumbered along the narrow, winding road clogged with men and wagons moving south. The night before, a raging storm produced torrents of rain, drenching the earth. Continuous passage of artillery pieces and thousands of troops had churned the road into soupy mud. The rain-swollen creek impeded our advances at Mitchell's Ford, making our crossing most difficult. At times, I felt I was going to sink out of sight in the water-filled holes. George told me to hold my breath, in case I went under. I hoped he was joking.

Supply wagons frequently stalled; others bogged down and had to be abandoned. The mud created a suction so great even a fresh team of mules, unless helped by several soldiers, could not pull our wagons from the sticky substance to get them rolling again. Mud, mud, mud!

Colonel Strange rode up and pointed to me. "You, Corporal, get your men behind that wagon and give a hand." I wondered if he remembered me from guard duty. I called upon several men, who waded in to help dislodge the wagon. We crowded around the wheels and used brute strength to push forward, while others pulled from the front. We were up to our knees in mud when suddenly, with a suction-like sound, the wagon moved forward. So did I, with the exception of my feet, which were firmly stuck. I fell face down in the mud. Charlie and Hungry pulled me out. I brushed off what I could and sloshed on through the muck, through ruts, through dizziness and fits of vomiting. With each step of the way, the drying mud caked onto my clothing a little more. As we progressed, I felt as though I were carrying a few more pounds. My feet grew heavy with drying mud.

The further south we traveled, the more I noticed spring was arriving. Clustered along the roadside in the meadows and thickets were bluebells in full bloom. Pink and white clover covered the nearby grasslands and fields. Ferns hanging from the edge of the Rappahannock River formed a carpet along its rocky cliffs. The river enchanted me as it flowed rapidly along its way. The smell of honeysuckle filled the air. Larks soared above, chirping their melodic notes, tsee-titi. In the adjacent forest, a white-tailed doe with two fawns stood silent and erect watching our every move. The hills and valleys offered a panoramic view. I thought the visionary enchantment would never end.

Someone whistled a song. Someone else began

to sing, and soon the whole column joined in. We were acting so cheerful that an outsider looking in could hardly imagine how much we were suffering.

As we grew tired, there was less talking from everyone, until at last it became quiet. Each man was preoccupied with his own thoughts. What a deplorable-looking group we were. I had never seen such a mass of filthy, strong-smelling, rough men. Our march had turned into a blurred and painful day. When we forded a river or crossed a creek, nothing was more enjoyable than to bathe our feet, hands, and faces in the cold water. Taking a break for a few minutes was pleasant, but the rewards could be short-lived. When the march resumed, my limbs were stiff and sore for the first mile or so. I tried to remember to just put one foot before the other.

After ten days and some one hundred miles, we still had not reached Culpepper. We tightened our belts another notch and continued shuffling along. Half-fed horses died in their tracks or simply laid down, refusing to go any farther. Men asked questions of the officers such as, "When are we gonna camp? How much further is it? Have you seen our supply wagons?" Our mess group had nothing left to eat except for some wild berries we had picked along the way. I longed for just one biscuit. We were so hungry that a Persimmon tree halted our entire column and detained it until the last persimmon disappeared.

I glanced over and saw George picking something up from the ground and setting it in the tree. Later I asked what he had picked up. George replied he had returned a baby bird to its nest.

Shortly after dark, we arrived at Culpepper. Over the next few days, we received rations and much-needed rest.

"Sure was a long march to make on corn and green apples," drawled a solider. "Wonder how far we're a-goin."

Buzzard stretched his lean and weary frame in an effort to relieve the pain of his rheumatism. "I reckon they'll let us know when we get there."

Word came down the Yanks had overrun Camp Mitchell after our departure and had burned some of our wagons before they could be moved. To lighten our load, several of us had placed our belongings in the supply wagon and, except for the clothing on our backs, we had lost everything.

That evening I noticed Charlie appeared troubled. He kept checking and rechecking his rifle. I could tell he was nervous.

"What's the problem, Charlie?" I asked.

"Sounds like we're finally gonna get to fight."

"I'm ready," George said. "I'm sick of this wet weather, and we can't end this-here war until we whip 'em badly."

"It looks like you're about to get your chance," I said.

George shook his head. "I don't think the war will last much longer. I hear tell those Yanks aren't as brave as us."

Charlie asked, "What do you mean by that?"

"The difference is with their officers," George said. "I hear the Yankee officers are mostly foreign mercenaries who have no interest in the war; they're fighting only for the money."

Charlie wiped down his rifle again. "Don't believe everything you hear. I've read where their officers have been displaying a lot of bravery on the battlefield to encourage their men to fight. You'll soon be seeing that for yourself."

"Reckon so, but I still think we have a stronger commitment for our cause." George stretched and chuckled. "We could lick `em with cornstalks, but damn `em, they won't fight us that way."

"We'll soon see," I said. "How about you, Charlie?"

"I guess I'm afraid I might become a coward. Might be seized by uncontrollable panic and run. God knows, I prayed about it. I want to do my duty and make my wife, Pa, and Ma proud of me. Daniel, if I do run, I wish you'd shoot me down."

I felt like a chaplain, calming everyone else, but I felt as nervous as they did. "It's only natural to be scared, Charlie. Everyone shares your feelings. No one wants to be killed."

"Yeah, but with mini balls screeching all around me and cannons thundering I may panic and run."

"If you're not nervous, something's wrong with you. I'll be right beside you all of the way. We can help each other. Draw on the strength of God."

That evening, we slept under the pine trees. Wood ticks crept from winter refuge to tunnel into our bodies. The next morning, we all stood and rubbed against rough trees, in an attempt to scratch the ticks off our backs.

Soon we were called by the long roll of the drums. The clouds were thick, and gray patches of fog lay all around us. We received orders to strike our tents and prepare to march. Although our destination was unknown it was obvious we were heading toward Richmond.

George, overjoyed at the possibility we would be bivouacking in Richmond, formed plans for that evening, but at Richmond, we didn't halt. Concerned for the safety of Richmond, we proceeded directly to the docks, where we were informed we would be moving to the peninsula to reinforce Yorktown, because a federal breakthrough was inevitable.

We boarded boats that throbbed and thrashed as they floated down the James River past the quiet rolling countryside of large plantations nestled among the live oaks. Although the boat ride was a welcome reprieve from marching, the weather was windy and horrid. George grumbled the entire way.

At Kings Mill, tobacco and cotton had been put to the torch. I was glad my father wasn't there to see it. The sight would have broken his heart. He always took pride in his tobacco; his whole way of life depended on it. I recall one time in particular we were in town picking up supplies when Papa met a Mister Shoop at Paxton's general store. He expressed a keen interest in the tobacco business and asked Papa what all it entailed and how long it took to produce a crop. Without cracking a smile, Papa told him it took fourteen months every year to grow a crop. The stranger looked puzzled, until he noticed Papa smiling; then he laughed. He indicated he might be interested in investing in a parcel of land. Papa, always willing to discuss tobacco, got serious.

"There is no rest, if you own a tobacco farm," Papa told him. "One year's crop is barely shipped to market before the seed must be sown for the next. In January the crop is planted in seedbeds. Next, field hands clear sections of the land and build a fire over the area to kill the weed seeds. As soon as I'm sure the frost is past, the small tobacco plants are transplanted to the field. The next step is the most important and it occurs in late July when we top the plants by squeezing them between your thumb and forefinger. If you fail to prune, the plants will grow tall and thin; the market looks for a full-bodied leaf. By early September the tobacco is ready to be harvested. We cut the whole plant; stalks included, and leave them in the field to wilt. Later we carry them to the curing barn and hang them on pegs for three to six weeks. Once the tobacco is cured we wait for rain. After a rain, we take down the plants, put them in piles, cover them, and leave them to sweat. Later we bind the leaves and pack them in large casks known as hogsheads and transport them in flat-bottom boats to the auction in Lynchburg."

"Why do you ship by water? Wouldn't rail be faster?"

"Most planters ship by water, because tobacco is not a good traveler. The plant is fragile, and the rough ride over rail or land can damage it. I ship about 3,500 pounds to market for every five acres I plant. After all my expenses, in a good year, I clear about twenty cents a pound. Once I sell, the cycle of plowing, planting, and caring for a new crop begins again."

"I understand what you said earlier about the

fourteen months. I hadn't realized all the time and effort tobacco required. I'll give a lot of thought to all of this. Thank you for the information."

My thoughts returned to the present as we were ordered to disembark and take up a line of march for Yorktown. Traveling along Lee's Mill road, the brigade came upon the enemy's pickets, and quickly over powered them. A few miles farther, we encountered the Yanks' rear guard. They briefly made a stand against us but due to our overwhelming numbers and fire power they soon retreated. George was upset because the marching order of the brigade had kept our regiment in the rear and we didn't have an opportunity to participate in the skirmish.

At dusk, exhausted, we arrived at Yorktown; a narrow peninsula formed by the James and Warwick Rivers. We were ordered to lie quietly in a densely wooded area next to a stream, fringed by swamps. I was conscious that the hour for a battle was drawing nearer. Yes sir, a battle was coming; the men felt it. The signs were easy to read, like a storm brewing. Like Charlie, I questioned if I would run at the first sight of conflict. I promptly put that thought out of my mind and prayed for God to give me the strength to do my duty, as I was trained to do.

Volleys of rifle fire sporadically pierced the air. A shot rang out from a bushwhacker, hitting Captain Evans. His blood splattered across my shirt. I shook just thinking about the possibility that I could be killed or worse yet, be wounded and crippled for life. I was confident though that with God's help, I would find the courage to carry on.

The Yanks opened a most furious attack of artillery shelling. The thundering bombardment seemed close. I felt a shiver run through my body.

Soon their infantry mounted a charge. Waves of men swept out of the woods and advanced upon us. The fierce battle began taking its toll. Men fell dead and wounded, half buried by the swamp's slimy ooze. We successfully repulsed their advance, driving them back across the stream and beyond our range of fire.

Tension remained high, and we stayed on alert for quite some time, expecting the Yanks to re-group and attack at any moment. As darkness fell, our anxiety eased. My first battle was one I would long remember.

Buzzard soon arrived and shouted out excitedly, "Did you hear what happened during a Yankee charge?"

"I haven't heard a word," I replied.

"During a skirmish, a bullet from a Yankee rifle cut down a hornet's nest, which fell first on the heads of our boys, then burst open as it hit the ground. Well, let me tell you those boys came charging out of their trenches screaming and waving their arms about them in such a frightful manner the advancing Yanks stopped in their tracks, turned and ran. They thought a counter attack was taking place."

"Was anyone stung or hurt?"

"Over half the company had to report to sick bay with wasp bites. The captain said he was stung twice in every possible place."

That evening, Reverend Starnes announced he would hold a special service. Quite a few soldiers wanted to hear the word and get right with his Maker before another battle. I asked George if he planned to attend.

"Daniel, you know, and I know; I ain't very religious, but I ain't unreligious, and I know that, too, but I reckon I need all the help I can get, so yeah, I'll go with you."

"Be careful, George. One of these days, it may rub off on you."

We assembled to offer prayers for those killed and wounded in the day's action. Reverend Starnes with stretched out arms, ended by reciting the twenty-third Psalm.

"Yea, though I walk through the valley of the shadow of death, I will fear no evil: for thou art with me; thy rod and thy staff they comfort me."

Afterwards, many of the men wrote sentimental letters to loved ones, while others preferred silent prayers and meditation.

At the first light of day, facing insurmountable odds, the brigade was ordered to fall back and form a line of defense at Williamsburg. We hastened to torch what cotton and tobacco was on the docks at Yorktown. Warehouses were filled to capacity with supplies. We took what food we could and opened all of the commissary warehouses to the local people to salvage what they could, before the Yanks returned. For men who had been living and marching on fruit and berries, being allowed to take what they wanted was a stroke of good fortune. It was like turning children loose in a candy store. Soldiers raced through the streets with delicacies unknown to our commissariat. We gorged ourselves on canned oysters, turkeys, and game birds, washing the food down with wine.

One building contained sacks heaped full of corn, wheat, and rye left unbolted, so it could be baked with a better texture. It made the sweetest and best-tasting bread one would ever eat.

We found fresh horses in the corrals to replace our worn-out, starving animals. After loading what few wagons we had remaining, we set fire to York-town's huge warehouses. The flames cast grotesque shadows across the city.

My company was to hold our position to provide cover for the brigade's retreat from Yorktown. I felt uneasy crouched among the trees, thinking only a handful of men were expected to hold back thousands of advancing Yanks.

"We'll get swallowed up if they charge us," said George.

Luckily, they didn't know how few of us there were. We lay concealed in the dense underbrush of the forest, waiting for their deadly charge.

Throughout the evening as the enemy drew near, I could hear the quick popping of rapid fire and see gunpowder flashing in the dark, from across the field. A bullet hit a tree next to me with a dull thud. I didn't see anyone but I returned their fire.

The darkness of the evening caused the Yanks to halt for the night and regroup. Their delay gave the time needed for our brigade to reach Williamsburg.

Dawn at last came, and soon our cavalry came charging at a break-neck speed, to assist with our retreat. Carefully, we fell back through miles of countryside where the guns from both sides had earlier mowed the ground like a giant reaper.

With the Yanks slashing at our heels, firing rifles that sent their lead messengers whistling past my ears, I dashed through the rainy dawn across the muddy fields and swollen creeks toward our lines. I passed through smoldering woods from the previous day's fighting. Everywhere lay wounded and dying men from both sides. The screams and moans of brave soldiers and the sounds of mangled and dying horses horrified me. Buzzards drifted lazily overhead; their sharp eyes fixed intently upon the dead men and animals below. The reality of it all was heinous. I'd never been so distressed in my life.

Two days later, after floundering through the rain and mud, we rejoined the brigade in Williamsburg. The men had been busy erecting ramparts around the city in anticipation of an attack. We arrived, barely in front of the Yanks, who were struggling along the muddy roads. Cheers broke out as we exited the woods onto the open fields in a mad dash for our lines.

Sleepless, fatigued, and dispirited, we took our position in the trenches. A sense of fear built even more, when I spotted the Yanks approaching from the east. The order was given to fix bayonets. I thought to myself, surely God will, in due time, deliver us from the hands of our enemies.

Soon all the fires of hell broke loose. A furious fight erupted. Until then, I never had a clear under-standing of the horrors of war. Terrified men, horses, and mules dashed about in confusion. Incredible numbers of men on both sides fell dead and dying. Blood was calf-deep within the trenches. I expected at any moment to hear a plunk from a bullet entering my body. If I ever prayed earnestly in my life, it was during those hours. Cannons caused mass casualties and made the earth tremble beneath my feet, as if an earthquake were taking place. The Yanks fell back into a strip of woods we had crossed earlier. They were as much afraid of us as we were of them.

They reorganized and formed a counterattack. Through the haze, I could see them steadily but cautiously advancing through a solid sheet of smoke as our batteries continued to inflict heavy casualties upon them. My heart raced, and I was filled with a mixture of panic and dread. The sound of hot lead thumping into human flesh sickened me. With a dull thud, a mini ball hit my Bible, which was inside my shirt pocket. The Bible had saved my life.

We were determined to hold our position at all costs. I never imagined anyone could survive such a storm of lead as we continued to pour volley after volley of fire into them. I was too scared to think. I guess that's what all the training does for you. You learn to react, rather than question orders.

Their cannons continued firing mercilessly at us, tearing limbs from trees and throwing rocks and dirt in every direction. Using our bayonets, pieces of wood, our fingernails, or anything else we could find, we tried to dig deeper and deeper into the earth.

I could see the wheels of their big guns coming closer and closer.

"Steady now," was the order. "See those horses

pulling the big guns? Aim at their knees." Our cannons fired swiftly. A direct hit tore a horse to pieces. Soon the ground was covered with dead horses and men.

A heavy force of infantry advanced toward us from the South and through the clouds of smoke and dust. I could see a number of Union flags approaching from the woods on the East. The men were on top of us before we knew it. A voice from our trenches cried out, "Don't load boys; they're too close to you. Let them have the cold steel."

We launched into hand-to-hand combat using bayonets, rocks, fence rails, and anything else we could get our hands on to repel them. We were determined to fight to the bitter end. The scene turned into total chaos. Hundreds of wounded and dying men covered the ground. The carnage had reached its climax. Bewildered, the Yanks hesitated, their ranks broke. The course of the battle had reversed. Their retreat soon evolved into a disorderly rout from the field.

Having gained the apparent advantage, amidst the thick smoke and musketry fire, we sprang forward from our trenches. Screaming like a demon with our blood-curdling, Rebel yell, Wa-oow-eey, we swooped down on them as they rushed across the open field, back to the thick forest. The sounds of grape canisters bursting over my head and the screams of dying men all around shook my senses, but I kept on advancing, firing, reloading, and firing again.

Charlie was hit by a musket ball as he charged beside me. He dropped to the ground. Blood gushed from his mouth, and I knew he was mortally wounded. I reached down to help him, saw his lacerated flesh and found myself screaming, "Stretcher bearer!"

"Daniel, am I hurt badly?"

"I believe you are."

"Will you pray for me?"

"You know I will."

He seemed comforted and reached out to me. He spent his last moments cradled in my arms as I gently rocked him back and forth. His death hit me hard. I wanted to stay with him, but I knew I couldn't. Others depended on me.

Filled with panic and dread, covered with dirt and Charlie's blood I moved forward. I gasped for breath when I saw Hungry on the ground. My stomach lurched and my legs went weak. I knelt beside him. Lying in a pool of blood, he had turned the color of bleached bones. The top of his head had been blown away, and his brains poured out onto the ground. I vomited; retching until nothing was left inside me. I was in shock, disbelieving what had happened.

"Tell me, God, he isn't dead. Please tell me he will be okay."

The shadows of the night soon began to fall. Darkness ended the slaughter and brought the action to a close. I turned aside, sobbing over my fallen comrades; I dragged myself to my feet and slowly walked back to our lines.

Other than a scrimmage that was my first battle. The sight of soldiers, mutilated beyond recognition in many cases, overwhelmed me. I pray that time will erase some of the memories. The elation I had experienced during anticipation of battle had left me. I thought to myself about how indifferent I had become toward my fellow man. Charlie's and Hungry's death stimulated me to seek revenge. My God, what kind of person had I become?

I began to have doubts and wondered if I could return home after the war and live life as I once did. I asked God's forgiveness for ever wishing to see or hear a battle.

George approached, excited. "We whipped `em. The war is over. Did you see `em skedaddle right after we leaped out of the trenches?"

"George! George, both Charlie and Hungry died out there today."

George shook his head in disbelief. Slowly, he sank to the ground and leaned his head back against a tree simply to rest his mind.

"There's no time to grieve, the wounded need tending to."

We were never out of hearing their groans and cries for help. Some cried out for us to have mercy on them by killing them. Many cried for a drink of water. God must have been listening because the heavens opened up and the rains came.

George and I went out onto the battlefield in search of our comrades. We found one fellow crying in pain. He groaned as he reached out to grasp my hand. "Please help me," he said. "I could bear all this alone, but my wife, my children." He paused as large tears rolled down his grimy face. Overcome with grief, he could only add, "Oh God! Oh God! How will they endure this?"

I held his hand tight. "Some way, God will provide and comfort them."

He looked at me with gratitude and whispered,

"God bless you, kind stranger."

George and I gently lifted him onto a blanket. We became confused in the cavern-like darkness and rain and weren't sure of our location.

"This way, George."

"No, I think it's this way," he said. We both attempted to pull the blanket in different directions. We finally agreed on a direction and carried our soldier toward some woods.

A guard hollered out, "Who goes there?"

"We are carrying a wounded man to the hospital," I answered.

"Well, you're going the wrong way. You're behind Union lines."

"We are?"

"Yes, you are. Turn around, and you'll run into your lines about five hundred yards straight ahead."

"Sir, you got a heart in you," George said as we turned toward our own lines.

That evening we carried wounded Yankee soldiers along with our own to farmhouses in the area. The good people had lost almost everything to the war. They could see the ruins of their neighbors' farms and knew the enemy was responsible. Regardless, the farm families received the injured kindly and bound their wounds. As one farmer said to me, except for an imaginary line that separates the North from the South, those young men could have been his own sons.

Colonel Gantt rode up to inform us to fall back and form our line directly behind the Wren building at the campus of William and Mary College. We were told to fortify our position by digging deep ditches on the Northeast corner of the campus.

I had read about the old school, but that was my first time to actually see it. Unfortunately, it wasn't the best of times to tour, but I felt drawn to view the halls and walkways that many famous Americans had traveled along. Presidents Thomas Jefferson, James Monroe, John Tyler, and George Washington all attended that school. I felt inspired and could feel their presence as I walked along, touching walls and rails they must have once touched. The majestic structure must have been nearly two hundred years old. I prayed the enemy wouldn't destroy it.

George and I returned to our lines and gathered a few twigs to build a small fire. I placed my battered tin cup over the flames to brew a cup of coffee. With my knife, I sliced off a piece of corn pone and dipped it into the coffee before eating it. Afterwards, I filled my pipe and settled down beside a tree stump to smoke. My thoughts turned back to home. I knocked out the ashes, laid down in the damp, muddy trenches, and thanked God for sparing me that day. The awful scene of death and suffering haunted me. I prayed that the war would be over soon and that both sides would be allowed to return home in peace. I asked God to watch over me in the days to come and to please take Charlie and Hungry into His arms.

I had seen the reality of battle, its bloodshed, its despair and desolation, the wounded, the dying, and the dead. I was too sickened to rejoice in our victory. I lay awake through the long cold and rainy night, wide-eyed, staring at the sky, experiencing the depths of depression. Sleep never came.

W △ 10

SECOND DAY AT SEVEN PINES

◆

Most of the fighting on the second day of the Battle of Seven Pines (Fair Oaks), occurred near here on 1 June 1862. Confederate Maj. Gen. Gustavus W. Smith, who had assumed command following the wounding of Gen. Joseph E. Johnston the evening before, resumed the attack in the morning. When the Union defenses proved too strong, the Confederates disengaged and retired to their original lines. Gen. Robert E. Lee, who already had been assigned to command the Confederate troops in front of Richmond early in the day, assumed that command when Smith collapsed from exhaustion during the afternoon.

DEPARTMENT OF HISTORIC RESOURCES, 1994

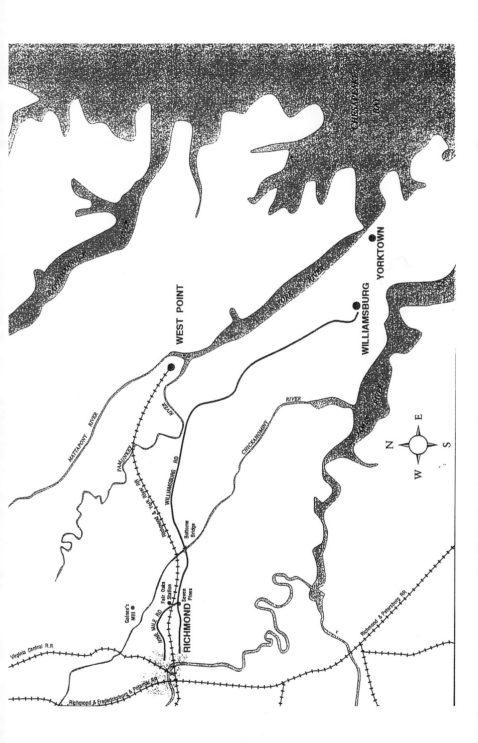

Hold Your Ground

⋞⋟

*R*eveille sounded at the first light of day. The morning was crisp, and cool in Williamsburg, but as the sun burned off the thick blanket of fog, the temperature rose considerably.

We assembled. Captain Rieser said, "Stand at ease men." We waited for our orders. Soon the quartermaster wagon pulled up and each man was issued forty rounds of ammunition. We were dismissed to make ready to march.

I tried not to think of what lay ahead. I rolled my blanket and shelter, tied our pots and pans about myself and hurriedly grabbed a johnnycake George had made the night before from cornmeal, water, and sugar.

I noticed Bullet was deep in thought and appeared troubled. I paused and offered to help.

"Daniel, do you think by falling back to defend Richmond, this could be our biggest fight?"

"Can't rightly say. The Yanks have assembled a lot of soldiers."

"I'm not sure I can survive another battle. Lately I've been having thoughts of dying and nightmares about the war. I reckon I'm not ready to die just yet. I wonder if we can defend another assault, after losing so many men at Williamsburg."

"I think everyone, including our officers, are scared, and that's probably true of both sides. It's not a sign of weakness; it's a sign of being human."

"Yeah, but, ain't you afraid of being killed?"

"Of course. I'm not really afraid to die; it's just how I die that worries me. I'm not sure I could handle the suffering that sometimes accompanies dying."

"It's good to know others have the same concerns I have," Bullet said as he smiled in deep gratification. "I'll be okay now."

The bugle sounded abruptly and demanded a quick response. We gathered our possessions and hurried to assemble. The order to march was given. We wheeled into columns with other companies, and trudged across an open field on to a clay road. It soon became common knowledge we were heading in the direction of Fair Oaks.

We tramped westward along the swamp-bordered Williamsburg road winding and twisting toward Richmond, until we reached Bottom's Bridge on the Chickahominy River. There we found the bridge and the railroad tracks had been destroyed. The Chickahominy was out of its banks, about forty feet wide from the recent rainfall. Fringed with a dense growth of trees, the river was bordered by low, marshy bottomland. Our engineers hastily built a temporary bridge for us to scurry across.

As we approached a tollgate between the railroad and Williamsburg road, we stumbled upon a Yankee brigade and quickly spread out for cover. From across the road, a Yankee officer shouted out in defiance, "Who are you?"

"Virginians!" we shouted back.

"Well, what are you boys fighting for?"

"We're fighting because you're down here," George yelled.

"Don't you fellows have anything better to wear than those rags?" the Yank shouted back.

Buzzard said, "Well now, do you think we put on our Sunday clothing to go out hunting vermin?"

George had heard enough. He leaped out from behind a tree, and pulled down his pants and flashed his derriere at the Yanks. "Look," he said, "we don't even wear drawers."

The Yankee officer called out loudly to his men, "Don't shoot! The Virginians will surrender."

That did it for us. Without hesitation, we responded with heavy fire, striking the officer several times, killing him instantly. The fight lasted almost an hour, before the Yanks retreated.

That evening, we bivouacked in an area near Fair Oaks and hastily constructed a line of breastwork to shore up our defense. A drenching downpour filled our trenches with water as quickly as we dug them. We remained on high alert, fearing the Yanks might attack at any moment.

The duty roster was posted; I had drawn guard duty. Tired, hungry, and covered with grime, I reported as corporal of the guard. I was told by Sergeant Ratchford to maintain a state of readiness. He directed me to alert the pickets that we were expecting a visit from high-ranking army brass later that evening.

An hour had passed when I heard the clattering of a horse's galloping hoofs. I looked up, and spotted a lone rider approaching from across the field. Dressed immaculately in a gray uniform, he sat squarely at ease on a magnificent black stallion. His posture and his rise and fall in the saddle were flawless as he drew near, I shouted for him to halt, but he continued toward me, showing absolutely no fear.

I thought he was going to run into me, but within a few feet, he reined up and wheeled sideways, brushing me with his horse. "Soldier," he said, "take me to General Johnston's headquarters immediately." He sat tall in the saddle and spoke with such authority and composure that I couldn't refuse his request.

With a great deal of prudence and watchfulness, I escorted him at musket length to the general's tent.

Once there the rider cut a leather button from his coat. Apparently he had earlier removed the stuffing from the button and in its place, inserted a waded piece of paper. When I presented the paper to General Johnston's staff officer, he read the note and promptly ushered the soldier inside. The meeting lasted only a few minutes. The stranger exited the general's headquarters, mounted his horse and road off at a full gallop.

Additional chairs where hurriedly brought into

the general's tent. Officers brushed off their uniforms as best they could. Our guests soon arrived and needed no introduction. Escorted by a company of men, President Jefferson Davis and Generals Robert E. Lee and D. H. Hill came riding directly toward me. I stood dumbfounded, frozen at attention.

As I had pictured him to be, Lee was a distinguished soldier with gray hair and moustache and a neatly trimmed beard. He was dressed in a gray uniform, and his boots had been spit polished. He looked calm, but his eyes pierced through me, instantly earning my respect. I was so overcome and in awe of meeting General Lee face to face, that I hardly remember what President Davis and General Hill wore. I knew that a meeting of great magnitude was about to take place. The matter had to be serious, for them to travel out to our camp. I thought to myself, "Wait until I tell Papa about this."

The entourage of men moved quickly toward General Johnston, who stood outside his headquarters to greet them. The men quickly dismounted and moved inside.

I stepped up to the guards who accompanied the generals and asked if General Hill's troops would be arriving any time soon.

They looked at me doubtlessly questioning my reason for wanting to know classified information. "What you want to know for? The captain asked."

"My brother Sam, serves under Hill's command. I was hoping to locate him. Its been a year since we've talked."

At first he was reluctant to discuss anything with me, but I soon convinced him that my brother was in the 49th under Hill's command.

"We must be careful," answered the Captain. "Spies are everywhere. But I can tell you, there was a battle nearby today, and General Hill's Infantry and Jeb Stuart's cavalry took part in it. So one can assume they are both here."

"That's great! My brothers Paul and Marcellus are in Stuart's Brigade. Looks like all of Mama's boys were probably going to be in one place at the same time."

The buildup of troops was impressive. The next battle could be the deciding one for the war. Maybe if we "ripped `em up" real good, the war would be over, and we could all go home.

President Davis and Generals Lee and Hill emerged from Johnston's tent. Once again I snapped to attention as they drew near. General Lee looked right at me and said, "You're doing a fine job of soldiering, son. Keep the faith, and thank you for serving your country."

"Thank you, Sir," was all I could say, surprised as I was that General Lee had spoken directly to me. Soon the entire entourage was off.

The trees began to sway in the soft breeze, as the rain came with renewed intensity. A rider came by and said the bridge we had built over the Chickahominy had washed out. The Yankees would need time to rebuild it. The delay would give us more time to prepare for a fight.

"Prisoners coming in," someone cried out. Our skirmishers had come upon a small group of enemy soldiers on a reconnaissance mission, surprised them, and captured them without a fight. Still on duty, I was present when the prisoners admitted that General McClellan had sent them to confirm the number of our artillery pieces.

Several companies of men had spent the day cutting down trees and gathering logs, which were painted with black tar and set in place to give the appearance of a battery of artillery cannons. After every tenth log we installed a real field piece that would ultimately be fired to draw attention. The fake, or Quaker guns as we called them, looked so real the Yanks believed they were overpowered and advised McClellan to postpone any attack. It helped him justify his position to halt his army until replacements could be brought up.

When I was relieved of guard duty, I set out to locate the whereabouts of Sam's regiment. Mama's letters had said that Sam was a lieutenant in Company F of the 49th Virginia Infantry, General Hill's Division. I learned they were camped less than a mile down the road from us. Because of the high alert, no one had permission to leave camp that evening, but I had to see Sam, if only for a minute.

When nature calls, one heads for the woods behind the camp, so I took a stroll in that direction. Once out of sight, I made a quick turn toward the area where the 49th was camped. I was fortunate in locating my brother's regiment. His company was on the edge of a wooded area near a fast-moving stream. Sam was outside his tent deep in conversation with his sergeant as I approached. He wore a slouch-hat with a battered brim and a weathered gray jacket over frayed jeans. He looked up and smiled. I was so glad to see him; I grinned from ear to ear. That was my first contact with any of my brothers in a long while. Sam dismissed the sergeant and ushered me inside.

"Sam, it's good to see you," I said as we hugged. "It's been a long time. Have you heard any news of Paul or Marcellus?"

"Not a word, Daniel."

"I heard about the battle the 49th was in today. I worried about you."

"You should have seen us. Colonel Smith ordered us to tear our undergarments into pieces and tie strips around our arms, so we could recognize each other."

"Did it work?"

"Yeah, many of our boys were wearing pants and jackets from dead Yanks, we might have shot each other, if we hadn't done that."

"Where are the Yanks now?"

"On the other side of the Chickahominy River. The river was flooded, and we chased them across, with our rifles held over our heads, to keep our powder dry."

"I suppose some powder got wet but you can always dry it out tonight."

"Fact is the artillery battery spread their powder out to dry and some fool soldier walked by with a lit pipe. A spark ignited the ammunition. Blew up a cannon and sent pieces of the boy flying all over the field."

"I'm glad you weren't hurt."

"Enough about me, how about some coffee and chicken fixin's?" We were lucky enough to capture a Yankee supply wagon during the battle."

I dug right in and almost choked while trying

to chew, drink, and talk, all at the same time. "Sam, I'm not angry at any one. I just want it all to end. I'm tired and want to go home."

"I agree, but the truth is we got a major fight shaping up. You heard Jeb Stuart's Calvary arrived today, didn't you?"

"Yeah, I heard about that. Maybe we'll get to see Paul and Marcellus."

"How come you didn't join the cavalry like they did?"

"The Calvary's just not my niche."

"Well, I do declare, I find that rather strange, after Papa spent so much time teaching you to ride."

It was getting late. We talked a while longer, before I told Sam I had to return before someone discovered I was gone.

"I understand, it sure was great seeing you. I was surprised when I saw you coming up to our camp."

"Want to get together tomorrow evening?"

"Sure. If we camp here tomorrow night, I'll come over to see you."

"Maybe we'll be able to spend a little more time together."

"I wish you could stay longer tonight, but I understand."

"Hey! Let's try to find Paul and Marcellus tomorrow."

"That would be great, and Daniel, if you write home tonight, tell everyone I send my love."

"I will. Oh, one last thing. Take care of yourself tomorrow. Being an officer has its disadvantages."

"Yeah, I know. Everybody shoots at me." Sam

smiled and waved good-bye as I hurried out of sight.
Before retiring that evening, I sat down and
wrote a short letter to the folks. Some sat around
cleaning their muskets, smoking their pipes, or
thinking of their families and loved ones back home.
Others read their Bibles. I suspected the possibility of
a battle loomed on everyone's mind and accounted for
the somberness.

I wrote, *"Dear Mama and Papa, sorry I haven't
written sooner, but I've been marching or in a fight since
last I wrote. I've been engaged in three fights, but have
escaped so far. My clothing was hit with mini balls twice,
but I remain unhurt. We are currently under marching
orders, and I do not know where we will be going next.
I'm sure the local newspaper will describe some of the hard
fighting to you in a few days. Some good news, I met up
with Sam today, and he provided me with a good meal. I
understand Paul and Marcellus are also in this area, but I
have not yet seen them. I plan to do so tomorrow. Sam sends
his love to all. I must close for now, as we will be marching
at first light. Give my love to the girls and Stephen. I
remain your loving son, Daniel."*

I folded the letter, sealed it, and delivered it to
our quartermaster. He promised to send it out in the
morning.

Returning to my tent, I noticed in the distance
the sky was ablaze from the thousands of enemy

campfires miles away. It produced a dawn-like effect that gave me an uncomfortable feeling. A wind lashed out as clouds rolled up from the northeast and darkened the sky. A low muttering of thunder sounded in the distance as men scrambled to gather their possessions before rushing to their shelters. Lightening bolts quickly replaced the lights of the campfires. A thunderstorm of unusual violence shook the heavens. Just as I reached our tent, a bolt of lighting struck the tips on our rifle bayonets stacked outside. I jumped as though I had been shot. I quickly crawled into my bedroll and lay there, staring through the tent opening at the ashes of our hissing campfire.

Reveille sounded, and we hurriedly assembled in an eerie daybreak. Every man was aware of the hardships he would soon endure. In the distance, I heard the continuous rumbling of cannon fire. Bibles had replaced dice and cards in soldiers' pockets. Many men softly said prayers. I found it absolutely amazing how quickly nonbelievers became believers. Some of the men had written their names on small pieces of paper and pinned them to the backs of their shirts in hopes that someone would notify their families if they were killed.

General Pickett addressed us. "Men we have been ordered to attack the enemy today. Major Sadler reports that your commissary failed to draw meat rations. You men will have to go into battle hungry. Before marching, check your ammunition. If it's wet, have ordnance issue you new powder. When the order comes down to double quick march, move quickly, We cannot move on the enemy until every brigade is in position.

"Today is the day we have all been preparing for, to defend not only Richmond, but also the Confederacy. Make sure you are within range of the enemy before you fire. Stand erect, fire a volley at fifty yards, rush forward, crouch, load, then rush forward again. Attempt to shoot their horses, to limit the movement of their artillery and block the roads. Next, try to shoot their officers, it can cause panic and confusion within their ranks. When ordered to charge, do so without hesitation. Do not stop to help wounded men or take them back to our lines. We have men assigned to care for the wounded. The best way of helping a wounded friend is to drive the enemy back from the battlefield. Finally, I want you to remember you are to oppose to the last extremity any attempt upon your position. God be with all of you."

The order to march, by General Pickett, was given. The General rode to the head of the column. We were reduced to marching single file, because both sides of the road were waist-high in water. However, men occasionally broke ranks to wade through the water and pick a handful of cherries from the trees along the way. As the sun rose and the morning mist retreated, the heat began to take its toll.

George nudged me to look at Buzzard. He was bent over in pain, although he continued to march.

"What's the matter, Buzzard?" I asked.

"Got a God-awful stomachache."

"You been eating too many of those cherries. Better stop, or you'll get the old soldier's disease."

"Already got it. All I got to do now is learn how to fight from a squatting position."

"At least it'll be more difficult to shoot you

down there," George said.

We arrived at Seven Pines shortly before noon and formed our battle lines. The yanks were in full view across the field. The regimental colors were unfurled, and a long roll of the drums alerted us to prepare for battle. Surgeons made ready their operation facilities, and litter bearers folded bandages while they waited. Ammunition wagons busily distributed cartridges to the regiments. Whips cracked on the backs of mules that strained with wagons and artillery pieces as they raced forward, jockeying to get into position.

Cannons roared in quick succession, causing the earth to tremble beneath our feet. Shells shrieking overhead burst, cutting a path of destruction throughout our ranks. Bullets whistled through the trees ripping them into kindling. I felt as though we had arrived at the very gates of hell.

The command to form our battle lines was given by Colonel Garnett, followed by "Double Quick, Foooorrrr." Rushing forward in a solid mass under a hail of bullets, we charged through puddles of water, splashing and bellowing out our ear-splitting Rebel yell. The sight and sound must have instilled terror within their ranks, because pandemonium broke out. Yanks abandoned their water-filled trenches.

Many of us were barefoot and left a trail of bloody footprints from stepping on the pieces of jagged iron and shell fragments that surrounded us. We were possessed with an enormous determination to whip the enemy. "Glory" or "greatness," as described in the newspapers, never entered my mind. Our thoughts were to kill or be killed. I said to myself, "Lord, please commit these Yankee souls into your kingdom, because I'm about to kill as many of them as I can."

I came upon a young wounded Yankee soldier about my age lying in a watery trench. His face was pale with fear. He reached out for my help. I raised my musket and made ready to fire, but as I looked down the barrel, I couldn't help but look directly into his eyes. I raised up slightly, still pointing my musket directly at him. I asked, "Are you hurt badly?"

He had fear in his voice. "Yes, I am. Are you going to kill me?"

"Well, that's the purpose I came here for." I couldn't shoot him, though. I slowly lowered my musket. "Your own men will be here soon. They'll carry you back to your lines for treatment." I wished I could do more for him, but I didn't know what to do.

The ground shook with the thunderous sound of pounding horse hooves. A heavy cloud of dust accompanied their approach. A bugler sounded the charge. Jeb Stuart's cavalry, its battalion flag popping in the morning breeze, galloped over the ridge in columns of four, sabers drawn and glistening in the sun.

I jumped up when I saw my brothers Paul and Marcellus. Caught up in the emotion and excitement, I leaped out of the trench and ran forward. To pause would invite instant death from a bullet. In the distance I saw a Yank rush to grab the bridle of a horse, in an attempt to pull the animal down. With one swift swing of his sword, the rider severed the man's hand.

The cracking sound of rifle and pistol fire came from the cloud of dust. Paul's horse reared up. A mini ball had struck his front leg. I watched as the animal spun around and went down on his knees. With enormous effort, the horse stood and tried to run. He limped a few yards, but could go no further. Forgetting my own danger, I stood riveted, looking on helplessly shouting at the top of my lungs, "Paul---Paul!" Blood ran down Paul's leg and into his boot. A bullet had shattered his knee. Paul passed out and fell from his horse. He was surrounded by the Yanks. I could do nothing to prevent his capture.

A rider approached at breakneck speed. As he drew nearer, I saw it was Marcellus, coming to Paul's aid. I could tell by the way he was slumped over in the saddle that he, too, had been shot.

When Marcellus drew close enough to see Paul had been captured he wheeled about, drove his spurs into his horse's flanks, and galloped away, rather than risk death or capture himself. I felt a painful emptiness in the pit of my stomach. I froze, when the Yanks pointed their weapons at Paul, as he lay on the ground. I was grief stricken watching him slowly get up and drag himself, under guard, to the rear.

Regaining my composure, I dropped to my knee to reload. I grabbed a bullet pack, quickly bit off the end of the paper, poured the powder into my musket, inserted a mini ball, rammed it in with a quick thrust, stood, and rushed ahead. Roaring, shrieking, struggling masses of men and horses lay dying beneath my feet. I had to think clearly. I pushed on more than ever, to avenge my brother's capture. I fired, stopped to reload, and discovered I was out of ammunition. I rose to my feet, with my bayonet in place, I continued on.

Ahead of me our flag bearer was shot in the arm, but refused to go to the rear. He continued to lead us, carrying our colors. His gallant, undaunted action inspired all of us. Others, who had emptied their cartridge pouches, continued their pursuit swinging their empty muskets wildly at the enemy.

The yanks paused, then began to run in disorder and confusion. The battle, was a severe one, but we had successfully driven the Yankees from their stronghold and captured their artillery.

Completely weakened from exhaustion, I could go no further. I fell to the ground on my knees. I had to catch my breath before returning to our lines. Painstakingly and sadly, I dragged myself from the carnage and started back to camp. Others had stopped to gather food and cartridges from dead Yanks; some gathered clothing. I plodded on until I reached our lines. Paul and Marcellus weighed heavily on my mind.

Within a few minutes, George came in. Black gunpowder residue covered his face, but he was truly a wonderful sight to see.

"Hey George, over here." I said.

"Are you okay, Daniel?"

"Yeah, I'm just sitting here against this old tree, trying to keep it from falling."

Before uttering a word, George dropped to the ground with a thud. He reached into his pocket and produced a pouch of Bright tobacco.

"I suppose you found that on a dead Yankee," I said.

"Yep, I did." He poured a small amount of tobacco into a sheet of paper cupped in the palm of his hand, snipped off the protruding ends, and lit his smoke with a red hot-twig from the fire. Settling back against the tree, he took a deep drag and slowly released the smoke through his nostrils. "We licked 'em today, Daniel, on all points. We captured three batteries of artillery, but I'm not so sure I can make it tomorrow. It took just about every bit of life out of my body."

"Maybe they'll pack up and go home."

"They would if they could, I'm confident of that. In fact, I read somewhere that a Confederate private told the press that if he could sit down with a Yankee soldier for thirty minutes, they could solve the problems that caused this war, and we could all pack up and go home."

"I agree with that." I rubbed my neck. "I'm feeling mighty sad right about now. I saw Paul and Marcellus both get shot today."

"Yeah, I saw the cavalry and figured they were here, but I never saw your brothers. Are they alive?"

"I can't rightly say. Paul's horse got shot out from under him, and he was captured. Marcellus was wounded and had to ride away or be captured."

"Those Yankee surgeons will patch him up. Heck, he might get to go home before we do. Sometimes they trade prisoners, if they think the men won't be able to come back and fight again."

"I hope you're right."

"I'm sure he's gonna be okay."

Buzzard and Bullet arrived with blankets wrapped around what they called delicacies left by the retreating Yankees.

"Spoils of war," Buzzard said. "Corn, cheese,

fruit . . ."

George interrupted, rubbing his stomach, "Who's night is it to cook?"

Buzzard grinned; "It must be yours George."

"We repulsed `em today," said Bullet. "They literally screamed with fright when we jumped into their trenches. They were in such a hurry to leave; we found rifles, cooking tins, and their knapsacks on the ground. Some of 'em leaped onto departing wagons."

"Yeah, some even clung to the sides of their ambulances," laughed Buzzard. "There sure enough wasn't any room for their wounded."

That evening we ate corndodgers, cheese, crackers, and apples. We drank coffee and enjoyed a good bit of tobacco.

We decided to boil some peanuts we found at the Yankee campsite. We boiled them in their hulls in salted water. Before long, Captain Cookson showed up at our fire. He reached into our pot with a long spoon and withdrew a peanut. "Mind if I sample one of these, boys?"

"Please help yourself, sir."

He took one, broke it open carefully, let the salty water from the hull drip into his mouth, then ate the pea and sucked the damp shell until its salty taste was gone.

"I'm here to tell you, boys, that's good eating," he said as he broke wind. Fortunately we were outside. Using the butt of my rifle, I pulled myself up. I was stiff all over from running such a great distance that day. I looked around. "George, I'm concerned about Sam. He told me he was coming over this evening. I know I gave him good directions."

"Don't go getting yourself upset just yet. Being an officer, Sam more than likely had to fill out and file battle and casualty reports from today's fight. Sam's tough; he'll be along shortly."

"I'm gonna try to find him. I'll be back as soon as I can."

At the headquarters of the 49th, I met with Colonel Smith. He was sitting in his tent writing a battle report of today's action.

"May I see you for a minute, sir?"

"Please come in."

"Sir, Lieutenant Samuel Hill of K company is my brother and I haven't heard from him. Could you tell me, is he missing?"

"It's too early to tell. He may just be late returning. There's a lot of men sill out there. Maybe he's been wounded. You can inquire at the field hospital, about a mile down the road."

"Thank you kindly, sir, I'll check with them."

Our field hospital tents housed more than two hundred sick and wounded. At each tent, I received the same answer: "No one by that name here."

To be sure, I lit a candle, went inside, and called out his name. Shattered and bandaged forms moaned and cried out. The candlelight flickered in the faces of the dead and dying. I could tell at a glance if a person was dead, because his eyes didn't blink at the light.

"Sam, are you in here?" I called out again and again. I began to wonder if I was overreacting. Sam was probably at camp looking for me.

I was just about to end my search, when an

orderly's voice answered me. "If you mean Lieutenant Hill," he said, "he's in the last bunk in the back of this-here tent."

I rushed in, fearing the worst. The smell of chloroform nearly gagged me. The buzzing of flies pervaded the entire tent, and the nauseating odor of body after body of the dead, dying, and badly wounded assaulted my nostrils.

I held the candle out in front of me. Abruptly, I stopped in my tracks. There was Sam, as white as a piece of marble. His body had swollen to twice its size, and although I was barely able to recognize him, I knew I had found my brother; then I saw his boots. Papa had given them to him two Christmases before. On Christmas Eve, I wanted the boots to look especially good, so I polished them before Sam ever saw them. They were still on my brother's feet.

When I put the flame near Sam's eyes, he didn't blink. I dropped to my knees and cried, "Why, Sam, God, why?"

I wanted Sam's boots to take home with me, but Sam's feet were so swollen, the only way to get them would have been to cut them off. Better he should be buried with his boots on, I thought. I stayed riveted to the ground, next to where my brother had died, overwhelmed with grief.

From across the room, I heard someone call out to me. I wiped my eyes and turned to see who called.

"Over here, Corporal."

I turned in his direction.

He paused for a moment, a look of bewilderment on his face. "I don't rightly recognize you. Did you know Sam?"

"Yes, he's my brother."

"I'm Cabell, Lieutenant Robert Cabell. I was with Sam today."

"Can you tell me how he died? Our family will want to know."

"I'll tell you as best as I can recollect." His gaze grew distant as the memories came back. "This morning we were making our way through a trackless forest, among the brush, bramble, and swamps, encountering the enemy at most every step. After a mile or so, we cleared the woods and entered onto an open field. We crossed the field without receiving any fire and entered the next body of timber.

"The Fourth North Carolina was on our right and the Twenty-seventh and Twenty-eighth Georgia boys were on our left. Because we hadn't drawn any fire in the open field, we weren't sure the Yanks were nearby, but all at once, from the tree line, they opened up on us with an enormous amount of rifle fire. General Garland's brigade was cut to pieces, but the Forty-ninth continued to charge.

"Men were falling fast from the rifle fire of an unseen foe. Several fell in the timber as we passed through, but Sam's company gallantly continued on, all the way to the enemy's rifle pits.

"Never before have I seen men behave more bravely. We were under heavy fire from our right flank and also from the rear, by our own boys trying to shoot over and around us. We screamed to the fellows behind, and told them to hold their fire.

"In the meantime, through the smoke and the haze, the boys from Georgia had lost their sense of direction and cut right across the front of us, causing us to have to hold our fire. We soon entered the open field. The Georgians, recognizing their error, fell back; leaving Sam's company entirely exposed. By that time we had been in battle for some three and a half-hours. We were running out of ammunition, having used up more than sixty rounds a man. The Colonel informed us that we could not be supplied additional ammunition; we would have to fall back to the ordnance wagon for replenishment.

"I ordered my company back, Sam said his men would stay and hold the line until we returned. At the wagons, we filled our cartridge pouch and pockets and moved back to the battle line, but Sam was nowhere to be found. I didn't know if he had been killed or wounded. Later I learned Sam had been shot and taken to the rear. A few minutes after that I took a bullet in my arm and leg and had to be carried from the battlefield myself.

"We were cut down to a mere handful. Of the seven officers shot, during the battle, only one was killed, your brother Sam. Colonel Smith said it as well as anyone could. He said, 'I have no language of praise enough to bestow on Lieutenant Sam Hill.' "

"Thank you kindly, Lieutenant Cabell I'm grateful to you for telling me about Sam's death."

The events of the day had taken their toll. I could go no farther. I fell into a heavy slumber and spent the night beside Sam.

I arose before daybreak to dig Sam a grave under the shade of an old oak tree. As I dug, I clearly remembered our last conversation. "Take care of your self tomorrow, Sam."

"Yeah, I know. Everybody shoots at the officers."

There was no minister to conduct a service, and no family members present, except for me. My grief was so great that I wept. When I regained my composure, I said a prayer. "God, I know Sam is in a better place now, and he's not suffering anymore. I don't understand why you felt it necessary to take him, but I'm sure you had a reason I'll understand someday. As for me, I'll try to continue to lead a Christian life and serve you. Amen."

With my pocketknife, I carved Sam's name on a piece of wood. I unfastened my diary and wrote:

May 31, 1862, in the prime of his life, Samuel Hill was killed today at the battle of seven pines.

I cried until no more tears would come.

Dawn appeared. I returned to my unit, a gnawing feeling in my gut. George couldn't get a fire going; the rain had saturated the wood, so we ate some odds and ends collected from the battlefield.

Gradually the fog lifted, giving a clear view of the battlefield. Still numb from burying my brother, I stood in disbelief and shock at what I was seeing. Hundreds of corpses of dead men and horses littered the ground. I closed my eyes and stood there in silence.

෩෪

Later that afternoon we were told General Johnston was severely wounded in battle the day before and General Robert E. Lee had been named to replace him. General Lee's orders were simple: "Maintain your position and hold your ground at all costs. You are to succeed in defending Richmond or perish in the attempt. To lose Richmond is to lose Virginia"

We desperately needed ammunition and replacements. I hoped our officers were telling that to General Lee.

The rains created new lakes that worked in our favor. The Yankees, strengthened with reinforcements, regrouped and were attempting to organize a charge on their own trenches, which we now occupied. They had bogged down temporarily. Some waded waist-deep in water; a few of their artillery pieces had slid out of sight under the water. Their cannons couldn't be moved into position.

In the distance, I saw teams of unhitched horses barely moving around. In some cases, wagons were buried in the mud up to the axles and had to be left behind. Still, the Yanks refused to stop advancing. We were determined to hold our position, and did so with a tenacious defense. I placed a double load in my gun. I had fired so often the red-hot barrel had bent out of shape. The Ramrod got stuck in the barrel.

George watched me as I attempted to remove the ramrod. He hollered, "if you fire again your gun will bust!"

Well I did. The gun went in one direction and I went in the other. Just across the field a Yankee raised his head and shouted, "where'd ya get that cannon?"

For six hours, the enemy bombarded us with everything it had. Our ammunition was close to being exhausted. The fate of Richmond and possibly the

Confederacy hung in the balance. We knew we were expected to hold as long as we had bayonets and stones to hurl at them.

The church bells in Richmond began to ring loud and clear, as if God were sending us a message. We were more determined then ever that Richmond would not fall. We dragged rails, logs, tree roots, bushes, and anything else we could find, to help fortify our defense. In an intense hail of musket fire bullets ricocheted off the trees and rails as the boys in blue drew nearer. I heard a bullet strike a soldier to my right. I glanced in that direction and saw Bullet lying face down on the ground. I reached out to help him, but a shower of mini balls sent me scurrying for cover. With great difficulty, I was able to drag Bullet out of range. The mini ball had grazed his scalp. I felt certain he would be okay. Before long, he came around, threw his arms around me, and wept for joy.

I had to leave, because we needed every man we could muster at the trenches. I told Bullet I would be back as soon as possible.

We had just been given the order to go onto the field and retrieve the cartridge boxes from the dead, when our wagons loaded with supplies and reinforcement arrived. With additional troops, and a supply of ammunition we were able to turn the Yanks back.

For now Richmond was saved, but we were too exhausted to shout or cheer. The reverberations of cannons ceased, as darkness brought the action to a close. It was a crushing defeat for the enemy.

That evening, casualties had to be tended to.

The local citizens turned out to help us bandage the bleeding soldiers and carry them back to the wagons for transportation to Richmond. Hospitals were filled to capacity, resulting in almost every home in the city becoming a private hospital and every woman, a nurse. Hundreds died simply because their wounds went unattended. We had also taken many prisoners that had to be treated. Caring for their wounds was one thing, but feeding them from the city's dwindling food supply added to the anxiety of the town people; however, they never complained.

That night was another cold and rainy one as I returned to a mud-soaked trench. I shuddered, pulling my shirt tight around my neck. I sat with my gaze fixed on the battlefield, numb to all feelings. I thought about how to write and tell Mama. Paul was wounded and captured; Marcellus was wounded, and Sam was killed.

From the depths of my soul, I prayed, "Lord have mercy!"

Would morning ever come?

The Battle of Gaines' Mill

✦

$\mathcal{W}$e had repelled the Union forces in a furious fight at Seven Pines, but the enemy's tenacity caused us to maintain a state of readiness by developing a formidable line of earthworks. Richmond was only a stone's throw away, so we could fall back no farther. The dense forest, muddy roads, and approaching nighttime prevented the Yanks from attacking. We rested as best we could, fatigued, and weary in our mud-soaked bivouac area, knowing the possibility of a battle still existed.

After a night of driving rain, we began the morning by scooping out the muddy wallows from our trenches.

Word came down that the Yankees had abandoned their position. A loud cheer followed the announcement. We were to be given a much-needed breather while waiting for reinforcements.

George wiped the perspiration from his forehead and grumbled, "More than likely we'll get a dozen or so boys. Sending a handful of green men into battle is like dropping a cat, clutching a raw steak, into a barrel of bulldogs."

That night, the rains abated, and we built a blazing fire to dry our clothing and blankets, which were scattered about.

Wood was in great demand and hard to come by, but George was persistent in gathering twigs, pine cones, and leaves. He lit the fire and fanned it with his hat. It soon blazed up, and he cooked some beef, onions, and mushrooms he had gathered from the haversacks of dead soldiers on the battlefield.

After the last biscuit was gone and the frying pan wiped clean of bacon grease, I poured myself one last cup of coffee. I packed my pipe with tobacco, pulled a red hot branch from the edge of the fire, touched it to the bowl, and took a deep draw. The blue smoke rose in wreaths and curls from my mouth as I stared into the flickering flame of our campfire.

I shouted to several to come join us for an evening songfest. Ed Drawdy, who played a fiddle, was always eager to join in. Soon Earl Reith showed up with his banjo. The music brought Bill Snell to his feet, and he danced a jig as well as any one I had ever witnessed. Others joined in, and before long, I suspect half the regiment showed up.

Old Bobby Lee once said, "I don't believe we can have an army without music."

What started out with just a few at our campfire turned into a powerful group. We went from singing "Home Sweet Home" and "Rock Of

Ages" to "Amazing Grace," followed by "Sweet Hour Of Prayer." We were having ourselves a sure enough revival, like a spiritual renewal. Reverend Starnes arrived, and silence quickly prevailed as he led us in a closing prayer. One by one, men slipped away to their blankets.

※※

Toward the last of July, we were back to full strength and eager to return to the brigade. Colonel Strange told us to prepare rations for three days. Our mess group didn't have three days of food left. If we had, George would have eaten it all at one time. He never worried about tomorrow. In fact the one Bible verse George quoted often was, "Eat, drink, and be merry, for tomorrow you may die." I used to tell him that not only had he overused it, he also had taken it out of context.

That evening, the quartermaster issued us a small amount of corn meal, some meat, a few potatoes, and some Louisiana chicory coffee. We built a fire that served two purposes, to cook our meal, and to cause smoke, to keep the mosquitoes at bay.

Bullet, having fully recovered from his head wound, had returned to camp. He and Buzzard went in search of fire wood. I made a slosh that consisted of salt, water, and corn meal. I formed a thick paste, rolled it up into small balls, slid them onto my bayonet, and laid them over the open fire. The blackened balls soon became as hard as rocks and made a clanking noise as I guided them onto a tin plate. I boiled some water and added potatoes and meat in an attempt to make a stew. I couldn't cotton to the coffee. It turned out so strong I spit it out on the campfire, which caused a blaze to rise up. I reckon a person has to develop a taste for chicory. You could stand a spoon up in the middle of the coffee, and it wouldn't fall over.

I could tell George had something on his mind, because he was unusually quiet that evening. Finally, he could contain himself no longer. He turned in my direction, spit across the room, and blurted out his thoughts.

"I'm going to tell you one thing I plan to do when I get home. I'm gonna grow wheat, 'cause I never intend to eat cornbread again. And another thing, that meat we had for dinner was mule meat."

"Are you sure about that?"

"Sure as shootin'. I found a mule shoe in the bottom of the kettle," he answered. He walked across the room and reached in the pot with a long handle spoon in an attempt to stir up another one from the bottom.

"No wonder it was bad," I said.

"It's about as bad as gray grits, but I ate it, 'cause I was hungry. Reckon I've had about all I can take of this here army life," he said, as he walked out the door slamming it behind him.

"George sounds a little upset to me," said Bullet, returning with an arm load of firewood.

"He'll get over it," I replied.

I found some writing paper George had confiscated from a knapsack left during a Yank's hasty departure. I sat down next to a large boulder to support my back and wrote a letter to Mama. The stars were bright that evening, and I found myself drifting into space. Staring directly at the heavenly bodies that illuminated the night, I got caught up in the tranquilly of the moment, and I wondered if back home they could see the same stars. Maybe, at that very moment, Mama and Papa were sitting in the swing on our front porch looking at the same star I was looking at. The possibility made me feel close to them.

I thought about my sister, Althea. I could always talk to her, if I had a problem. I thought of Paul and Marcellus and prayed they both would soon be going home. I was still haunted over the death of Sam and wondered how well Mama took the news. I wished I could have been with her to help ease her pain, when she received my letter telling her about Sam's death. God, how I missed everyone.

Morning came. A thick fog from the Chickohominy River covered the ground like a blanket. I packed my gear in the pre dawn light.

Shortly after sunrise, we broke camp and moved northward. Wearily, we shuffled over hilly terrain covered in dense, gloomy forest. The area was sparsely settled with a few small farms. The corn and wheat normally found in the fields had long been laid to waste from the invasion of both armies. We desperately needed rations; we had nothing to eat except for what we could plunder from an occasional turnip patch here, or an onion patch there. By noon, my canteen was empty. Given a brief pause, several of us dashed down to a nearby tiny brook to grab a quick mouthful of cold mountain water and refill our canteens.

We regrouped in a matter of minutes and silently resumed our march; each man deep in his own thoughts as we dragged our feet along the winding road. I could hear the rumbling artillery fire growing louder with each advancing step and was aware of the impending battle looming in the distance. My stomach began to churn.

As we approached the Chickohominy River, I noticed its swollen banks from the recent rains. Our column was ordered to stand at rest until our engineers could determine if it was safe to cross. Just beyond us, amid the smoldering ruins, were the remains of a plantation. There among the large oak trees, facing the river, were majestic columns and steps going up to nothingness. How beautiful it must have been. Several huge trees had been split in half by cannon fire; others were riddled with bullet holes. Large limbs had broken away and fallen to the ground. A fire had destroyed most of the roof, and the entire front wall had been blown away. Mini balls lodged in the remaining brick walls and crumbling chimneys. Windows had been shattered, and several shutters were missing. The once-beautiful home lay in ruins, deserted and forsaken in knee-deep grass among clusters of yellow and blue wild flax. I recall Papa making rope from the fibrous stem of flax, although hemp had long since replaced it in popularity. I recall Professor Palmer telling us flax was man's oldest crop. Egyptians used it more that four thousand years ago to wrap mummies. The Romans called it linum, meaning linen. Women spun and wove it into linen fabrics and laces.

A lean boy with sandy hair in a faded butternut uniform approached. His face was pale in color. As he passed by me I asked, "Do you know who lived here?"

He answered in a dispassionate voice wiping his nose on the back of his hand. "Reckon I do, this was my home. My name is Joseph."

"Mine is Daniel." I accompanied him through the rusty iron gates, down a brick path bordered with purple and rose geraniums, to the back of the house. He paused to point upstairs. "I was born in that corner room on the second floor. My brothers and I used to hunt in the nearby woods. This is the first time I've seen our home since we left."

We continued down the path through what had been the garden, covered with running blue-violet myrtle. We came to a stately magnolia tree in full blossom. Abruptly he halted, removed his hat, and stared down among the lilacs at his mother's grave. He didn't speak a word.

It seemed a pity. The perfume of the earth surrounded her grave as double rows of daffodils formed a border. It was so peaceful, one could not imagine a battle had just recently been fought here.

We returned to our ranks and noticed the general and his staff of engineers were frantically reviewing maps and charts, trying to determine the depth of the river and the safest place to cross. Joseph walked over and unhitched a horse from a caisson, jumped on it bareback, and rode out into the middle of the river, where the rushing water came up just below his horse's knees. He yelled, "If you aim to cross it, it's about this deep, General."

Captain Howe turned in his stirrups and hollered to the wagon drivers, "Follow me." The lead driver removed his whip from its place in the socket beside the brake and popped the backs of his mules, fording the river among the buzzing of dragonflies and a host of birds that filled the air with fluttering wings. Our artillery, supply wagons, ambulances, blacksmith shops, horses, mules, cattle, and anything else we would need to sustain us in a battle, followed.

I heard a loud commotion followed by a string of profanity, and turned in time to see a mule driver floundering about in two feet of water. It was obvious he couldn't swim. At first I thought he was a goner. The captain guided his horse into the water, spurred him lightly, splashed through the river to the man's side, and fished him out safely. The man coughed and spit up half the river. He looked up at the captain and said, "I don't rightly believe in immersion, I ain't no Baptist, but thank you kindly."

At the top of the rise, the wagons stopped to rest the horses. We hesitated only long enough for the brigade to complete its crossing after which we continued on, creaking along the winding river road amid the dogwoods.

❧

West of Trotopotomoy, we passed over the Central Railroad and came across an advance post of Yankee cavalrymen that fled on our approach. Late that afternoon, we reached a creek and found the bridge in flames. A regiment of the enemy blocked the road on the opposite side. The 18th gallantly crossed over and engaged the Yanks. A light artillery piece was brought forth and after a few rounds, dispersed the enemy. The bridge was rebuilt by our engineers. We crossed, continuing on the road to Pale Green Church at Hundleys corner. There we bivouacked for the night. A furious cannonade in the direction of Mechanicsville indicated a severe battle was going on. That evening we slept under the stars, without the benefit of a fire or tent.

Before dawn the next morning, we were on the march, our regiment in the lead. We reached Gaines' Mill about mid afternoon, and were promptly led to the right in the direction of heavy musket fire. Passing through the woods, we reached a large, open, undulating field with heavy timber on all sides. We formed a line of battle. The enemy fire became so heavy with grape and shell that we halted and were ordered to lie down. We remained there for more than one hour, while skirmishers were sent forward.

By noon, our artillery was in place. The roar of the big guns sounded, shelling their position. The federal batteries replied. Late in the afternoon, the engagement became extensive, and Colonel Hunton gave us the order to charge. We drove the Yanks from their trenches at Beaver Dam. Unopposed, we forded the river and captured a battery of well-preserved Parrot guns in good working order.

We then encountered the enemy, dug in and fortified, in a row of defense: first, from deep ditches; second, from a barricade upon the top of the hill. Our color bearers moved into position and unfurled the battle flag as we stood in a double-ranked formation and steeled ourselves for the upcoming ordeal. The hill in front of us was sloped and flanked with ravines infiltrated by infantry protected by the crest and ridges.

The command came, "Forward," followed by the sound of the bugle. Because of the impenetrable thickness, we had to claw our way through the tangled ravines ascending the bluff on our hands and knees to reach the enemy. The Yanks stubbornly resisted our charge. The fighting intensified.

Our flag bearer was killed instantly. A soldier threw away his musket, and raised our fallen flag; he led a splendid charge with shouts of victory, as he scrambled up the bullet-swept hill.

Although a gallant effort, our first charge was futile. The Yanks received re-enforcement, and the whole Federal line attacked with vigor. Men abandoned the field in every direction. Two regiments from Louisiana actually marched back from the fire, skulking in shame.

George shouted to no one in particular, "Backsliders, you been telling us about what a sweet place heaven is, and now that you got a chance to go there in a few minutes, you're running away from it. Go on and leave. We need us a little wiggle-room, anyway."

I turned and shouted, "George, quit running behind me. Your stepping on my heals."

"Sorry I was watching those fellows marching down the hill."

"Well you run like an old cow."

The captain ordered us to go over or through the Yanks, which we did. The Texans came up and joined us on the left of our line. Georgia, Mississippi, Alabama, and North Carolina advanced with the line and charged the ravine, yelling like people gone mad. Near the crest, another regiment of Yankees, supported by well-served batteries and a heavy force of infantry, lay in wait with full view of our movements. Concealed and protected by the ravine the boys in blue poured a destructive fire on us. We suffered severely and gained nothing in our attempt to scale the bluff. It was unlike anything I had ever seen in my life. Scores of men were wounded or killed.

The momentum of the battle soon changed when "Stonewall's" brigade arrived and entered the thickest of the fight. I had heard many stories about him. A soldier in his First Brigade once told me, it had taken forty years for Moses to lead his people through the wilderness but if "ole Jack" had been there, he would have double-quicked them, and made it in three days. I felt a shiver run through my body. That was my first encounter with the general. Some say his feats had elevated him to mythical proportions, because he feared no enemy, was stubborn, hard-hitting, and made of pure iron. He wore a faded uniform and a dingy military cap. A rusty sabre hung by his side. He was a master of the attack and sat astride his horse like a ramrod ready for action. Apparently not fearing for his life, he remained in plain view, refusing to dodge bullets. He once was quoted as saying he had confidence in God, not man.

"Now listen up, men," he said. "When I give the word, we'll charge the rest of the way up the hill. I want each and every one of you to yell like the devil, run a dozen paces, drop down on your knee and shoot. Then load, get up and do the same thing over again. Now charge, men!" He yelled harshly. Enthusiasm replaced fear, and with a loud, bloodcurdling rebel yell, we responded in a second assault on the bluffs, releasing a volley of fire with such destructive effect, it caused the Yanks to break and flee from their stronghold, leaving many dead on the field. We were relieved shortly before dark and ordered to return to our bivouac area for the night.

Exhausted, several lay on the ground and fell asleep with their weapons in their arms; others assembled in the open air, on an intimation that Reverend Starnes would be preaching.

The Reverend said he never found soldiers too weary to assemble in large numbers at an evening prayer meeting. We sat through the services with the deepest interest, notwithstanding the fact that a drenching rain was falling at the time. We gave thanks that our lives had been spared, and offered prayers for our fallen comrades. After services Reverend Starnes said, "Daniel, I just preached to one of the most solemnly attentive congregations it was ever my fortune to address."

"Reverend, each man knew that may have been their last message of salvation. It appears we'll be in another battle tomorrow.

Before dawn reveille sounded. We were informed the Yankees had made it safely across White Oak swamp, destroying the bridge behind them. They had assembled at Frayser's Farm, south of the Charles City Road. We would have to find another place to ford the river in our attempt to stop them from attacking Richmond. At Willis Church, on the Quaker road, we caught up with them. The bloody encounter of Frayser's Farm began.

Jackson's column appeared at the northern end of the destroyed bridge and opened fire with heavy batteries. Cheers rent the air. Jackson desisted from making a further attack, but he continued to support us with his artillery, keeping the Yanks pinned down.

We had formed a line of battle along a fence bordering a cornfield. Colonel Hunton ordered us to advance across open ground where we encountered heavy fire. We rushed forward, but found the Yanks toughly entrenched behind broad belts of fallen trees and wide swampy grounds. We took a heavy toll before falling back to the woods.

Word reached us General Lee, in command of a division, was advancing along the New Market road toward the Charles City Court House. We renewed the conflict, charging forward through fallen timber and tangled underbrush, causing their skirmishers to fall back to a place called Turkey Run.

Meanwhile, Colonel Hunton had relinquished his command back to Colonel Strange, who had recovered well enough from the wounds he had received. He was in conversation with a group of officers when a solider, about my age, wounded in the hand and arm, approached him looking for a surgeon to care for his wounds. A surgeon came forward accompanied by a gentleman in civilian dress who inquired about news of the battle.

"Our regiment was cut to pieces, and we can't hold out much longer without help," the soldier said.

A Lieutenant cut in. "He's a beardless youth and excited I wouldn't pay him much attention."

Looking the officer directly in the eye the soldier replied, "Sir, you would be excited, too, if you had been over where I was."

A colonel tapped the boy on the shoulder, told him to hush, and informed him he was addressing President Davis.

I watched as the lad declined to let others hold his arm while the surgeon removed the bullet. "You're a better soldier than they thought," the surgeon told him.

The young soldier reasserted that without re-enforcements, they would all be killed or be repulsed. There were troops in the rear, and President Davis advised his staff of his desire to rally these troops and lead them into the fight himself. A presidential advisor convinced Davis to allow a member of his staff to lead the charge. Having agreed, the men rallied and charged bravely across an open field in time to save the rest of the regiment. Colonel Strange ordered us to advance. We captured a battery and requested permission to turn the guns on the retreating enemy. We were denied, because we didn't know the exact position of our own troops. Right before dark, when all companies were accounted for, permission was granted. Our boys fired continuously until nightfall, when our bugler sounded recall. When darkness came, the Yanks, took a line of retreat back to the James River, where they received aid from Union gunboats. The conflict came to a close. Richmond had been relieved from siege.

The following day, we were ordered back to Richmond for a rest. George was overjoyed at the thought of spending time in Richmond.

༺ঌৎ༻

On July 10,1862, at a camp near Richmond, I sat down under a large oak tree and wrote a letter to Mama.

Dear Mama, I take the present opportunity of writing you a few lines this evening to let you know I am yet alive but am worn out. Have been marching for thrice weeks in two hard fights and living on fat meat and crackers and that boiled on the coals. I am completely burnt out poorer than I ever was in my life. I would give anything for a few weeks furlough, though we have driven the Yankees out of the hearing of Richmond 35 miles by land, 70 by water. I do not know how it was that I was not shot, for the bombs would bust and cover me up with dirt. Our 3rd Brigade charged a battery of eight guns, and they just poured the grape and canister shot into us. I suppose it was by the hand of God. I would give you a list of killed and wounded, but I know you heard all about it before now. Mama, you must make me a pair of pants and send me as soon as you can, for mine is nearly worn out, and I have not got a cent of money, not even to pay postage. Tell Papa by the first chance Rev. Williams might come down to bring me something to eat. It would not cost much. I have given you all the news I have, and I will close. Give my love to girls and to Stephen and Richard also, and accept a full portion yourself. I still remain your affectionate son.

D. C. Knight

I saw Capt. Whitehead not long since--he said Paul was well and that Marcellus's horse give out somewhere near Charlottesville and that he had gone home. No such luck as that for me.

Camp Near Richmond, July the

Dear Ma, Ma,

    I take the present opportunity of
writing you a few lines this evening to
let you know I am yet alive but am wore
I have been marching for three weeks un two
[   ] fights and living on fat meat and [   ]
[   ] that broiled on the coals I am completely bro
[   ] spirited than I ever was in my life I would
[   ] any thing for a few weeks furlough though
we have driven the Yankees out of the hearing of
Richmond 35 miles by land 10 by water I do [   ]
[   ] it was that I was not shot for the bombs [   ]
[   ] and cover me up with dirt over the 63ed
[   ] gade charged a battery of eight guns and they just
[   ] the grape and canister shot into us I sup
[   ] the hand of god I would give you a list [   ]
[   ] and wounded but know you heard all about
[   ] be fore now M Ma you must me a pair of [   ]
[   ] send me as soon as you can for mine is near
[   ] out and I have not got a cent of money
[   ] even to pay postage tell [   ] some by [   ]
[   ] chance Br William might come down an
[   ] me some thing to eat it would not [   ]
[   ] I believe I have given you all [   ]
[   ] I will close give my love to girls
[   ] to pea to Stephen and accept a full [   ]
your self I will remain your affectionate son
and Richard also
            Dr E [   ]

ORIGINAL LETTER FROM DANIEL.
SEE PAGES 149 AND 150

The Second Manassas

❦

O n August 22nd, one year to the day since I enlisted, we were given the familiar order, prepare three day's provisions, and make ready to march. I sat down and wrote a letter to Mama. I closed by saying:

I must hurry to pack my haversack, as we will be marching soon, I know not where. I will write as soon as I can, your loving son, Daniel.

We boarded a train heading northwest to reinforce General Jackson, who was engaged with the Yankees at Gordonsville. On arrival we moved across the tracks to a creek and took up a position in a ravine. From here we engaged in a splattering of musketry fire. Finally we were successful in driving the enemy back across the field, to the edge of the woods. Because of the reinforcements, I suppose the Yanks decided to think twice about committing to a larger engagement. That evening, we camped near Bowlers Mill.

After three days, we departed Gordonsville and

marched strenuously for four days, before reaching the Rappahannock River. There we stopped to rest and replenish our supplies before heading north along the western slope of Carter's Mountain. On we walked through Thoroughfare Gap to Bristow station, where we came under intense fire. Not being able to see friend or foe through the pines, we were ordered to lie down while Colonel Strange sought a view of the enemy. Returning, he ordered us to proceed through the woods towards Sudley Church.

Emerging from the woods into the open field, the regiment came under heavy attack. We advanced firmly, under the enemy's fire, and not until we began firing did the Yanks retreat to the hills. We continued to pursue them, across a meadow, following their tracks toward Manassas. With night approaching, the bugler recalled us.

The next morning, a blanket of fog covered the ground. We marched across a stone bridge below Lewis' Ford until we reached the rail tracks. From here we followed them south to Manassas Junction.

Our regiment, along with the 18th, was ordered to secure the depot. We were victorious in our efforts and successfully captured a Yankee train loaded with provisions and supplies. A fierce battle broke out. A brigade of Yankee infantry charged our position, attempting to recapture the supplies. A detachment of Jackson's Black Horse Cavalry led by the General himself charged forward and the Yanks rapidly retreated.

Our supply wagons arrived, and after loading what supplies they could hold, we set fire to the train.

We hadn't eaten for several days, except for a few ears of corn taken from the fields near the road. The vast supply of captured food was rapidly gathered up, and divided among us.

Jackson soon returned and ordered his artillery to commence firing at the advancing Yanks. A courier rode up and informed Jackson the general's cannons were wet with rain and could not be used. "General Branch would like to know what he should do if attacked, Sir."

"You tell the general that the rain is falling just as hard on the enemy. If they attack us and our guns cannot be discharged, then use your bayonets. Hold your position."

The battle carried us to Plains, a village on the Manassas Railroad. That evening we spent the night near Salem. The next day, Lee's army arrived and joined up with Jackson's corps. At that point, we were in a position to attack the Federal armies with full force.

Approaching the open fields of Manassas, we heard the sounds of a heavy battle. A Yankee regiment rapidly moved up against our right flank. Fighting became so severe Colonel Strange called up reinforcements. The battle raged fiercely, it seemed impossible to hold our ground much longer. I had serious doubts any of us would survive. I was out of ammunition, but stood ready to defend my ground with only my bayonet to afford me protection.

Captain Duncan's six-gun battery came dashing up at a full gallop. He wheeled his company into position and directed them to open fire against the enemy. The enemy line faltered for an instant, started again, and then as Shoop's artillery pounded into them a broadside, the Yanks broke ranks and ran.

A young soldier from Georgia rushed up to me with his two middle fingers shattered. "Could you use your bayonet, please, to cut off these fingers? The boys are going into another battle directly, and I want to be with them."

I stared in disbelief. "I can't do that!"

"I don't care a darn for those fingers, they warn't of no account, no how. But the fingers on my right hand are a different story. They're good 'uns, and I hate to lose 'em, especially my trigger finger."

I directed him to the rear, where he might find a surgeon. Shortly thereafter, I saw him running past me to rejoin his company.

We sprung from the woods, sweeping down upon them, driving them back until darkness brought our action to a close. Our losses were heavy, but at least for now the battle was over.

That evening, we camped near the edge of the woods. Bullet was nowhere about. George and I grew worried and set out to find him.

"Don't worry," George said. "He survived a head wound at Seven Pines, and he'll survive this. I bet he's out and about looking for supplies."

We didn't have to go very far before finding Bullet, lying in a spreading pool of blood, holding his chest. Blood oozed between his fingers. Still conscious, he looked up and smiled. "Couldn't outrun this one," he said.

I tried to remove his hand and apply pressure to stop the bleeding. The shot had blown a gaping hole in his chest.

"Let's get him back to a doctor," George said.

"No don't move me. I reckon my hours on earth are about to run out. Tell my parents I died happy." Bullet's eyes sparkled as he spoke his final words; "Jesus is with me now." Bullet went limp; breath had found its way out.

George and I both had to fight to hold back our tears. George clenched his fist and cursed the Yankees.

When Bullet died that day I truly believe he was not alone.

With our bayonets, George and I dug Bullet a shallow grave on the battlefield of Manassas.

That evening, George was somber as he fried some meat. Mini balls from sharpshooters whistled around us. One struck our fire and threw ashes in the frying pan. George simply moved to the other side of the fire and continued his cooking.

"Plague on those ignoramus," he said. "I expect they'll spoil all my grease, before they stop their madness."

The service that evening was especially impressive, one that I shall never forget. It was a beautiful Sabbath eve, but a fierce artillery duel was going on somewhere in the distance. A shell occasionally burst near us, but the service continued. As we sang the last stanza of "Amazing Grace," a huge shell fell in the very center of the congregation, burying itself into the ground. Fortunately, it failed to explode. Of course, some commotion broke out but quiet soon returned and the preacher finished the service.

At dawn, the Yankees, having been routed

from their position, began to fall back. We pursued them across Mitchell's Ford, up Bull Run, and past Sudley Church. They were heading for Centreville, where we had spent the winter of '62, digging a strong entrenchment of breastwork surrounding the city.

George looked over at me and hollered, "Now I'm really upset. Those Yanks are using the trenches and houses we built. I don't recall offering them my shelter. I'm gonna make 'em pay for this. It's enough to make a preacher cuss."

I remembered that when we first arrived at Centreville George had grumbled. "We need to be fighting. I didn't join this army to dig." Now we were on the way back to Centreville—months later, after much more digging and a great deal of fighting.

As we approached the rampart, I felt a tug on my right pants leg, followed by a thud. Feeling a warm sensation in my foot I paused for a moment. I glanced down and saw that a mini ball had passed through my pants leaving a perfectly rounded hole. Blood trickled down my leg and saturated my pants. My Lord, I thought, I've been hit. I continued forward, expecting at any moment to be killed. Another bullet tore at my foot, flinging me to the ground. I felt a sharp, stinging pain, unlike any I had experienced before. I struggled awkwardly to get up. The air was heavy with the odor of smoke, sweat and blood. Breathing hard, feeling light-headed and dizzy from the loss of blood, I could go no further.

Our color bearer waved our flag in defiance of the enemy fire. "Rally to the flag, boys," he shouted. A rush of perspiration and pain came over me; I fought it off.

Although exhausted, I managed to draw strength from God. I rose, pushed myself on, and engaged the enemy, reloading and firing, until at last I was out of ammunition. I paused only long enough to fix my bayonet, then moved forward once again.

I reached the trenches, crawled over the top, landed on my left foot, and fought like a person possessed. A Yankee officer attempted to engage me with his sword. With the butt of my rifle, I was able to knock him down. I was engaged in a life-and-death struggle, breathing hard and feeling light-headed and dizzy from the loss of blood.

The Yanks, convinced they were surrounded and outnumbered, became disorganized. We soon routed them from their trenches; they broke ranks and ran in a full retreat. Some of our boys kept on chasing them, continuing to fire as they withdrew. I could go no farther. I collapsed on the battlefield.

George turned and saw I was down. Without hesitating he returned to my side, using my musket for support, I struggled to get up. "Are you hurt?" he asked.

"I don't think so, but I'm as scared as I've ever been. I think this was the worst battle of the war for me."

"There's blood, a lot of it, on your britches leg."

"Guess l got nicked, but I'll be okay."

"You sure?"

"I'm sure." I could tell George was uneasy with my answer. I was not sure who was worried the most, George, or me.

Nervously George blurted out, "Look at this

fine cigar I found on a dead Yankee officer. I plan to save it for a special occasion."

The blood loss began taking its toll; I felt profoundly exhausted, confused, and disoriented. An intense stabbing pain shot through my leg; cold perspiration formed on my forehead. I tried to keep as calm as possible, but a rush of dizziness caused me to lose my footing. The ground rushed up to meet me; I must have passed out.

When I opened my eyes, a distinguished gentleman with salt-and-pepper hair was examining me. His white, bloodstained coat told me he was a surgeon, and I must have been in a field hospital. Seeing that I was still confused, he touched my hand and smiled, as if to say I was going to be okay.

"How long have I been here, Doctor . . . . ?"

"It's Doctor Madani, and you were brought in about an hour ago. You're a lucky young man. A ball shattered a bone in your foot and at least two other shots passed through your leg. Your wound is an ugly one, but you'll live."

"I want you to promise me before God that you won't take off my leg. Will you promise me that?"

"I can't say for sure, but I won't remove it for now. If infection sets in, though, I'll be forced to amputate."

"When can l go back to my regiment?"

"I'm afraid you won't be returning for a while. You'll have to keep your weight off that foot until it heals properly; otherwise, you'll reopen the wound, and you may indeed lose the foot. I'm sending you home on furlough to recover."

"Home?"

"Yes, I want to give it some time to heal. You'll be able to return in a few weeks."

My emotions soared at the prospect of returning home. To bathe; change clothing; sleep in my own bed and not hear the sound of reveille or taps; sit down at a table with flapjacks, bacon, biscuits, I could barely comprehend all those experiences.

An orderly arrived with a probe and a pan half-filled with bloody water. I gritted my teeth and held on while the doctor dug out the ball without giving me chloroform.

I tried not to concentrate on the sounds of the men around me crying out for help. The smell of the dead and the dying filled the air. The pain and fear of death were more than some could deal with. Doctors amputated legs and arms without the benefit of anesthetic. I was fortunate the surgeon didn't cut off my leg.

The flap on the hospital tent opened and let a ray of light into the dingy room. The brightness quickly drew my attention. "George," I cried out. It was sure good to see him.

The doctor nodded and walked away, to help another soldier.

"I'm over here," I shouted.

"You really gave us all quite a scare," George said as he approached.

"I'll be all right; in fact, I'm going home on furlough. Tell me, how did I get here?"

"I carried you."

I was overwhelmed. I didn't know how to

express myself, other than just to say, thanks.

"Look who's coming."

I turned my head. It was Ossen.

"How did you know l was here?" I asked.

"George sent word. Are you okay? What did the doctor say?"

"I'll be okay, but he's sending me home to recover."

"That's great news. Mama will get you back on your feet in no time."

George was quick to respond. "Well, l think I'm going to get myself shot, so l can go with you."

"You don't want to do that. Instead of wounding you, they might kill you. The difference between dying today or tomorrow isn't much, but we all prefer tomorrow."

"Fiddlesticks," George cut in, "hadn't thought about that but I guess it makes sense." He smiled at me. "I better go and let you get some rest. Good seeing you again, Ossen." With a wave of his hand, George departed.

"Ossen, don't go just yet. Stay with me a little longer."

"Get some rest. I'll be here, if you need me."

"Did you get a chance to see "Stonewall" in action today?"

"Yeah, I saw "Ole Jack." Some say he has the finest, most disciplined army in the Confederacy."

"It sure appears so. I understand he hurled his troops at the Yanks, refusing to be denied a victory today."

"Little brother, why don't you quit talking for

now and try to get some rest."

"You're right, I'm really tired. I think I'll close my eyes for a little while."

The next morning, the sun was already peeking through the trees when I awoke. Ossen had gone, but he left me a note.

Daniel, had to get back. I understand my unit is marching sometime today. Give my love to everyone back home. Your big brother, Ossen.

I had mixed emotions about going home. I wanted to see everybody, but at the same time, I didn't want to leave the men who depended on me. I wasn't offered the choice. Space was limited, and soon my space would be needed for the day's incoming wounded. By noon, my papers had been processed. An orderly applied a fresh bandage, and l was given one crutch to help keep the weight off my foot. I regretted not being able to say good-bye to everyone.

Yankees had destroyed the railroad tracks between Richmond and Manassas, so the army used a supply wagon with wrought-iron wheels to transport many of us to the railroad station in Richmond. The ride was rough. Traveling slowly and laboriously over axle-deep-mud roads, we must have hit every pothole along the way.

In Richmond, the sound of Yankee cannons firing in the distance rattled the windowpanes of nearby buildings. The city was in an uproar; everyone's face held a look of dismay. A scene of frenzied activity had taken hold; panic seized the people. Many thought the Yankees would break through any minute, and they were moving what belongings they could out of town in a futile search for sanctuary from the invaders. Our wagon made its way through the crowded streets at a tedious pace. Women ran from house to house with the latest rumor. "The Yanks are coming! What shall we do?"

Carriages, buggies, ambulances, and a continuous line of wagons with drivers whipping startled mules jammed the narrow streets. In an attempt to flee Richmond, they fought their way over Mayo's Bridge in a mad rush to cross the James River. Numerous vehicles with broken axles sat abandoned along the way.

An older gentleman with a long gray unkempt beard held a Bible over his head and preached to no one in particular. A woman by his side shook a tambourine to a steady beat. "The Lord will pity his people. I shall remove from you the Yankee army, and will drive them into a barren and desolate land." No one stopped to listen. People had only one thought in mind: escape.

Straggling lines of newly arriving troops marched to the tunes of regimental bands and headed east into another day of battle.

A whistle signaling an approaching train drowned out the rumbling noise of wagons. The sound meant the rail south was still open and operating. The train, a tremendous shower of sparks blowing from its smokestack, came to a hissing stop. Soldiers rushed forward to unload cannons and other supplies that had arrived on flatbed cars. Wounded men were unloaded and placed on the ground shoulder-to-shoulder, stretched out in endless rows.

Swarms of flies hovered over their wounds, crawling and buzzing about. Everywhere I looked, I saw blood and dirty bandages. Over the sounds of the train, I heard groans, screams, and curses from pain. The smell of blood and sweat, unwashed bodies, and excrement rose up in waves until I became nauseated.

Civilians shoved and pushed in an attempt to board the overloaded southbound train. All the seats had filled in a matter of minutes. Women held small children on their laps, while older children ran around like wild animals. I managed to maneuver myself onto a flatbed car and prop up my wounded leg. My foot throbbed with pain. I tried to concentrate on the fact that I was going home. I knew the ride would be a long, slow, noisy one, and I wasn't thinking very Christian thoughts at that moment. Instead, I decided if one of those unruly kids tripped over my foot, I was going to shoot him. I pushed the thought aside, but my foot was sure hurting, and the thought of someone kicking it didn't sit well with me. In my struggle to board, I had torn my wounds open. The bandage showed a growing bloodstain.

The train whistle sounded. An official walking down the platform waved a lantern. With long squeaking groans and a soul-shaking jerk the locomotive gathered it's strength as it lunged forward. We passed a column of weather-beaten troops with fife and drum playing a marching tune. The iron horse belched out sparks and puffs of dark, black smoke as it picked up speed. My thoughts returned to those I had left behind. I prayed to God to keep them safe and to help me recover quickly, so I might soon rejoin them. I want to be there with them, to hear the shouts of victory, when this war is finally over.

Lumbering along, we stopped at every small town and railroad crossing to pick up peddlers, carpetbaggers, and women with small children. Slowly pulling into the station, I could see, little hope for the future reflected in their faces. After each stop, barefoot children ran alongside the train until it gathered enough speed to outrun them. Although I felt like an eternity had passed since I had left home, it had been only a year. I felt a growing sense of excitement as we continued southward.

I must have dozed off. A blast from the train's whistle startled me. We were clamoring along somewhere between Richmond and Charlottesville. A Yankee patrol swarmed over the station in front of us. They fired at us; instinctively I reached for my rifle, lying next to me. The engineer opened the throttle, which sent the train thundering forward under a full head of steam, through a volley of enemy rifle fire. We crashed into a barricade of railroad ties and I felt a tremendous jolt, but the cowcatcher managed to plow through, providing our escape. The jarring almost blinded me with pain. I felt sick and shaken. The pulsating ache in my leg became increasingly sharper.

From around the distant bend, I saw the light of an approaching train. Traveling at great speed, it failed to heed our engineer's warning. A loud blast from our whistle and flashing lights failed to slow the train down. With tremendous force, the iron steed passed us and collided with the debris and scattered ties laying across the northbound tracks I could see the engine rock, then overturn and plunge, down an embankment into a ravine spilling passengers and soldiers alike. The boiler exploded, adding fire to the destruction. To return to the scene would have been suicidal. A sickening feeling came over me as we continued on. The wreck happened so quickly I didn't have time to load or fire my rifle. I thought to myself, the Yankees had performed yet another malicious act deliberately aimed at innocent civilians.

⫷⫸

Soon I recognized the countryside, with its pastoral settings. Fertile farmlands and flowing streams stretched out from the great Blue Ridge Mountains. In the distance, a settler struck long furrows with a plow. Black dirt streamed on the restless winds. The farmer paused at the wail of the train whistle to watch us go by.

Waist high tobacco plants had ripened and their golden-green leaves seemed like a page from a book of health as they rustled in the breeze. It was the first week of September and schools would be closed for the harvest and curing of the tobacco leaves.

An occasional farm or white clapboard church with a tall wooden steeple dotted the countryside, and I realized we were passing the fields that Prince and I had romped over many a time.

I thanked God the echoes of war had not yet penetrated here. At last I was home.

A Time To Heal

❧

*P*apa had received my telegram and was waiting at the depot. I spotted him right away, standing very ridged with his hands clasped behind his back. His eyes peered into each car as it passed by, searching to find me. The train slowed and gave out one final hiss sound before coming to a stop.

My father was a statuesque man, more than six feet tall. He was the grandest person I knew. As I grew older, I gained even more respect for him and his wisdom. He always answered my every question and appeared to think before he spoke.

"Papa, Papa, over here," I shouted.

He turned in my direction, and his normally solemn face beamed with a smile when he saw me. After sitting in one position too long I struggled to pull myself up. The pain nearly blinded me. Papa quickly came to help me. We embraced for a long time, which in itself was a rarity, because Papa never showed emotions in public. We gathered my belongings, and with Papa's help, I managed to hobble to our buggy.

"How is everyone?" I asked excitedly.

"Everyone is doing just fine. Ma wanted me to come by myself, so she could stay at home and fix you a decent meal." Papa snapped the reins and shouted, "Giddy-up, Commodore." He turned toward me. "Ma didn't say so, but I think she wanted to give us some time alone. Tell me truthfully, son, how is your leg and foot?"

"They're gonna be okay. I just need to stay off them for a while, so they can heal properly. I should be able to return to my regiment shortly."

"Don't you think you've sacrificed enough?"

"I don't rightly know how I feel. I've been thinking about that a lot. Sometimes I wish I didn't have to go back, but an awful lot of folks are depending on me. I know I wouldn't be able to forgive myself, if I didn't go back."

"I suppose you're right. I'm real proud of you, son."

Papa snapped the reigns once more, turning west on Stagecoach Road. Commodore was soon in a brisk trot.

As we traveled toward home, I recalled memories of when I first left amid the cheers and farewells. I had been proud to become a soldier and defend my country, but that seemed so long ago.

The countryside along the three-mile ride had changed. As we passed each farm, I noticed tobacco plants had disappeared or were greatly reduced, in favor of corn and wheat. In some cases, once-beautiful plantations were in disrepair. "What happened, Papa? I didn't realize the war had produced such an effect this far south."

"Without farm hands, folks had to cut back on the amount of crops they could manage. We had to plant corn and wheat, in place of tobacco, to help feed our armies. Military wagons come by regularly, and we must give a portion of our grain, meat, and other edibles in support of our army. Don't get me wrong, everyone wants to do whatever he can to help, but its hard to break old habits or change old ways of life."

"I'd heard the war touched everyone's life in some way, but I hadn't realized how much."

"I've had to go back and work in the fields myself, to try to save what little I could. Ma and the girls have been right there beside me. Sort of like the old days, except then, I was a lot younger."

I looked in Papa's direction. The forbearance he once possessed was clearly diminishing, and he looked exhausted. For the first time ever, I feared for his health.

"Papa are you well?"

"I'm just fine, Daniel. Indestructible. I may appear to look tired, but you know I always fall asleep in my chair about this time every day."

I could tell his levity was forced, but I thought that was not the time to bring it up. I'd discuss it with Althea as soon as possible.

Papa didn't notice my concern. He continued. "With the blockade imposed on us by Europe and the northern states, it's getting nearly impossible to find parts for plows or wagons. Even if we had the money, there's no place left to buy any replacement parts. I've had to rely on makeshift parts I find discarded in the fields."

"Do you have any help at all?"

"Just our family. With the men gone, women have learned to plant and cultivate the fields, chop firewood and feed livestock, but I think the best thing they've done is their work at the hospitals when they can. They also meet three evenings a week at homes or churches to sew uniforms for our troops. I've never heard one complaint from any one of them. Sometimes I think our women are making greater sacrifices than some of the men."

"I never dreamed it had gotten that bad here."

"Indeed it has. Our savings were converted to Confederate money, and I hear the situation may get worse, before it gets better. Inflation has made the Confederate dollar almost worthless."

I could see our home in the distance. As we approached the gates, my old dog, Cass, ran out to greet us. Immediately she recognized me, and jumped up and down as if to say, I've missed you. Cass, a black Labrador, was about fifteen years old and could no longer leap into the buggy, although she certainly tried.

Althea heard Cass barking, and she rushed from the house down the hill to meet us. Mama, a thin, slightly stooped woman with a frail profile paused to wipe her hands on her apron. Her white hair was neatly parted in the middle and pulled into a bun. She stood waiting on the porch. With Papa's help, slowly I climbed down from the buggy.

At long last, I was home. I was thinner than when I left, in a uniform that was worn and threadbare. For a fleeting moment the war was but a bad dream from which I had just awakened. Home was never so sweet. I hugged both Althea and Mama for what seemed like an eternity.

"Oh Daniel," said Mama. "I'm so glad your home, you look all done in. Althea, get Daniel some cold buttermilk. Why I declare, if you ain't dirty son. Althea, put some water on the stove to boil."

"Mama I know you want to hear all about Sam."

"I do, but come in the house and rest first."

"Where are Stephen and the girls?"

"Stephen will be home from school shortly. He wanted to stay home today, but your father said no. Victoria's at the hospital tending the wounded, but I'm sure she'll high-tail it home as soon as her replacement shows up.

"How about, Sue?"

"I guess you hadn't received word, but Sue and Cyrus Paxton got married last November," said Papa. "He was drafted in the army, shortly thereafter he was sent to Richmond, so she's running the general store by herself. She'll be here by supper."

"Appears that you've lost a lot of weight," said Mama, "but, I reckon I can fix that. Tonight we're having your favorite meal: chicken fixings with dressing, kale, hominy grits, corn bread, and sorghum syrup."

"Did you put some cracklin in the corn bread?"

"You know I did, and we eat just as soon as your brother and sisters get home. You got just enough time to get in a tub. Althea made you a pair of jeans, and Papa got you some brogans. Those clothes you're wearing can go straight to the trash. They're not even fit to be mended."

Althea hugged me again. "As soon as you get dressed, call me, so I can bandage that foot myself. I've been trained at the hospital on how to do that."

"Okay, but first I'd like to go out to the barn and see Prince. I promise I'll only be a few minutes." I whistled for Cass to come. It was painful to walk, but with the help of the crutch, I hobbled to the barn.

Prince recognized me; he flared his nostrils and pawed the ground to indicate he was ready to go. He loved to run and stretch his legs. Personally, I don't think horses were meant to be penned up. I reached around his neck to hug him, and he in turn responded by laying his chin on my shoulder. I rubbed his neck and told him, "Not now, boy. Soon we'll be together racing over the countryside as free as a bird." He always loved his ears to be scratched, and as I rubbed them, he raised his head and nuzzled against my neck. I picked up his brush and slowly brushed him down. I could tell Stephen had taken good care of him in my absence. I sensed Prince could feel my frustration when I turned to walk out of the barn.

I entered the house; the aroma of fresh-baked bread filled the room. Crocks of milk sat cooling in a tub of water, and the scent of fried chicken wafted from the cook stove where Mama always put the meat to keep it warm. A jar of strawberry jam and the remnants of a ham were on the table. I grabbed a slice of ham before heading for the tub.

Sis had boiled water for me, which she carried one bucket at a time to the back porch and poured into a large tin tub. A hot bath did wonders for me. Layers of dirt melted away as the steam rose from the tub. I didn't want the sensation to end. Sis brought in another kettle of hot water to re-heat the tub. At first she thought I had died, because I was submerged up to my chin in water and lye soap, fast asleep. You learn to sleep any chance you get, in the army.

I had not slipped into clean clothing in a long time, and I had forgotten how good it felt. Papa emptied the tub. "There's enough dirt in here to plant potatoes," he said.

"I suppose so, Papa. I haven't had any soap to use in a long time."

The front door slammed and I knew Stephen was home. I heard him dash through the house to find me.

"You're home," he said as he hugged my neck. "Can I see your pocket knife? Did you carry it into battle with you?"

"Sure, I did; in fact, I never went anywhere without it."

"Maybe you'll come to school with me one day and tell us all about the battles you were in."

"I will, as soon as this foot heals up."

"Can I see your bullet holes?"

"Not now. Sis just put new bandages on them, but the next time she changes them, I'll make sure it's when your home, okay?"

"I guess so, but I can't wait until I tell my best friend Billy at school tomorrow. Maybe he can come over and see your bullet holes."

"We'll see."

Victoria and Susan arrived as I was making my

way toward the kitchen table. I had managed to get the jeans on but the foot was still too swollen to wear the brogans.

"Susan, I understand congratulations are in order. So you and Cyrus Paxton got married. Wasn't he the fellow who came by every Sunday and escorted you to church?"

"He was indeed. I'm surprised you remembered him."

"Yeah, I hear tell he got drafted in the army. Sent him to Richmond, I understand?"

"They did. That's not too far. Maybe I'll get to go see him or he'll get a furlough home soon."

I thought to myself, not anytime soon, Sis. It'll be least a year, and the chances of him staying in Richmond are slim.

"Victoria, what's happened in your life, since I've been gone?"

"Not much. Between the hospital and working part-time as a dressmaker I stay busy. There's a soldier at the hospital I've grown fond of. We'll just have to wait and see what happens."

"How's the shop doing?"

"We're about out of cloth and can't get any more, so l don't know how much longer I'll be able to stay there."

"Supper's ready," Althea called. She didn't have to say it twice. Mama had cooked fatback in the kale, which gave it a distinct flavor. I believe I could live forever on kale and hominy grits. I sopped up the last bit of sorghum with my bread, before calling it quits. The sweet potato pie would have to wait.

After our evening meal, the girls threw a large thin cloth over the food left from the meal, so the flies would not attack it. We lingered at the kitchen table and swapped stories until Althea suggested we all move to the front porch. Mama, Susan, and Victoria cleared the table before putting out the lamp and joining us. As Mama walked outside she said, "Look Stephen, in the northwest sky, there's the Big Dipper, spilling not a drop."

"We were studying about the stars this past week at school," Stephen said. "At night, the stars can be used as a guide to find your way. Look at that bright one; it's the North Star. "

"Daniel, can I get you anything else to eat?" Althea asked.

"I'm full as a tick, Sis. If I were any fuller, I couldn't stand myself. What I'd really like is something to drink and for Mama to play the piano for me."

Mama smiled and nodded. Papa lit his pipe before moving to the parlor.

As Mama played some gospel hymns, her face glowed from the light of a nearby oil lamp. The final hymn was Papa's favorite, "Nearer My God To Thee." We all joined in as Papa led us in song.

As was the custom in our family, Papa read to us from the Scriptures, then began his prayer by thanking God for delivering me home safely. He asked God to watch over Paul, Marcellus, Ossen, and Cyrus in the coming days.

The night was a hot, stifling one, but I couldn't hold my eyes open any longer. Climbing stairs to my room was out of the question, so Mama made me a comfortable bed on the sofa.

"Night, Son," said Papa.

"Good night, Papa. It's good to be home."

I lay staring at the ceiling and thinking how we take for granted so many things, such as a safe home with a dry roof over our head, until we leave home and face the real world. The last thing I remember was hearing the grandfather clock in the hall ticking a rhythmic pattern. The sound was a wonderful one; at last I was assured I was not dreaming. I was really home.

I slept peacefully until awakened by the orders to charge. Amid the rattle of musketry, roar of artillery fire, explosions of shells and hoof beats of charging cavalry, I gave the rebel yell and sprang forward off the sofa, knocking over a lamp. Covered in perspiration, I came to my senses when I heard Mama call out, "Daniel, are you okay?"

"I'm okay now. Guess I was dreaming."

The summer crept by. During the day I sat on the front porch and tried as best I could not to apply any unnecessary pressure to my foot. I read a lot, especially <u>American</u> <u>Farmer</u> magazine. I enjoyed reading <u>Moby</u> <u>Dick</u> by Herman Melville. I looked forward to reading <u>Uncle</u> <u>Tom's</u> <u>Cabin</u>, a highly controversial book. If nothing else, at least my mind was being challenged. Eventually though, I became restless.

Between volunteer work at the hospital and chores at home, Althea spent what time she could listening to me ramble on about all the places I had been and the things I had seen and done.

"Tell me about Papa," I said. "He doesn't appear well."

"He's under a lot of stress right now. He had a mild heart attack, but after he survived the crucial first week, Doctor Jones said more than likely he would be just fine. Papa didn't tell you, because he didn't want you to worry. The doctor did tell him he had to slow down but you know Papa. He's as stubborn as our mule. Lately he's felt exhausted, but he's convinced himself it's his imagination, even though he falls asleep in his chair in front of the fire every evening."

"Promise me, Sis, you'll get word to me, if he takes a turn for the worse."

"You know I will."

The family wanted to hear about Sam, how he died, and whether he had suffered a great deal, but it was still too painful for me to talk about. I refrained from going into details.

Mama was concerned with replacing the twenty or so pounds I had lost.

Throughout my recuperation, Cass was my constant companion. In the evenings, she slept on the floor next to me, where I could reach down and pat her on the head or scratch behind her ears, whenever I wanted to. She often sat and stared at me with her big, sad eyes, as if she understood what I had been through.

"Breakfast is ready," came the call from the kitchen. Both Cass and I sat up at the same time to smell the coffee and eggs. It was time for me to start moving around some. I hobbled to the kitchen and made a less-than-graceful entrance, plopping down in a chair with a thud. Mama was already up. She had stoked the fire she had banked the night before, and had fixed Papa's breakfast. She had good reasons for not letting the fire go out from the previous day. First, the stove got hot enough for cooking much faster, and secondly, the warmth overcame the morning chill in the kitchen.

As a child, we always hit the floor running, clothing in hand, to dress in the warm kitchen. I can still remember the shock when my bare feet hit the cold floor.

"Where's Papa," I asked.

"He has already left for the fields," she replied.

"It's hard to believe Papa must leave so early."

"You forget, September is when he begins to pack his tobacco for hauling to market."

Mama had fixed biscuits and eggs that morning with cold buttermilk and coffee to drink. I had only been home a couple of weeks, but already had gained at least five pounds.

I never realized how much there was to do around the house. Besides tending to the fire and cooking, Mama and the girls washed the clothes, made tallow candles, cleaned, and sewed everything from clothing to bed linens and draperies. They had other chores, too, such as churning butter, preserving foods by salting the meats, and so on.

The time had come to pack the peaches Mama had dried in the sun. She moved them to the breezeway between the kitchen and the storage room and hung the dried fruit in cotton bags, so the air could circulate and keep them from molding. Over the next few days she would also make peach brandy. With my sisters' help, she would begin preserving blackberries, snap beans, cucumbers, watermelon rind, and the rest of the peaches. I was beginning to get an idea of just how hard Mama and the girls worked around the house.

Our home was comfortable. Papa had acquired our furnishings before the war. The parlor was furnished in early Victorian and contained Mama's piano, a spindle-back Boston rocker with the latest issue of Harper's Bazaar placed in the seat, a green velvet wingback chair, a marble top end table that held the family Bible, and a multi-colored kerosene lamp with gold fringe. Our sofa had an arched top rail that Mama called a serpentine back. The walls were covered with an elaborate pattern of wallpaper. Bookshelves lined both sides of the fireplace; the mantel displayed a Currier and Ives lithograph of a landscape and a daguerreotype portrait of our family. A large framed mirror hung across from the window and reflected light into the room. The carpet, with its red and tan diamond pattern, added a final touch of elegance to the parlor.

Papa used to grumble, "Our parlor is only used to entertain guests. We furnished a nice room in the house to look at once a week. Unless Mama plays her piano, or we all gather for evening prayer, we're not allowed to enter the room. What's the use of having such a nice place?"

When Mama wasn't playing her piano or doing chores, she sat in her rocker in the back parlor, next to the potbellied parlor stove and worked on her quilting. Papa sat next to her in his overstuffed easy chair, reading his newspaper. A smoking stand beside his chair held his pipes. To my knowledge, no one ever tried to sit in Papa's chair when he was home.

The rest of our furnishings throughout the house were either antiques or hand-me-downs, except for our kitchen table, which Sam and Ossen had made from a fallen walnut tree. That table had to be the most used piece of furniture in our home. That's where the family and close friends gathered.

❧

On Saturday, Papa finished his chores at the barn early and returned to the house. I suppose he could tell I was becoming restless and depressed from sitting around day after day.

"Daniel," he said, "would you like to go to town with me this afternoon?"

"Yes, sir," I replied. "I do need to get out of the house for a while. I'm ready to go, right now."

Papa laughed, "Let's have a bite to eat, then we'll be on our way. I'll hitch up the wagon; that'll give you time to change."

The swelling in my foot had gone down. It was a struggle but I managed to get my boots on.

As we pulled out of the path onto the road, I heard Mama shouting, "Be careful, Daniel, you don't want to undo what we gained."

Once on the road, Papa reached behind the seat and retrieved a cane for me. "This was Granddaddy's. I packed it away in his old trunk when he died."

I was glad to get it; my arm was sore from using a crutch.

❧

New Glasgow hadn't changed much. A hotel with a tavern and the town's only cafe stood next door to the general store that Cyrus and Susan owned. Uncle Howard and Aunt Dorris, as they were affectionately called, owned the hotel where the stage line stopped overnight. They were no relation to us but everyone called them uncle and aunt. If you wanted a good hot meal, you asked when the next stage was due. That's when the food was ready.

Next to the hotel was the dress shop where Victoria worked. Farther down the road was St. Mark's Episcopal Church. Only a few Episcopalians lived in our area. Mostly the town was made up of Methodists and Baptists. St. Mark's was a beautiful old church built entirely out of bricks in 1816. Mama told me in one of her letters that it had grown in membership.

On the other side of the road was a tanyard that sold leather goods; the wheelwright shop that repaired wagon, coach or carriage wheels; and Mr. Gladermear's funeral home. Although unpaved, Main Street was well kept. Perhaps because it didn't have the thousands of troops, wagons, and artillery pieces running back and forth on it daily, the way Richmond's roads did.

Papa pulled up at the general store. "Son, let's stop off at Cyrus' place first."

Once inside, I looked around and found everything as if time had stood still. The potbellied stove with six hard-back wooden chairs surrounding it was the focus point for the town's unofficial meetings. You could always find a group of elderly men there who were the authorities on any subject. Under the stove was a sandbox, allegedly to protect the wood floors from catching fire. I suppose it worked, but the men knew its real purpose was for spitting tobacco.

The shelves behind the counter contained a varity of homemade preserves, jellies, candles, lamps, and oils. Beer, whiskey, and molasses were dispensed through spigots from barrels. Of course, the pickle barrel, which was always my favorite, was still popular. It stood in front of the counter, where anyone could reach into the brine and withdraw a whole, large pickle for two cents. The waist high counter, stained by countless dirty hands that had leaned on it, still contained the old penny-candy jar that I had reached in many a time to fetch a handful of peppermint sticks. Next to the candy jar were several containers of dried beans.

Across the room was a pile of homespun overalls and shirts the local folks had made and traded for items they needed, such as eggs, butter, or meat.

Scattered around were a few farm supplies. Before the war, you could find all kind of hoes, rakes, nails, wire for fencing, plows, stoves, pump parts, and hand tools, but most of those items were long gone. In the back was the post office.

The musty smell of cloth in bolts along with the scent of smoked meats and fish permeated the wooden floor that still squeaked when I walked across them.

The men all stood to greet us, offering me

a chair. I brought fresh stories straight from the battlefield, or as Papa would say, straight from the horse's mouth. My badges of honor were my wounds and grandfather's cane. A year before I would never have been offered a chair in Paxton's store with the elders of New Glasgow.

George Mays Senior pulled his chair closer and asked about his son. Ishmael Jackson did the same. Almost everyone there had some relative to inquire about. I attempted to answer all their questions as best I could.

Sis brought me a cup of cider, and as I sipped on it, I couldn't help noticing a group of young boys gathered outside, pressing their faces against the window. A lady entered with a basket of eggs, which she exchanged for a slab of bacon. As she turned to leave, she looked in my direction. "Why Daniel, I heard you were home. It's good to see you."

I stood and tipped my hat, but I must have looked puzzled. She reminded me she was Sarah Smith's mother.

"Oh, yes, Sarah. I haven't seen her since she went away to attend Lynchburg Female Seminary, Light brown hair with pigtails, I recollect. Please forgive me. How is, Sarah?"

"Well, she no longer has pigtails. She's doing fine. I think she would enjoy talking to you, and you may be surprised when you see her." She smiled and turned to leave.

Henry, a man of color who had refused to leave his home and go north, when the war started, entered as Mrs. Smith was leaving. He held his hat in his hands as he approached. His cropped white hair stood like stubble on his head. Henry was a respected old Negro who worked as a blacksmith. He could fix just about anything having to do with iron. He delighted in talking about the past. Often he would shake his head and tell anyone who would listen that some folks were not like they used to be. Over the years, he had saved enough money to buy his freedom and, most recently, the freedom of his entire family.

I enjoyed watching Henry forge and shape horseshoes and nails, and make parts for tools, plowshares, and other implements. Some days, I'd stop by to watch Henry work. He often appeared to be dozing, but would wake with a start and say, "I'm not sleeping, I'm just resting my eyes."

His understanding of horses and mules grew as the years passed and helped him be content being a farrier. He would bring his son, Jerome, along when he came to work on our horses or wagons. Mama used to take two biscuits left over from breakfast, poke a finger in their sides, and fill the holes with syrup. Jerome and I would each grab one and high-tail it to the river to fish. We developed a competitive friendship, each trying to catch the biggest, and most fish. In all honesty, I think his Pa enjoyed seeing his son enjoying himself.

Henry squinted his eyes as he turned in my direction. Age had caught up with him. "Do tell, is that you, Mars Daniel?"

"It's me, Henry."

"We sho-nuff missed you. I hear tell you was home."

"It's good to be home. Where's Jerome?"

"He didn't know you was a comin to town today, or he'd be here. He done gone a fishin."

"I'll make it a point of seeing him before I go back. In the meantime, tell him to stop by any day he wants someone to go fishing with him."

"I sho-nuff will, Mars Daniel. Miss Susan, if you'll put one of them big pickles from that barrel on my bill, I'd sho be much obliged."

"Your credit is always good here, Henry. Need anything else?"

"No, Ma'am, I reckon not. I be on my way."

I rose to excuse myself. I wanted to go over to Pryor's tanyard shop to see Dan. He had always been good with his hands, and I knew he could fix Prince's halter, where the stitching had torn. Because of a childhood illness that caused him to walk with a limp, he was unable to join the army. I bid my farewells from the men in the general store and hobbled across the street to the tanyard, only to learn Dan had gone to Lynchburg for supplies.

"I know he'll be sorry he missed you," his father said. "I'll tell him you were in."

I rested on a deacon's bench outside Pryor's shop. It felt good sitting there by myself, people-watching. I thought about how our priorities change as we grow older. When I was in school, I couldn't wait until the bell rang, and when it finally did, I ran home, picked up a cane pole and dashed down to the river where I was content to fish and dream until supper time.

I began to see the impact the war had on everyone. Few men my age were left in New Glasgow. The youth had gone off to war.

Many of the local citizens, with stern faces, stood before the newspaper bulletin-board, in silent apprehension, searching for information about those wounded or killed in yesterday's battles. Wives and Parents trembled at the thought of bad news. But there was no news of the war this day.

My Sweet Sarah

❦

*O*ut of the corner of my eye, I caught a glimpse of a young lady crossing the street. From my vantage point, I was able to view her inconspicuously. She was tall, slender, and quick-footed; her full skirt, its hem girlishly high, left her long limbs free to measure her swift steps. Her blouse enhanced her bosom, and her blue skirt, accented with blue trim, narrowed at the waist. A palatine, lined in soft blue satin and trimmed with lace, draped casually across her shoulders. A simple gold medallion on a blue ribbon adorned her neck. Her honey-gold color hair was held in place by combs that allowed ringlets on either side of her face. She turned in my direction; I recognized Sarah Smith. She smiled, and I found myself fumbling for words. As she drew nearer I gazed into her gray-green eyes. I rose to greet her. "Sarah, I can't believe it's you. You look great . . . I mean, it's great to see you, again," I stammered.

"Hello, Daniel. Mother told me you were in town, and I've been looking all over for you. I heard

191

you were wounded in the war. Is it bad?"

"It hurts at times, but if I could just lean on you, I'm sure I could make it back to my wagon."

Her laughter was spontaneous but friendly. "Sakes alive, you haven't changed a bit since school."

"But you have, and I must confess you're the prettiest girl in Amherst County. Okay, I admit it. I can walk without help. You wanna get a soda?"

"Why, thank you, Daniel. You always did know how to charm a girl and yes, I'd love to get something to drink."

I hadn't had the pleasure of escorting a girl in a long time. Her presence lightened the room as we entered Paxton's store and caused those still sitting to turn and greet us.

"Two lemonades and ten cents worth of fudge, Sis."

I whispered in Sarah's ear. "I bet they're saying, 'back when I was a young man, times were different. You had to get permission to court a girl.' "

Sarah blushed and smiled. "But we've known each other since the first grade. It's not like you're courting me."

"Makes no difference to them. We're here together, unaccompanied by a chaperon."

"Hi Daniel, Miss Sarah," Bob Brown said as he entered the store. "Sarah, your mother is looking for you."

Outside, Mrs. Smith explained she promised her husband she'd be home before dark, so he needn't worry. I held Sarah's hand as I helped her into their buggy. I didn't want her to leave. I thought, I can't just let her go; it's was now or never. I blurted out, "Mrs.

Smith, I hope you don't think it presumptuous of me to ask so quickly, but may I come to call on your daughter?"

"Do you mean the tall skinny one with pigtails?"

Embarrassment turned my face red as I fumbled with my cane. "Yes, Ma'am."

She looked at Sarah who, without saying a word nodded slightly. Mrs. Smith looked back at me. "You may. Would you like to come over next Wednesday?"

"Yes, Ma'am, I would."

"Good, then plan to stay for dinner. Mister Smith is looking forward to seeing you again." Sarah's mother shook the reigns as she turned, "Giddy up, Chelsey," she said.

As Sarah's horse trotted down the road, I completely forgot about the pain in my foot, and I hurried to find Papa. On the way home, I tried to put into words how I felt about Sarah. "She is like a stalk of corn in July. Tall and straight up, somewhat thin in the middle, but open in full blossom at the top."

"Son, I hear you, but I don't think you should use that type of description to describe her to others."

⊷⊱⊰⊶

Wednesday was a delightful day as the fiery red sun climbed into the sky. My priorities were changing. I began to think more about Sarah and less about the war. Both my leg and foot were healing. I knew soon I would be returning to the war, but for now I didn't want to think about that. I was able to ride Prince, and he was eager to stretch his legs. At the barn, I brushed him until his coat had a sheen. When I reached for the saddle, he knew we were going for a run across the open fields. He whinnied his approval. Shortly after noon, we were on our way.

He was all business, ready to go at my command. It felt good to ride again. He pranced and bobbed his head up and down along the pathway leading from our house, to the front gates. At the gates, I gave him his reins, and we left the road heading across rolling green, unfenced fields in a long free lope towards Sarah's house. The countryside was as I remembered, with plenty of open space surrounded by wooded forest and an occasional stream along the way. The wind was in my face, and I felt really good. I stopped only once to pick a multitude of colored wildflower for Sarah.

As I rode up the magnolia tree-lined driveway, Sarah rushed out to greet me. She looked even more ravishing than I had remembered. She was wearing her hair differently, brushed straight back without a part, which allowed it to fall long and full down her back. A large red bow held it all together. I was truly smitten, "hook line and sinker."

"Daniel, are those flowers for me? They're beautiful."

"I thought of you when I saw them and had to bring them to you."

"I've been looking forward to your visit, but I must warn you, Pa has insisted we limit our visits to the parlor."

"If I had a daughter as beautiful as you, I would say the same thing."

Sarah's father stepped out onto the porch. "Daniel, good to see you," his voice roared like a bull.

Mr. Smith was a big man, broad-shouldered, with a rugged face, gray beard, and a moustache. He wore bright red suspenders, and a short gold chain connected his pocket watch to the buttonhole of his pants. I remembered, he strongly opposed the Union long before the war.

Sarah hurried inside to help her mother. Her father and I stayed out on the front porch to talk.

"It's been awhile. Tell me, what's the perception of the people in Richmond about the war? I learned a long time ago you can't believe everything you read in the newspaper."

"Everyone appears to be in a state of panic, concerned for their safety, right now."

Mister Smith filled his pipe, then took several puffs until he was sure it was lit properly. He finally responded. "I'm sorry to hear that. What the newspapers are saying must be true."

He looked at me seriously. "Daniel, I've always thought highly of you. I've known your Pa for many years, and I'm aware you attend church on the Sabbath but I was a boy once myself and I understand young men's feelings. I understand you wish to call on my daughter, Sarah. I want you to think about her, still living here in New Glasgow, after you return to the army. The last thing you want is to have people talking about either of you after you've left. All I ask is that you consider Sarah, if you wish to court her. If you will, then you have my permission to come a-courting, but I must warn you that Sarah's Aunt Emma will be present when you and her are together. Is that understood?"

"I not only understand, but I completely agree with your decision, sir." Although I verbally agreed with her father I hoped that, as the evening progressed, Aunt Emma would be tactful enough to withdraw to the kitchen and visit with Mrs. Smith.

"There's a barn raising over at Bob Wiley's place this Saturday. May I have your permission to ask Sarah, and of course Aunt Emma, to accompany me?"

Mister Smith grunted but somewhere within the sagging folds of his face a smile formed then quickly vanished.

"Let me think about that awhile," he said.

"Dinner, "Mrs. Smith called.

Mister Smith removed from his pocket his timepiece. "Let's eat," he said as he noted the time.

I could tell Mrs. Smith had given some serious thought to the meal. In the center of the table were a huge pot roast, new potatoes, onions, turnips cooked in hog's lard, and cabbage. For dessert, she had baked an apple and a pecan pie. I thought Sarah's Ma was nice to seat us opposite each other at the table, so we could steal fleeting glances during the meal. Sarah tried but could not conceal the blush and purity in her flushed cheeks when our eyes would meet. Her eyelids would flutter, ever so slightly in the lamplight.

I ate, until I was miserably full. I felt guilty

wondering what George and the others had to eat that night. I tried not to think about it, but it continued to haunt me.

After dinner, Aunt Emma showed up. Her timing was perfect. Sarah, Emma, and I retired to the parlor. I felt awkward and apprehensive with Emma's presence. After all, I had never courted a girl before. "How have you been, Aunt 'watch us', uh, I mean Aunt Emma?"

Sarah spoke in a low tone. "Daniel, why are you so nervous?"

"I don't rightly know, but I am."

"You have one thing in your favor. Aunt Emma can't hear very well."

"Then can we hold hands?"

"I said she can't hear you, but she can see you."

"Could we possibly step outside just to get some fresh air without Aunt Emma?"

"Daniel Knight, you make me blush at such thoughts."

"Aunt Emma," Sarah shouted, "I believe there's one more piece of pie left. Why don't you help yourself. We'll be on the front porch in the swing, for a spell."

A slight chill blew through the air. I draped Sarah's shawl around her shoulders. We sat in the swing talking for almost two hours, always under the watchful eyes of Aunt Emma. The wind began to swirl around, and the temperature dropped rapidly. We decided to go inside. I had close to an hour's ride home, so I bid everyone good-bye. Mr. Smith gave me permission to ask Sarah to accompany me to Saturday's barn raising.

"That'll be a lot of fun. I'll be ready early," Sarah replied. Leaving, I stole one last glance at the up-stairs window. Sara was standing there waving goodbye.

The ride home was cold and dark. The clouds had hidden behind the moon. The only sounds I heard were the sounds of frogs from the near by swamps. A storm was brewing. I shrugged down in my saddle, pulled my collar up around my ears, and let Prince take us home. Soon the rain came with blinding flashes of lightning that stabbed the earth like bayonets.

Everyone was in bed when I arrived. I entered the dark house and stood by the fireplace with my hands out to receive the warmth from the dying embers. I noticed a letter addressed to Susan on the mantel. Rather than wait up Papa must have placed it there before turning in. Susan arrived home late and failed to notice the letter. It was from a Captain Cox. My happy thoughts of the day turned dismal. I had seen that type of letter before and assumed it contained bad news. I couldn't go to sleep thinking about what the letter comprised. I poured myself a cup of coffee. It tasted bitter from roasting on the fire all day. I sat somberly gazing at the flickering fire in a hypnotic state as it flared up, then faded again. The night would be a long one. Susan was due with child, within a month; she didn't need bad news now.

Susan rose early. Surprised to find me in the kitchen, she sensed something was out of order. She asked, "What's wrong?"

"I hope nothing, but there's a letter on the mantel, addressed to you from the army. Here, you need to open it." I stepped onto the back porch, giving her a few minutes alone. When I returned, she was sitting with the letter crushed in her hands. I took it from her fingers, praying for the best. Possibly Cyrus had only been wounded. I read the tear-stained words.

Dear Mrs. Paxton, I regret to inform you that your husband, Cyrus Paxton, was killed in action today during the battle of Frederick, Maryland.

I didn't need to read any further. I reached out and held Sis tight in my arms. "I'm so sorry."

∽⟨⟩∾

I had just polished off a stack of Mama's buckwheat griddlecakes and some cold buttermilk when Jerome came by the house.

"Massa Daniel, I hear tell dem catfish are chomping at da bit. I ain't been a fishin with you in a coon's age. Wanna go get a mess?"

"Sure, Jerome, let me tell Mama we're going. I'll be right with you. Maybe today will be the day we catch "The Boss." I know the cove where he hides, and I been a hankering to see if he's home. Come on, Cass, we're going fishing."

I saddled Prince. Jerome, Cass, Prince, and I set out through the thick woods to the riverbank. Once there, we headed east, following it, as it wound down from the Blue Ridge Mountains. Soon we reached the shaded banks where the water slowly rolled over the mossy rocks. "This is the place, and "The Boss" lives right over yonder in that tall grass," I said.

I flung myself down under the shade of a large

oak tree. Lulled by the river sounds, I lay with my hands locked beneath my head while Jerome dug for fishing worms. The sky was vivid blue, unblemished by clouds. Papa would say we were experiencing a typical Indian Summer that only comes every few years and soon it would turn cold. I watched the water rush by and savored the soft breeze blowing across my face in the cool shade. I began to relax. I rolled over on my back and nibbled on a twig.

Jerome soon returned and baited a hook he had made from a thorn. With a flip of his wrist, he accurately cast his line to the spot where he believed "The Boss" to be.

I checked my line and sinker before baiting my hook. Then I swung the line through the air and let it drop into the water, by the tall grass, near a rotting tree that had fallen into the edge of the river. I stuck my cane pole firmly into the ground and slouched back against a fallen tree that had lain there so long, moss had covered it completely.

"Jerome, I don't think God ever made a more calm, quiet, or peaceful place than an old fishing hole. Here there's no one to tell us what to do, no bands playing, no creaking wagons, soldiers shuffling, or canteens rattling, or people shooting at us. I think it's about as near to heaven as anybody can get on this earth."

"I reckon so, Massa Daniel, but I ain't never heard dem sounds afore."

"Once you do, you never forget them."

"Massa, I'm worried 'bout you going off and fightin and all."

"I'll be careful. Besides, I've put my faith in

God."

"We all heard where slaves was free now, but we don't wanna leave our home. Everyone in my family cried just at t' thought of leaving. My family only got a one-room cabin, but it's cozy, 'cause we got us a fireplace to keep us warm in the winter. T' other Negroes that left and come back say they had a hard time 'fore they was free, but it wasn't as bad then like it is now. They couldn't get no work from nobody. Wouldn't any man hire 'em.

"Here at home, we get together with others on Saturday nights and have us a Juba."

"I know that's a dance of some kind Jerome, but how do you do it?"

"You pat your hands on your knees, then pat them together, then hit your right shoulder with your left hand, then your left shoulder with your right hand all the while singing and keeping time with your feet."

"Someday I'd like to see that.... Uh oh, I think I've got 'em. Look at that cork and how deep it's running, Jerome." I jumped up and swung a huge catfish onto the bank. It flopped briefly before I unhooked it.

"Don't lose em. Be careful. He sure is a big un. Reckon you done caught The Boss."

"Would you look at that, Jerome? It's The Boss all right. You know, he's lived here a long time. I don't rightly believe we should cut his head off. I'm gonna toss him back, give him a second chance. There's plenty of others out there."

"Well Massa, at least I can say I seen The Boss

up real close."

"I reckon it's time to leave," Daniel said as he tossed the fish back into the river. "Supper should be ready soon."

Jerome picked up a flat stone and sent it skipping across the surface of the water. It made it all the way across to the other side.

Saturday I got up early, went to the barn, and brushed Prince before leading him to our carriage. "Today, you get to pull the buggy for Miss Sarah and me," I said as I finished harnessing Prince. Papa came out to the barn and handed me a small bottle of his homemade apple brandy.

"Here, take this, just in case Miss Emma gets cold. I mixed in a little Winslow's baby syrup, which contains morphine. It'll take the chill out of the air."

" You look nice," said Mama. " You need to use some of Papa's bear grease to slick down the cow-lick on the back of your head."

"I think not, Mama. Sarah might like to run her fingers through my hair."

"Young people. You're too forward, today."

"Oh, Mama, this is the sixties. Times are different. I'm also aware you used to walk five miles through the snow to school every day. I promise I'm a very honorable person, and I can assure you I intend to remain that way. You can be sure the old spinster Emma will be with us every minute."

I arrived at Sarah's house shortly after eight

that morning. Sarah and Aunt Emma were waiting for me on the porch swing. Sarah's green velvet dress lay in graceful folds about her and a gold locket on a velvet ribbon rested against her throat. She looked stunning. I was pleased they were ready. After all, if we were going to raise a barn in one day, we needed a full day's light.

Aunt Emma climbed into the buggy and leaned forward, her back as stiff, and apparently as hard, as a board. I draped a blanket over Sarah's shoulders and another across Aunt Emma's lap as she mumbled to herself about how cold it was, and that all of us were sure to come down with chills and fever.

"Here, Aunt Emma, take a little swig of this. It'll help take the chill out of your bones." The magic began to work immediately. After a few minutes, I turned around and saw Aunt Emma was fast asleep on the back seat. I drove holding the reins with one hand and Sarah's hand with the other, overcome with love.

We were soon at Bob Wiley's house. Some twenty wagons and buggies had already arrived. Aunt Emma woke up, took one last swig of brandy, dropped the empty bottle on the floor of the buggy, and headed straight for the house. As Sarah and I entered, I overheard someone say, "Sarah has set her cap for Daniel." That was okay with me.

Several men were already at work on the barn. I immediately went out to help. The job took the best part of the day, but by early evening, the women lit candles and the fiddles and banjos warmed up. The dancing commenced. The women had prepared a mess of chicken, along with barbecued mutton, plenty of bread, milk, and pound cake for desserts. Bob had brewed a new batch of apple brandy, and Aunt Emma was testing its mixture, to make sure it tasted right. We all nibbled, laughed, and chatted as if there were no war. A square dance line formed. I left my cane under a chair and grabbed Sarah's hand to join in. The music and the thought of holding Sarah in my arms excited me.

The dance opened with the Virginia Reel. Six couples in our circle twisted and turned, changing partners at the caller's request. How gracefully Sarah responded to the step and the timing of the music. We danced until the "wee small" hours of the morning. My injured leg was on fire, but I continued to dance. Sarah noticed I was favoring it and asked me to stop awhile, claiming she needed a breath of fresh air. We decided to take a stroll. Aunt Emma could not have cared less that we were not being chaperoned. We were alone at last.

We stepped outside, and walked down a path lined with large oaks. I reached for her hand. We stopped for a moment, and I turned toward her. Lifting her chin slightly I looked into her eyes. She was more beautiful than I had ever seen her before. The sparkle of her eyes beamed brightly as the moonlight splashed softly on her face. I ran my fingers through her hair, then held her close. My heart leaped with hunger for her. I slid my arms around her and felt the soft warmth of her body as we kissed. We were in love, and there could be no other for me. I whispered, "Will you wait for me to return from the war?"

"I will Daniel, I will, however long it takes."

The time came to leave. With great reluctance, we bade everyone good night, as we helped Aunt Emma out to our carriage. It began sleeting. We snuggled under a pile of blankets, and I stole a few kisses on our moonlit ride home. Only the thought that my foot was healing and that I would soon be returning to my unit spoiled the day for me.

Prince trotted in a steady gait down the road to Sarah's home. Aunt Emma slept in the back; Sarah laid her head on my shoulder. In a soothing, caressing way, she ran her fingers through my hair. We talked about our dreams and expectations along the way. Sarah and I made plans to attend church together on the next Sabbath. Maybe we both revealed our feelings for one another rapidly, but time was not in our favor, and as young people often do, we were eager to make the best of the time we had left together.

Once home, Aunt Emma awoke, gathered her knitting, stuffed it into her tapestry bag, and marched inside. Sarah lifted her face to the stars and ran her arms about my neck. With a gentle kiss, I bid her good night. She turned and rushed into the house, watching me from her bedroom window as I drove away. I knew that I loved her and that my life would be changed forever.

⊸᭤᭥⊱

On Sunday, I dressed in my go-to-meeting clothes. The early morning air had a chill about it, as Papa and I harnessed a team of horses to the big wagon. Papa drove, and Mama and Stephen rode up front with him. I sat directly behind Papa. Althea sat next to me. She, Victoria, and Susan covered up snugly, under a blanket.

The horses with a steady rhythm, trotted along under a gray overcast sky. Papa called out to me. I leaned forward. "Yes, Sir?"

"Church has changed since you went away to war."

"In what way, Papa?"

"Well, the service is still the same, and Reverend Thomas is still our pastor, but in place of the covered dish meal, we now have a sandwich, so the women folks can spend the rest of the afternoon knitting and sewing clothing for our soldiers. In fact, you'll see the women all wearing a secession badge in support of our cause."

Althea leaned over. "You remember Ann Yancey?" I nodded yes.

"Well, she gave up her French and piano lessons and has most enthusiastically headed up a group of women to make drawers and socks for our soldiers. At first she was quite embarrassed to be sewing men's drawers. A lot of young women giggled while watching her, but now she's the best drawer-maker in our church."

"I can't wait to see all that. I don't suppose she'll want me to model drawers for everybody, do you?"

"I hope not. You didn't hear what happened to Clara Hoffman while you were away, did you?"

"No, what?"

"It was in all the local newspapers and even

took the headlines away from the war for a day. It seems as if Clara and her boyfriend, Tim Horsefield, went boating last June. The newspaper said she had placed full confidence in his honor, only to find out she was sadly mistaken."

"Did he kiss her?"

"No, but once in the middle of the river, he decided to go for a swim. He removed his pants and stood before her in his drawers. They said she covered her eyes and cried."

"Never seen a naked man, I suppose."

"Daniel, I'm trying to be serious. They said he paid no attention to her pitiful appeals and proceeded to disrobe, forcing her to bury her fingernails into her flesh and cry in a fit of hysteria. In fact she could hear him splashing about in the water, but I understand, she still refused to peek."

"Boy, that must have hurt."

"He did a dastardly thing. She claimed her heart was beating like a pigeon's wing when Horsefield climbed back into the boat, got dressed, and rowed to shore. Although he never touched her, she never recovered from the shock."

"I wonder why?"

"I guess she felt people would say unkind things about her. She brooded over the incident until her mind just gave way. They say, brain fever set in, and she became delirious."

"Because of his undressing?"

"I suppose so. The doctors did all they could for her, but to no avail. Finely, they informed the family the end was near but I understand two days later she recovered briefly, opened her eyes and, in a barely audible voice, she told everyone, she never peeked. Then she died from the shock of it all. They say the angel of death had beckoned her and reached down and told her to follow."

"Wow, What a story. I'm glad she never visited our camp. Tell me, Sis, would you have peeked?"

"In a heartbeat, and I think Clara did, too, which caused her to die for telling a story."

"That's my sister."

We soon arrived at the church. Its great wooden steeple and weather-board siding had recently received a fresh coat of white paint.

In the sanctuary, each family had its own pew. Papa and Mama understood that I would sit with Sarah and her family. Sarah was all smiles as I slid in next to her. We shared a hymnbook and joined in with the opening hymn of "Onward Christians Soldiers."

Reverend Thomas spoke from the heart. I can't recall him ever reading from notes. Throughout the sermon and until the benediction, Sarah and I stole quick glances at each other. Evidently Reverend Thomas noticed, because he came up to me after the service to shake my hand.

"What part of the sermon did you find most enlightening, Daniel?"

"Reverend, it was a powerful message, especially the part where you said the Ten Commandments so welded together religion and morality that one cannot exist without the other."

"Very good, Daniel, I'm impressed that under the circumstances, you were able to retain as much as you did."

As we turned to walk away, Sarah turned to me, "I didn't realize you were giving your undivided attention to Reverend Thomas today."

"I wasn't. I remembered that same sermon from camp last summer."

Papa, being a vestryman, was administering the affairs of the church. I was left to enter into discussions with the men who had gathered outside. Talk soon turned to the war. You would have thought I was a general rather than a corporal, as I attempted to answer questions.

During the ride home, it began to snow. It transformed an entire countryside into undisturbed tranquility, something magical and peaceful had happened to me. I was in love.

With less time demanded in the fields, Papa had taken a part-time job as Amherst County's snow warden. He was already at work by the time I poured my first cup of coffee that morning. As snow warden, Papa's job was to keep snow flattened on the local roads to ease traveling conditions. The county had a horse-drawn plow to clear drifts from the roads. Other times, Papa hooked up a team of horses to a large wooden roller, which packed down the snow. The job provided him with some extra money, in addition to keeping him occupied and mobile, during the winter months.

My foot no longer gave me any problems, except for an occasional pain when I turned swiftly. I mentally prepared for the day I had to return to duty, which would be soon.

Together, Stephen and I dispensed with the morning chores. We milked the cows, fed the animals, cut the firewood, and stacked it on the back porch. We were sitting in the barn and I was whittling on a stick, when Stephen said, "I'm so worried that you're going to go back to the war. What if you get killed?"

"I plan to be real careful, and I'll try not to let that happen. You shouldn't worry about things you have no control over. You have to put your faith in God. Besides, I have to go back because in every town I go through, I'm looking for a pocket knife just like mine, for you."

Reverend Thomas pulled his buggy into our gates. I walked out to meet him. "Good morning, Daniel."

"What brings you out here on a morning like this, Reverend?" I asked.

"Widow James died last night, and I'm looking for volunteers to dig a grave this afternoon."

"I'd be pleased to help, Reverend."

"Good. We're gonna meet at the church cemetery as soon as possible. We need to get her buried before another storm hits."

"Would you like a cup of coffee before you go, Reverend?"

"Thanks, but I've got no time now. I've got to round up a couple more men to help. Please give my regards to your mother and father for me. He turned his buggy around and trotted off.

Five men showed up to help dig the grave, and

we planned to stay until after the funeral to fill it in. We used to take a stick to mark off the size of the grave before digging, but Kenneth had made us a frame to lay on the ground and mark off the exact size.

The weather turned colder. The wind picked up and soon the air became so cold, we had to burn an old mulberry stump, just to keep warm. The wind whistled out of the North. I buttoned my thin coat around my throat as the first stinging slivers of sleet began falling. As I dug, I remembered that many years before, the Powhatan Indians had lived there, and as a boy, I had found arrowheads and other artifacts. I always kept a sharp lookout for such things.

Across the road was the Negro cemetery. I noticed a fresh-marked grave and remembered when they buried old Jesse. I was fifteen years old at the time, and it was the first Negro funeral I had ever attended. The preacher stepped forward and told the diggers to box Jesse before he started preaching. "Friends and neighbors! There he lays, a gen-u-wine chile of God, Amen." The diggers then lowered the coffin and took up the shovels.

Negro graves were always decorated with the last article the deceased had used. On Jesse's grave his family had placed bits of a broken pitcher and a colored glass. A patchwork quilt was laid at the foot of his grave, and a bell was mounted on the lid of the casket with a cord running through the casket and tied to Jesse's hand. Sometimes a physician pronounced a patient dead and he or she was buried alive. Occasionally the deceased miraculously came to during the funeral service and rang the bell. I also heard of placing shovels and crowbars in the deceased's casket so he could dig his way out.

❦

Papa handed me the Daily Virginian newspaper. Under the day's "News About The War" was an article regarding my unit.

'The Nineteenth Regiment was engaged in a savage battle today at Slaughter's Gap. After marching from Hagerstown, Maryland to Boonsborough the Regiment formed a line of battle on the top of a hill. The enemy lay concealed behind a stone fence, less than fifteen paces away. A murderous fire opened, killing or wounding over one-third of the Regiment. The Nineteenth resisted and held for some time against the fierce attack by many times their numbers. It was indeed bravery by all, in which they discharged their duties. Colonel John Strange, commanding officer of the Nineteenth, was killed.'

The shock was almost too great for me to handle. "Papa, I must return at once. I'll ride over and tell Sarah I'll be leaving in the morning; then I'll stop by the telegraph office and send a wire to advise them I am returning."

Papa nodded. "A man's life is the sum of his actions. He must do what he thinks is best. If that's your decision, so be it."

Mama had made me another cinnamon-hued uniform. Mrs. Mays stopped by and asked me to carry a package containing a pair of pants, a shirt, and some fruit for George. I was delighted to do so.

Susan had to open the store, so we said good-bye the night before. Victoria had committed to go to the hospital. Her presence was needed there more than with me at the depot. Althea would not listen to any reason; she planned to accompany me, as did Stephen and Mama.

On a cold, dismal morning, Papa hitched up the horses while I, with Althea's help, finished packing before setting out for the railroad depot.

Papa took his watch out of his pocket; it was eight-thirty. "It's time to go, the train won't wait for you."

I turned and took one last look at our home before rounding the bend in the road.

At the station, Sarah, along with her ma and pa, were waiting for us. Captain Decker's wire to the station had put me in charge of twelve recruits and instructed me to escort them to camp. The men were waiting and I saw in their eyes the same spirit I had when I first went off to war. This time, I knew what lay in front of me, and it was hard for me to share in their enthusiasm. I told them to stand at ease and visit with their families. "Say good-bye now, because we cannot hold the train any longer than necessary."

I gave each member of my family a hug and assured them I would be okay.

"Take good care of yourself Son," said Papa.

"I will Papa, I promise."

I turned toward Sarah and gently placed my arms around her. Her eyes were swollen with tears. She bit her lip as she reached up to hug me. In a whisper, she said, "I mustn't cry —I mustn't spoil this last moment together."

"Sarah, never forget how much I love you.

We've only had a little time together, but I'll always cherish those moments, and think about them every day. This war will be over before you know it. We're either gonna lick 'em or run out of bullets. One way or the other, I'll be home soon." I wiped away her tears with my handkerchief. "I'll never wash this handkerchief again. I'll always keep it close to my heart. I must go. Now don't you start blubbering," I said with a smile.

Standing on her tiptoes, she kissed me on the cheek. "Please be careful and take good care of yourself. I'll be here waiting for you as long as it takes. Nothing, nothing will ever stop me from loving you."

The iron horse hissed clouds of steam, let out a belch of black smoke, and whistled a loud blast to signal it was time to leave. I assembled the troops and quickly boarded.

With a piercing whistle and several jerks, the train slowly moved forward. I turned one final time in Sarah's direction. Her tears started anew as she stood pale and rigid in a light mid-morning mist. I can see to this day her pink cheeks and red nose as we waved good-bye to each other.

The train rumbled along, clattering and swaying over the rickety tracks, our destination Richmond. I was returning to all that I had tried to forget. The horror of war was back. I closed my eyes and whispered a silent prayer.

Death Of A Hero

❧❧

*A*s the train slowly pulled into the depot that evening, no bands played. No people cheered like they had before. Richmond had become a city of refugees. Torches lined the streets and sent shadows leaping against the buildings. In the glow of smoky oil lanterns, civilians and soldiers alike dashed back and forth. Everyone felt threatened by the advancing Federal army, which was stalled some fifty miles away at Fredericksburg. Life was in a state of turmoil.

In a cloud of steam and grinding metal, our train came to a halt. Vendors appeared hawking whiskey, or rotgut, as it was called by some. Peddlers offered newspapers, magazines, sandwiches, and other items. Regiments poured into town by all roads, and long lines of sunburned marching troops extended as far as the eye could see. Horses reared up on their haunches as column after column passed by.

The newspapers reported that we had held an entrenched position at Fredericksburg, and through sheer determination, had won a decisive battle. On five separate attempts, the Yanks charged our position, and each time, we repelled their advances. Still, the big question was, would they try again, as soon as they received additional replacements? The newspaper stated that President Lincoln was outraged that General Lee had outmaneuvered the Federal army, and the President had replaced General Burnside. It appeared the North was beginning to appreciate the brilliance of Lee as a great military leader.

While the new recruits waited tensely at the depot, I reported to the adjutant general's office for orders. I was informed my brigade had moved into winter quarters near Guiney's station, some twenty or so miles north of Richmond. That evening, we billeted in Richmond.

Early the next morning, we drew field rations consisting of hardtack and salt pork. After rolling up our ground cloths and securing them to our knapsacks, we moved out under gray overcast skies. Wagons shuttling supplies and wounded troops had cut deep ruts in the road, making our trip difficult. Wagon drivers, cracking their whips at braying mules, refused to slow down for anyone and would run you over if you got in the way. The road was littered with broken wheels, axles, ammo carriers, and dead animals.

We passed companies of ragged-looking soldiers standing guard to protect our supply route. The single thing we could not afford to do was to be cut off from our supply lines. Supplies were vital to our survival, and those soldiers knew the importance of their assignment. Looking tired and hungry they stared at us with hollowed, sleepless eyes.

We continued on, each man in silence with his own thoughts. I thought of Sarah and how she always had a cheerful smile for everyone. Memories of the time we spent together filled my every waking moment. I retrieved the tear-stained handkerchief from my pocket and touched my lips to it. The smell of lilac perfume filled my nostrils. I missed her so much. In terms of eternity, we had but a moment together, but God willing, I said to myself, we would have the rest of our lives to spend with each other after the war was over.

∽⋞⋟∾

We arrived at Guiney's Station; I located my brigade, then the regimental headquarters. I spotted Colonel Gantt in front of his shelter, and he recognized me. I was still deeply upset about Colonel Strange's death, but I also knew the army couldn't have replaced him with a better or more respected leader than Henry Gantt. He was not only knowledgeable, but also a fine Christian gentleman.

Colonel Gantt was from Scottsville, Virginia, and a graduate of Virginia Military Institute. Like

Papa, he was a tobacco farmer, before the war. We first had met at a tobacco auction in Lynchburg, and discussed farming and our faith. I wondered if our relationship would be the same, now that he had been promoted to the rank of colonel and been given the command of the nineteenth regiment.

"Corporal Knight with twelve replacements reporting for duty, sir."

"It's good to have you back, Daniel. How is that foot healing?"

"No problems, sir. It's as good as ever."

"We've had some major battles since you left, and we've lost a lot of men. I was hoping for more than twelve replacements, but you can't look a gift horse in the mouth. We need every man we can get."

"I wish there were more, sir, but there's very few young men left in Amherst. Where is the rest of the nineteenth camped?"

"You're looking at `em. We're down from a regiment of about four hundred men to fewer than fifty now."

"In the whole regiment?"

"That's correct. Of course, not all were killed. Several were wounded, but only a handful of those will be returning."

"I remember when the regiment first was formed. We had over eight hundred men."

"I don't think we'll ever have that many again."

"I reckon that's true sir, sad but true. But as they say, one Southern boy fighting is equal to three Yankees. Where is company H located?"

Gantt turned and pointed toward the river. "Right over there on Barefoot Avenue. You can't miss it."

The regiment had built shelters along the Rappahannock River comparable to the ones we had built the previous year at Centreville. Each one was constructed with logs packed with small stones and mud to keep out the cold winter winds. It was easy to find Barefoot Avenue. Each street proudly displayed its own name carved on a plank from a discarded crate.

I walked down the muddy street, and a wave of emotion swept over me. I felt as if I had never left. Smoke swirled up from every chimney as evening temperatures fell. I pondered which hut George was in. Some of the places had names carved above the doors. I passed "Growlers," "Holly Joe's," "Howlers," and then I knew in an instant which place was ours. Above the door was inscribed "Daniel's Den." I remember George saying to me as I lay in the hospital wounded that he would build a house for me to return to. He refused to give up hope that I wouldn't fully recover. "Naw," he would say, "you ain't gonna loose that foot."

"Hey, I'm hungry. Is supper ready?" I shouted as I opened the door. George was sitting on an empty ammo box reading an old newspaper. He turned, leaping to his feet in surprise. George was thinner than I remembered. He looked weather-beaten, but he sure was a sight for sore eyes. I grabbed and hugged him.

"George, your ma sent this package to you. Both your parents are well and send their love. Where's Buzzard?

"Buzzard hung up his fiddle at Fredericksburg.

I was beside him when he died," said George.

I felt as though I had been gut shot. Recovering my breath, I asked, "Did he suffer long?"

"He didn't know what hit him. After he was shot, he turned toward me as if trying to say something, exhaled, and fell down. I guess you heard about Colonel Strange getting killed and Gantt being promoted to Colonel."

"Yeah, I saw him when I first arrived."

"Well, I guess you can say Colonel Gantt is the biggest toad in the pond, now."

"Seems so." Although no longer in a party mood, I was keenly aware of George's hunger and handed him some bacon and corn meal along with the package his Ma had sent him from home. "Wanta cook it up?"

"You bet. I was fixing to have some homemade soup made from water, grass and a tad bit of flour, but it can wait. We'll have it tomorrow night."

"Tell you what. You cook the bacon while I find the twenty eighth and see if I can catch up with Ossen."

"He's on the next street over, Mudville Avenue. You can't miss it, but you better hurry, 'cause I ain't waiting for you, once the bacon's ready. Hell, it's been so long since I've had good bacon, I may eat it raw, before you get out the door."

"You'll enjoy it more fried, and I'll be back before you can cook it."

Ossen was glad to see me and wanted to hear everything about home. "We'll get together later tonight and I'll bring you up to date then," I said. "George is cooking, and if I don't get back soon he'll eat everything in sight."

I could smell the bacon frying a block away as the scent rose up the chimney and lazily circulated throughout the camp. A voice cried out, "Where in God's name did you Rebs get that bacon? There ain't a hog within thirty miles of here."

I wheeled around as if I was about to be shot. "Who's that?" I called out.

"Over here, across the river. I can tell by your uniform you're new here. Don't worry, we got a truce between us for now. We don't shoot you'en, and you'en agreed not to shoot us during this-here winter camp. Heck boy, we been reading each other's newspapers. We trade within a couple of hours after they're delivered from town. The papers let us know how we been doing in the war."

"One night last week our band was playing, 'The Battle Hymn of the Republic' when one of your boys shouted out, play something for us. Our band played 'Dixie.' Then the two bands struck up the same tune and men on both sides of the river, joined in singing 'Home Sweet Home.'"

"Well, I'm sure glad to hear about that. I'll be seeing you." Realizing how stupid that sounded I quickly added, "After the war I hope." The wind picked up, and I could smell the rain coming. I turned and increased my pace back to the shelter. I thought to myself, it's not as warm as back home, but it's my home for now, and I must think positive about it.

The rain began to fall and quickly turned to sleet. I dashed inside, completely drenched. George had already devoured his share of the bacon and was in his bed, with his eyes closed. I poured myself a cup of coffee and sniffed at the steaming cup. "It's raining again, George."

"Yes it is, but at least it smells like coffee," he replied, turning over in his bed.

"George, have you ever been in love?" He did not answer. I lay awake a long time; my gaze riveted on the ceiling. I began to think of Sarah, and thanked God for keeping her safe. I soon fell asleep.

In the morning we awoke to a heavy snow storm. Snow had fallen most of the night and continued to fall until we had at the very least, six inches of snow on the ground. During the next few days, we amused ourselves by playing cards, checkers, or chess. I loved to read, but poor lighting made reading impossible in the evenings. When the winds died down, we moved outside. I watched as George played mumbley-peg with a new recruit from Company "D." The two faced each other and threw knives as close as possible to their opponent's feet. If your blade stuck in the ground closer to his foot than his stuck to yours, you won. If your opponent flinched by moving his foot, he also lost. The loser had to pull the knife out of the ground with his teeth.

Over on Mudville Avenue, a serious card game of Monte went on. I didn't understand it entirely, but I watched and noticed the dealer laid out four cards, and players bet on the two top and bottom cards that would be matched before the others.

The following day was Saturday, and as Ossen and I walked along the riverbanks, we stopped and engaged in small talk with four Yanks across the river.

Although a verbal truce was in place, we still never fully trusted them not to attack. Pickets were posted around the clock.

Picket duty was a lonely, cold duty to have in the winter. To stay awake was torture; to doze was death. I once heard of a soldier who was found frozen stiff at his post as he stood looking across the open field. Icicles hung from his face. When I drew picket duty, I wrapped old newspapers around my feet before putting on my shoes, to help keep my feet from freezing. If I could find enough newspaper, I also wrapped it around my chest.

❧

February came and rumors began to fly that we would soon be moving out. Toward the end of the month, we received orders to make preparations for departure at the first light of dawn. Although the news meant giving up our shelters, we were excited to be on the move again. Boredom had set in from the dreary and wretchedness of winter quarters. We heard the Yanks had assembled a major force and, in all probability, planned once again to attack Richmond. We had beaten a force far superior in numbers than ours the previous December at Fredericksburg, and were confident we could do it again.

That evening, we were issued a ration of coffee. It was crisp and cool as we sat around the fire. I buried my face in the curling vapor of hot steam that rose from my cup and sipped the coffee slowly. The scalding liquid trickled down my throat and spread a warm feeling within my body. I became preoccupied with the usual thoughts preceding a battle. Night soon deepened into starry darkness. I sat staring through the green pines at the majestic sky, wondering if Sarah was also looking at the stars this very minute. I thought to myself, I must write a letter to her before dropping off to sleep this evening, but I didn't that day.

Drums and bugles sounded reveille just before dawn. I rolled out of my blanket and dressed hurriedly in the dark before leaving our warm shelter for the cold, damp morning. We assembled for roll call and were told we were heading south toward Petersburg.

With a major movement of the entire corps, it took time to assemble the men, pack the long trains of white-topped wagons, gather and hitch up the mules, and connect our field artillery pieces to the horses in final preparation for moving out. Many of the veterans, myself included, refused to be loaded down with a full knapsack. I packed essential items such as toiletries and what little food I had in my blanket, rolled it up, slung it over one shoulder, and tied the other end to my opposite hip. I threw the dregs of my coffee on the ground and took my position in line.

Columns of men formed in regiments, brigades, and divisions. Regimental flags unfurled and popped like the sound of gunfire in the morning breeze. Amid the clanking of gear, creaking wagons, cracking of the long whips, mules braying, horses snorting, and thousands of feet shuffling we moved forward. Our drummer boys beat a cadence for us to keep step with Ba-rum, Ba-rum, Ba-rum dum dum. At first we moved slowly, our pace measured by our creeping supply wagons, until they gained momentum. Then our regimental band played marching tunes. I wondered what the Yanks across the river thought, awaking to all of the noise and commotion. It must have scared the fire out of them, thinking we were attacking, as we marched forward, our musket barrels glistening in the morning light.

I worked a quid of tobacco around to the back of my mouth, then swung around to take one final look at our camp site. I realized there could be no retreat except to the grave.

Local town's people were out in force to cheer us on. Many waved Confederate flags in support of our cause. A group of young ladies came out with buckets of fresh water for us. The sight created an immense thirst within the ranks. Each man attempted to take a sip of water and asked a question, simply to hear the sound of a feminine voice. I have never seen such painful straining of necks and gawking in my life.

The longer we marched, the colder the weather got. I longed for the warmth of the shelter we had left behind. Any minute, we expected to turn off the road and camp in the woods for the evening. As darkness approached, we finally came to a halt and set about preparing for the night. Temperatures dropped dramatically and wind gusts whipped our camp so severely they lifted my tent from the ground and deposited it across the way. I was forced to sleep wrapped only in a single blanket, exposed to the sleet and rain that continued to fall throughout the night.

The next day we arrived at Petersburg totally exhausted, cold, wet, and hungry. Pickets were assigned to protect our perimeter; thank God our company did not draw the assignment. We gathered what firewood we could find, erected our tents, and prepared our evening meal.

"George, remember that farm we passed a little while ago?" I asked.

"Yeah, I saw it,"

"I bet if we pooled our money, we could buy something to eat from that farmer."

"You may be right, let's try it."

We waited until dark had fully set in. After resting, a bit, George and I went in search of the farm. Not wishing to alarm anyone, we approached the barn cautiously. We came upon the farmer butchering a hog for his family. Seeing we were Confederates, he welcomed us and offered us some chittlins and hoecakes, which we gratefully accepted.

"What brings you boys to my farm?"

"Well, sir, we would like to buy some of that hog you're butchering."

"His eyebrows rose. It's all we have left, but I believe I could sell you boys at least a shoulder."

"Yes, sir, we'd like to buy a shoulder." We closed the deal.

"Pa," a small boy shouted as he burst into the barn. "There's a Cavalry patrol heading this way."

"You boys better hide in the root cellar, until I find out for sure who it is and what they want. Ishmael, show `em the way."

We crawled under the house where we discovered potatoes, carrots, turnips, and onions being stored there. With a crunch, George bit into a turnip. "All we got to eat, my foot," said George. "By golly, I plan to eat my dollars worth right here."

"Shhh," I said. We remained still and listened. It was indeed a union Cavalry patrol that wanted only to fill its canteens and water its horses.

As soon as they were gone, we climbed out of the cellar, paid for our ham, and hastily departed.

The aroma of a ham cooking on an open pit soon filtered through the camp. Captain Clark just happened to be in the area and stopped by.

"Care to set in, Captain?"

"Thank you kindly," he said. "How did you boys come by a hog?"

"Well, sir," replied George, "it's kind of creepy. We came across a dead pig that one of our battery horses had kicked. I didn't think we should leave it lying in the road."

"Easy, friend," the captain said. Doubt showed on his face, especially after he bit down on a bullet, but after we assured him it was the head of a horseshoe nail, he continued to eat and enjoy the meat.

The incident reminded me of the time at Centreville when starving men, craving the fresh corn they had just marched past, returned that evening to confiscate a few ears. The next day, the farmer, complained to the colonel, who apologized for his men and assured him that he would take appropriate action. He did. He shared what corn they had taken, then sent them back for more.

∽⁀∾

May came, and the dogwood, in full bloom, flashed its spectral white in the woods. Wild honeysuckle scrambled across the ground to hug the tree trunks.

We received word General "Stonewall" Jackson was accidentally shot at Chancellorsville. He was on reconnaissance in front of his lines. When he headed back, his own men saw, mounted figures wrapped in overcoats galloping toward them, thought it was a federal attack and opened fire. A volley of musket balls hit the general, once in his right hand and twice in his left arm. Jackson was taken to a hospital near The Old Wilderness Tavern where the doctors chose to amputate his left arm. General Lee, upon hearing of the amputation, said, "He has lost his left arm, but I have lost my right arm."

Because the federal soldiers could possibly reach the field hospital, Jackson was ordered moved. When asked if he had any choice of destination, Jackson requested to be taken to Chandler's place at Guiney's Station, where he had earlier spent a few days.

He thought this a good choice, because it was close to the railroad and Richmond. The nineteenth, having bivouacked at Guiney's station earlier, was familiar with the area and being nearby at the time was ordered to dispatch two companies to the Chandler's plantation to provide security for the General's arrival. Our company, in addition to two others, was sent to the field hospital at Wilderness Run to provide escort for the general. To make the journey as comfortable as possible, a detail was sent ahead to clear the road of debris.

As we traveled southeast down Brock Road, people gathered to pay their respects, and watch in awe as the general passed by in an army ambulance. Tears filled many well-wishers' eyes. We passed Todd's Tavern on the way to the Spotsylvania courthouse, where we stopped awhile to rest by the village well. From there we continued southward, crossed the Ny River near the Massaponax Church, and moved toward Guiney's Station. We passed the railroad depot before coming to Chandler's Fairfield Plantation.

The Chandler's home was an appealing brick dwelling with four fireplaces. The main house sat back from the road in a grove of oak trees. Although ravaged by war, it still had a welcoming look. Next to the house was a small building, which I later learned was used as an office. As we approached the home, I saw several wounded Confederate soldiers sitting on the front porch. Saddle horses and carriages lined the road. High-ranking soldiers and doctors had arrived earlier and were busy making plans for the general's arrival. General Jackson, although semiconscious, noticed the home was being used as a temporary field hospital and said he did not want anyone moved for him.

Together with his doctors, he agreed the small office building would serve his needs very well. Servants scurried about moving a bed, chairs, and other items of furniture to make the cottage more comfortable for the general and his staff. The following day, Mrs. Jackson, their daughter, Julia, and several more physicians arrived.

Crouched beside a scant fire of twigs on

Saturday evening, soldiers who had served with the general told several stories. I felt honored to be present. Captain Blackford, a courier on Jackson's staff told the most memorable story.

"President Jefferson Davis called for a meeting in Richmond of Generals Lee and Jackson. With the federal troops within striking distance of Jackson's troops, Jackson was reluctant to abandon his soldiers, but felt obliged to follow orders so, with his staff at hand, he set out for Richmond. I was not privy to the discussions, but I do know the meeting lasted no more than thirty minutes. Once outside, the three distinguished gentlemen talked for a few moments on the steps of the President's house. They shook hands cordially and bid each other farewell. Jackson got on his horse, which I had been holding for him. Without saying a word to anyone he left in a gallop, with the rest of us close behind, toward the Mechanicsville Pike, which we soon reached.

"By his own orders to his corps, he strictly enjoined preservation of crops along the roads the army and its trains traveled. He had forbade all officers and men from riding in the fields next to the road side. He tried to remain on the road, but it was slow going, and I could tell the general was especially eager to get back to his men. Long wagon trains filled the pike. Some were going to Richmond, and others were headed out with supplies. Under such circumstances he found it impossible to make time and also obey his own orders. He had to dodge in and out among the wagons. His progress was slow, much slower than his needs demanded. He ordered us to fall in a single file, and then he rode out into an extensive oat field and struck a gallop. Several hundred yards ahead was a farm house. The owner, a fat little gentleman in his shirt sleeves, sat on his porch smoking his pipe. He had one eye focused on the morning's Examiner and the other on his beloved oats. When he saw us he threw down his paper, rushed down the steps, and raced along the path. When we reached the place where the path and the pike united, he was standing like a lion, puffing and blowing, wiping the perspiration from his brow and so bursting with rage that all power of speech seemed gone.

"The General saw him, and for the first time in his career, seemed inclined to retreat. By that time the irate farmer regained his speech and roared out obscenities as Jackson drew rein within ten feet of him.

"Why the hell are you riding over my oats? Didn't you know it's against orders?

"The general looked confused, fumbled at his bridle rein, and was as abashed as any schoolboy ever caught trespassing in a watermelon patch. Before he could get a word out, the man had another volcanic eruption: 'Damn you, don't you know it's against orders? I intend to have every damn one of you arrested. What's your name, anyhow?

" 'My name is Jackson.'

" 'Jackson! Jackson!' The farmer's voice showed great contempt. 'Well, Jackson, I intend to report every one of you and have you all arrested. Yes, I'd report you, if you were old "Stonewall" himself, instead of damn quartermasters and commissaries riding through my oats. Yes, I'll report you to "Stonewall" Jackson himself, that's what I'll do.'

" 'They call me by that name sometimes,' the general said.

" 'What name?'

" 'Stonewall.'

"By that time, several of us had ridden up pretty close to see the fun, and I think when the old fellow saw a smile playing on our faces, his suspicions got aroused.

"The gentleman's tone changed.' 'What name did you say, sir?'

" 'Stonewall.'

" 'You don't mean to say you are "Stonewall" Jackson, do you?'

" 'Yes, sir, I am.'

"I can give you no adequate description of the sudden change that came over him. His anger was gone in an instant, and in its place came an admiration that was adoration. Tears stood in his eyes. His speech came with all the vigor of his vernacular. He shouted and waved his bandanna around his head, 'hurrah for "Stonewall" Jackson! By God, general, do me the honor. Please ride all over my damn old oats!'

"It was a wonderful scene and one I shall never forget. The old man would not let the general pass 'til he and all us aides had taken a glass of cold buttermilk. He pressed the general to take every variety of strong drink, but buttermilk was all he would take. As we left his home, we made sure we traveled down the path to the pike."

≼֍≽

I placed a limb on the fire and watched in silence as the flickering flames engulfed it. We sat motionless, staring at the reflection of our fire, waiting and waiting. Word came down, that the general had taken a turn for the worse. Everyone was deeply disturbed, and several offered prayers.

"Damn it," George said, his lips quivering as his voice trailed off.

The half-darkness of the approaching day soon gave way to the morning light. It was the Sabbath. The doctors had lost all hope of Jackson's recovery, but as he grew physically weaker, he remained spiritually strong. It was said he had always desired to die on the Sabbath.

Mrs. Jackson, who had not left the general's side since she arrived, came outside. A death-like silence came over us. Our worst fears were soon confirmed. It struck our hearts a grievous blow. At thirty-nine years of age, General Thomas J. Jackson, one of the bravest, shrewdest and most daring soldiers, had died. It was Sunday May 10, 1863. By evening, reporters, as well as embalmers with a coffin, began to arrive. Word quickly spread, which produced a gloom across the South

That evening we gathered by our campfire. His aide told us that the Lord had sent his angels to escort the general to heaven, but they couldn't find him anywhere. They returned to heaven and were making out a report, when to their astonishment there he was. "Old Jack" had outflanked the angels and gotten to heaven before them.

Monday morning, our company, marching with reversed arms, escorted the general's casket down the walkway, over the terraces, to the railroad station. The whole South mourned the loss of its beloved general.

Thousands crowded the tracks, waiting for hours to pay their respects and gain a glimpse as the funeral train slowly rolled by, carrying their fallen champion.

As the train steamed into Richmond, I heard the bells tolling his death. Crowds had assembled lining the streets from the railroad station to the capitol. Carriages containing statesmen, military officers, and friends attempted to maneuver in the streets. Bands with muffled drums swelled the cortege following the hearse, drawn by four white horses. The general's coffin was draped in both the Virginia and the Confederate flags.

The pelting of rain on the carriages and umbrellas prevented us from hearing the speeches, but I'm positive Jackson's memory will live forever in the hearts of his countrymen. Stories will be told to children and grandchildren of all southern soldiers, and they in turn will pass them along to their descendants. I bet no one will forget the deeds and glory inspired by General Thomas "Stonewall" Jackson.

Later we boarded the train and continued our journey to Lexington for General Jackson's funeral. Services were held at the Presbyterian Church followed by his burial in the town cemetery, not far from Virginia Military Institute, where he taught before the war.

Dr. McGuire carefully noted Jackson's last words. "A smile of ineffable sweetness spread itself over his pale face, and he said quietly, and with an expression as if of relief, 'Let us cross over the river, and rest under the shade of the trees.' "

Divisions, Brigades, and Regiments,
with names of commanding officers in the First Army Corps.
June 22, 1863

FIRST ARMY CORPS
Lieut. Gen. JAMES LONGSTREET
DIVISION
Maj. Gen. GEORGE E. PICKETT

Brigade Brig. Gen. James L. Kemper	Brigade Brig. Gen. RICHARD B. GARNETT	Brigade Brig. Gen. LEWIS A. ARMISTEAD
1st VA., Col. Lewis B. Williams	8th VA., Col. Eppa Hunton	9th VA.,
3rd VA., Col. Joseph Mayo, Jr.	18th VA.,	Lieut. Col. J.S. Gilliam
7th VA., Col. W.T. Patton	Col. R.E. Whithers	Maj. John C. Owens
11th VA., Col. David Funsten	Lieut. Col. H.A. Carrington	14th VA., Col. James G. Hodges
24th VA., Col. William R. Terry	19th VA., Col. Henry Gatt	38th VA., Col. F.C. Edmonds
	28th VA., Col. R.C. Allen	53rd VA., Col. W.R. Aylett
	56th VA., Col. W.D. Stuart	57th VA., Col. J. Bowie Magruder

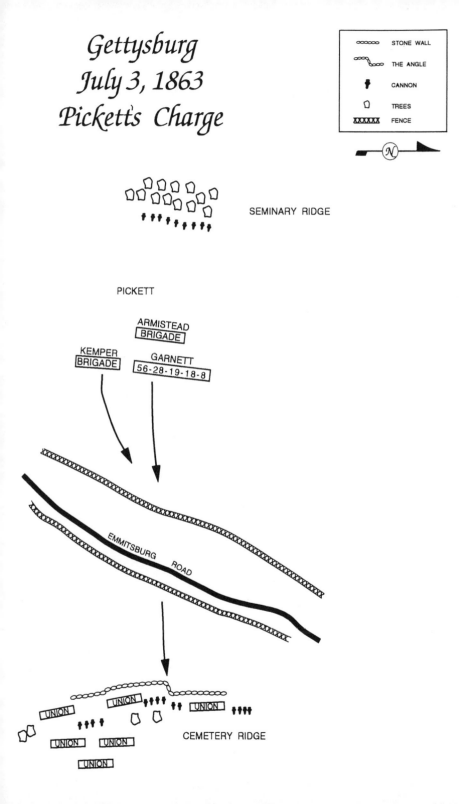

THE STONE WALL AT GETTYSBURG

OPEN FIELD THE CONFEDERATES TRAVELED ACROSS TO REACH THE STONE WALL. THERE WAS A DISTANCE OF APPROXIMATELY 1,200 FEET FROM THE TREES TO THE WALL.

Gettysburg

❧❧

On Thursday, the second of July, our division, by then five thousand strong, had our endurance tested. We marched, weighted down with our rifles and knapsacks, through choking clouds of dust that clogged our throats and nostrils. The day aged quickly with intense hell-like heat, drying the fields with brutal soaring temperatures. The sun followed us relentlessly. We cursed and itched, sweltering beneath our heavy uniforms. We marched through the woods and valleys, fording many streams, stopping only briefly to fill our canteens and pick some unripe berries that zigzagged through the fence rails along the way. I reminisced of the time as a young boy when I couldn't wait to grab a pail and gather blackberries for Mama to make a cobbler. Papa used to tell me to be patient that the berries would bloom about the same time the shad swam upriver, but I knew I had only a few days before the squirrels and the birds would gobble the fruit.

Three miles from Gettysburg, we halted to bivouac for the night. Thirsty and completely worn out, my whole body throbbed in pain. Our clothing and hair were matted with dirt and filth. We appeared as ragged a bunch, as you would ever want to meet. Slowly, I poured water from my canteen over my head and let it run down my face and into my eyes. It was cool and it washed away layers of dirt. I took a swig to clear my throat but spit out the muddy water. Gradually the rapid pumping in my ears eased up and the headache began to die down. I supposed it was only natural for men to drag their feet during a hard march, but it sure did kick up the dust. Although we had marched some twenty-five miles that day I was impatient to hear about what had happened at Gettysburg.

After a short rest, we secured our camp and pickets were posted. Harry went about gathering firewood. George prepared our evening meal, which amounted to green apples and potatoes boiled and mashed together then seasoned with onions and garlic. Rations had not been issued for several days, and we had been living on hard crackers and items we appropriated along the way.

I was slapping at my pants trying desperately to remove the dust that had penetrated them, when the driver of a supply wagon returning from Gettysburg shouted out, "We've driven the Yankees back." His words were greeted with loud cheers. It confirmed rumors that had been circulating all day; we had won a decisive battle at Gettysburg. The boys from Georgia had overrun a federal entrenchment and captured six Parrot guns. The Alabamians and Texans had captured hundreds of prisoners and forced an entire federal brigade to retreat. Although we had licked them badly, we knew they were assembling a massive force; they were far from defeated. I suspected a large battle was brewing for the next day.

We were told to remain alert and ready to move at a double-quick pace, day or night. Horses that pulled the guns and caissons were to be kept in harness and, except for a brief period when they were taken for water, they were to be kept hooked to the limbers ready to move at a moment's notice.

In the distance, the sky was aglow with a red blaze from the thunderous roar of cannons firing in rapid succession. I knew somewhere out there we were catching hell. I was convinced Gettysburg was not going be a small scrimmage.

I gathered the canteens and walked briskly down the slope toward the riverbank. At the edge, I squatted and plunged my head into the cool water. I heard a whisper-like voice from across the river. I was startled and quickly glanced at the opposite bank.

"Hey, Johnny Reb, I'll give you some Maryland coffee for a little of that Virginia 'chawing' tobacco."

I nearly jumped out of my skin. I had left my rifle stacked back at camp and was completely defenseless.

"How come you didn't shoot me?" I asked. "It's what you're supposed to do."

"Hell, boy, I just want a chaw. I don't want the whole damn Confederate army shooting at me."

I thought about what he said and decided he

was right, and besides I wouldn't want to kill someone I'd had a conversation with. "Stay put, I'll be right back."

He hesitated; I could feel his concern.

"Don't worry, I'm just going to get some Lone Jack. It's the best tobacco there is. My papa grows it back in Virginia."

To keep from alarming anyone, I walked slowly back to camp, even though I felt like running. I must have looked tense, because George asked, "What's up?"

"Nothing. You just get that water boiling; I'll be right back."

I returned to the stream with the tobacco. At first, I couldn't find the Yank. I thought maybe he had spooked and fled.

"Hey, I'm over here, Reb."

I wheeled around, startled at first. "I got you some tobacco."

"Well, I sure as hell ain't gonna walk over there. Pitch it over."

I tossed it across the creek, and wondered if he would skedaddle with it. I was relieved when he tossed back a sack of coffee, tipped his hat, smiled, and quickly disappeared into the woods.

"Well I'll be dang," said George. "Where did you get that coffee?"

"Don't ask," I replied.

I ground up the beans and poured a few into a cup filled with water, then placed the cup directly on the coals. Soon the delicious aroma of the coffee filled the air. I lay back against a large pine and watched as gray smoke from the fire rose skyward in the evening air. I took a sip of coffee and wished I was home on our front porch swing with Sarah watching the stars. I was deep in thought, half way dreaming, halfway listening to our regimental band, when they began playing, "The Girl I Left Behind." It filled my head with thoughts of Sarah.

When I get home, I thought, I'll marry Sarah and raise a family on that parcel of land Papa deeded to me. I've grown tired of this war and the camp life that comes with it, but it's for Sarah, Mama and the others that we must drive the Yankees from our southern borders before we can rest. I'm afraid if this war lasts much longer I'll be out of practice and forget how to kiss Sarah. At least, I'm not as bad as some. Last week a wash-woman came to our camp, and the whole dadburn bunch gawked at her.

George shouted from across the way, "Hey, Daniel, want to play cards?"

I was eager to get my mind away from home and the visions of what the next day might bring, so I nodded yes. I told George I could only play for a while; I wanted to get letters off to Sarah and Mama before turning in.

I was concentrating on whether to draw one card or three when I thought I recognized a voice from behind me.

"Is this where company H is bivouacked?"

"Sure is," George said without even looking up.

"Well, do you know where I can find Daniel...."

Before he could finish, I turned around. It was my brother Ossen. We saw each other at the same time.

"Ossen, you're back. How are Papa and Mama?

What's the news from home?" I had so many questions.

"Not so fast. Papa and Mama are both in good health. I did learn the 1st Tennessee Artillery Division arrived here this morning. Isn't Cousin Jerry in that division?"

"He sure is. I haven't seen Jerry in a long time."

"Well, with thousands of soldiers arriving everyday, I doubt you'll find him, but I guess anything's possible."

Deep in conversation, we were surprised when George announced it was time for the evening prayer meeting with Reverend Starnes. The reverend always held a special service on the eve of a battle.

"Want to come with me to prayer service before returning?" I asked.

"Sure, I'll make time for that."

That evening, many men re-affirmed their loyalty to God and the South as they stood in a circle, hands linked, as Reverend Starnes led them in prayer. Several had discussions regarding their concerns about dying and the families they would leave behind. One fellow wanted to know if a drunken hell-raiser had a chance of getting into heaven. Reverend Starnes reassured him that except for denying God, there was no sin too great for forgiveness.

The minister's message that evening was from the book of John, Chapter fourteen, verses one, two, and three. "Let not your hearts be troubled, ye believe in God, believe also in me. In my Father's house are many mansions: I go to prepare a place for you." The words seemed to comfort many.

The evening ended too soon, but I knew Ossen had to return to his company.

We embraced, "I can't begin to tell you how great it was to see you."

"Believe me, Daniel, it was equally great for me. I'm glad to see you're well."

As he was leaving, he turned to me and said, "The twenty-eighth's gonna be covering your left flank tomorrow. Don't worry about those Yanks trying to maneuver around you. We'll be right there. You just concentrate on the ones in front." He smiled, waved, and walked away.

I was exhausted when I finally laid down, but thoughts of Sarah kept me from falling asleep. The memory of her long blond hair and her beautiful gray green eyes filled my head. How graceful she was at Bob Wiley's barn-raising dance! She was indeed an angel on earth.

❧❧

On July 3, sleep was broken by the rumble of caissons on the road. I quickly shook off my drowsiness. All around me, men came to their feet. As the darkness gave way to light reveille sounded. I grabbed a hoecake and assumed my assigned position in the line. Our division prepared to move out.

Bustle and confusion reigned. Surgeons busily prepared their supplies. Litter bearers and ambulances stood ready and waiting. George and I renewed our pledges to seek each other out, if we were missing by nightfall.

Several men read their testaments; others muttered silent prayers. We were issued forty rounds of ammunition, plus rations consisting of one piece of salt pork, about the size of a thumb, a small amount of lard, and some hardtack.

By early morning light, with our regimental band playing, we marched toward Gettysburg. The weather was clear, indicating a day that would not be interrupted by the elements. I could already tell it was going to be a hot one. The steady tramping of feet kicked up dust as the sun climbed into the sky. Perspiration streamed down our faces. George bit off a chew of tobacco to relieve his tensions, then passed it over to me. "Want a chew, Daniel?"

"Not now. It don't mix well with the dirt and grit in my mouth, but thanks anyway."

The farther we marched, the more we discovered that the roadside and marshes were strewn with men and animals, lying among the swamp lilies. They had been killed or severely wounded during the previous days of fighting, and the dead were now decomposing in the sweltering heat. I heard groans, moaning, and screams from wounded men begging for water and calling out for their mothers. Others simply cried out, pleading for us to stop and help them. "For God's sake, please help me. Don't leave me here to die." Hundreds of muskets lay in the road, mixed with cooking utensils, personal possessions, blankets, and knapsacks. The walking wounded lined the roads, returning from bloody battles. Wagons and caissons lay overturned and destroyed. Artillery horses lay with their harness still on. The sight left little doubt of what we were about to encounter.

By ten o'clock we reached the field at Gettysburg. Our artillery had arrived the night before and posted hub to hub along a line of trees west of Emmitsburg Road. Our regiment was halted near the fringe of the trees, then ordered behind a hill overlooking our artillery,

Soon the Yankee artillery began the most severe bombardment I had ever encountered. It burst the silence like full notes from a church organ. The ground quivered beneath our feet as if it were about to be torn apart. Hundreds of field pieces were fired at the same time, accompanied with an equal number of explosions from shells. The fire far exceeded any I had ever witnessed. I found myself bleeding from both ears from concussion, as did many others.

A shell whistled over my head, exploding directly behind me. I was frightened. For once in my life, I tried to make myself as small as possible. Men who had been at our forward post staggered back toward our lines covered in blood and writhing in pain.

The deep roar of our artillery added to the clamor as we returned fire. I rose up to observe from behind a rock that I had tried to crawl under. The air was filled with projectiles, several bursting at once. Across the road, I spotted my cousin Jerry beside the 1st Tennessee Artillery. I had last seen him about two years before He had married a girl from Tennessee and moved to the wilderness to be near her ailing parents.

Tall and handsome with a rugged, weather-beaten look, he had dauntless courage. Jerry, a sergeant major stood rigid and unflinching, while missiles burst all around. As he turned to his waiting gunner, he gave the command, "Load, come to ready. Fire." The gunner pulled the lanyard, and the twelve-pounder solid brass Napoleon spoke with an ear-splitting blast, like a fire-breathing dragon. Flames and white smoke burst from its muzzle.

Each time the big guns fired, they recoiled. A log was used to mark the original spot for the artillery-men to quickly turn the guns back to their original position, before firing again.

Colonel Gantt tapped me on the shoulder. "Son, you better hunker down before you lose your head." I slid behind a rock, praying it was large enough to protect me.

Nervous and scared, I wiped the dust from my rifle and checked and re-checked my ammunition. My mouth was dry, my palms wet and clammy, and I was extremely thirsty. I knew I had to conserve water, but I felt compelled to take a sip from my canteen.

Around noon, we moved to the fringe of a nearby apple grove. At first we crouched among the trees then we were ordered to lay face down to escape the shells that passed over us from several directions. The bombardment continued. Shells screeched through the trees and burst with a thunderous sound, splitting limbs that crashed down around us. As I hugged and clawed at the earth, a pain exploded in my back. Fearing I was hit by shell fragments, I envisioned pieces of jagged metal lodged in my back, my life blood oozing from my body.

"George, I've been shot" I hollered out.

"Is it a serious wound?"

"I'm not sure, but it doesn't hurt much."

I lay motionless, calling for water, which I had witnessed many a wounded soldier do, but soon I realized I wasn't experiencing any pain. I carefully reached back over my shoulder, but I couldn't feel any blood. I realized I hadn't been shot at all; I had been pelted by small green apples. Now that I wasn't dead, I bit into an apple; I was starved. The fruit was sour, but filling. I remember Mama used to boil the tart apples with sugar to make crab apple jelly.

Word came down that General Lee had assigned Pickett's Division the post of honor. In turn, General Pickett assigned our regiment the forward point, which meant we would be leading the charge. General Kemper's regiment was on our right and General Armistead's regiment was on our left, slightly behind us. Our assignment was indeed an honor, but the thought of such responsibility was frightening. I felt apprehensive about the orders that could seal our fate. We had been eager for a fight, a fight it would be.

☙❧ THE BATTLE ☙❧

Upon the bugler's call to arms, followed by the long roll of the snare drums, every man instantly leaped to his feet and rushed forward to where the colors were being formed. The brigade was moved forward to the front lines. Our hour of glory had arrived. The unfurled flags fluttered and snapped as they danced in the summer breeze. We were ordered to cast off our haversacks. I believe George must have been one of the first to discard his. "Now I can shoot," he said. I stood there thinking that before that day ended, many soldiers on both sides would be killed or seriously wounded.

Awaiting the orders to march, I studied the field we would be crossing. We had about 1,500 yards of rolling terrain between us and a stone wall on the crest of a hill. I knew that once we reached the first hill, we would be in range of their rifles, and the real battle would begin. We would have to cross an open field, two fences, and a road before ascending the final slope. Climbing over those fences could be disastrous. General Garnett pointed out our rendezvous point, a cluster of trees, where the stone wall took a sharp turn and formed an angle.

General Lee soon approached astride his favorite horse, Traveler. He rode erect in the saddle. His keen dark eyes took in everything around him. Several men saluted. One shouted, "We'll lick 'em for you and Virginia, Bobby." I removed my cap and held it over my heart in deep respect for such a great man.

General Pickett, puffing on a cigar, rode behind Lee. He reined in his horse beside General Garnett, and I heard him say, "Once you get within rifle range, get across that field as quickly as you can. I'm afraid you're gonna catch hell today."

I turned to George and said, "If we don't meet again on earth, I'll see you in heaven." He looked at me and smiled.

General Pickett stood up in his stirrups and shouted, "Men, don't forget today you are Virginians." Few could hear him because our lines stretched out

SKETCH BY A.R. WAUD, LIBRARY OF CONGRESS

nearly a mile long, parallel to the enemy. "It won't be hard to reach that ridge. The hell of it will be to stay there."

George nudged me to glance up at the entrance sign posted over the top of the cemetery gate. It read, "All persons found using firearms in these grounds will be prosecuted with the utmost rigor of the law."

General Pickett raised his sword, and shouted, "Remember to rally around the flag! It's a-ways across the field so advance slowly, no firing until we get within range. His orders rang down the line. F-o-o-o-o-r-r-r-r-w-a-a-a-r-r-r-d M-a-a-r-r-ch.!"

It was nearing three in the afternoon; I had a gnawing feeling in my stomach. Was it nerves, the green apples, or was I still hungry and suffering from the intense heat?

The stirring rhythm of fife and drums signaled the command to march. My pulse beat rapidly as we began to advance, into the valley of death. The bloodletting had begun.

Our bayonets, flashing in the sun, must have sent a chill through the enemy as we steadily advanced toward Cemetery Ridge, ignoring the hellish roar of their murderous cannons.

The dust from the shuffling of thousands of feet, shells bursting, cannons roaring, soon obliterated all points of view. I was unable to see our regimental flag directly in front of me.

"Close up, men; close up." We were ordered to double-quick march, a severe test of endurance as the rippling heat rose from the earth. We continued in a straight line; several were killed or severely wounded, others moved forward closing the gap. Never in my life had I ever heard or seen anything equal to that. We were marching into hell. Shells burst all around. Jagged pieces of iron and shrapnel rained down on us like a hailstorm. The Yanks poured into us the most destructive fire I had ever witnessed. Human life was being poured out like water.

Soon we reached the crest of the first hill and were in range of their rifles. They commenced firing with such intense force, our wounded were returning to our lines in streams. Men begging for help fell in every direction. I wondered if anyone would escape the carnage. Projectiles tore up the ground, pinging and popping all around, covering me with dirt and gravel. Amid dense smoke and the never-ending roar of cannons, I became so disoriented that I couldn't tell where my regiment was. I saw flashes of powder rising from Yankee guns, and I moved in that direction.

Pandemonium prevailed. Bursting shells set the grass ablaze. Horses and riders were sprawled on the ground dead or dying. Our color bearers were being slaughtered, but in spite of the dangers, we pressed on.

No place was safe. I was never more scared in my life, as I continued forward, loading and firing, praying all the way. My rifle grew so hot I could no longer hold it to reload. I threw it down and picked up another one from a dead soldier.

I was next to General Garnett, when his horse was hit with a shell fragment. The horse spooked and reared. I grabbed the halter to steady the animal.

From over the hill, a courier approached. Spotting the general, he jerked his reins in our direction and headed toward us at a breakneck speed. He reined in his lathered mount beside the general and bent forward to steady his horse by running his hand over his horse's neck as he spoke.

"General Garnett, Sir, General Pickett wanted you to know our artillery ammunition is running low. He's not sure how much longer he'll be able to support you properly. He also wished me to sadly inform you that Colonel Gantt has been wounded."

"Are Gantt's wounds bad?"

"I understand he was shot in the face and taken prisoner. The general wishes to know if Gantt's men will continue to fight."

"Yes, like hell, if you give them the chance."

The courier tipped the brim of his hat, spun around on his wild-eyed horse, dug his spurs deeply into its flesh, and galloped away in a cloud of dust.

I knew that, without Gantt's leadership or artillery support, the battle would be disastrous, but there is no turning back. Our losses grew each step of the way.

We reached the first of two fences. The night before, our skirmishers attempted to tear them down, but they were too solidly constructed. We had to endure the briars and thorns surrounding the fence, beating at them with the butts of our rifles in a futile attempt to dislodge them. The order was given to climb over. With our rebel yell of Wa-ooweey we reached the first fence amid a volley of rifle fire and belching cannons and quickly leaped across. We heard sounds of pop! Bang! Whiz! Thud! Men went down en masse. Bullets passed through my clothing but I remained unscathed. Just when I was thinking it couldn't get any worse, a death-like silence fell over our artillery. My God, I thought, our cannons are silent. We could no longer depend on their support, and we were in range of their deadly grape and canister that could literally tear a man to shreds. The massacre had begun.

Like rows of corn in a field, men fell in straight lines. I thought my entire company had been killed or wounded, but I was determined to continue as long as I could. All regimental action had ceased. The outcome was up to each individual.

I scrambled over the second fence. The Yanks fired another explosive volley with deadly accuracy. I felt mini balls tearing through my shirt as I landed on the other side. Worse I heard the thumping sound of bullets tearing into the flesh of those around me. One soldier made a futile attempt to ease his fall by tamping his rifle butt on the ground, but he was clearly dead. Another soldier stunned by a bullet to his chest sat spread-legged on the ground. He looked up and promised God that if he could live, he would never drink or cuss again. I moved on wondering if he would live or die. In all the excitement, I forgot to remove the ramrod from my rifle. I aimed and fired, sending the rod flying through the air, and landing harmlessly in front of me.

Across the way I saw George. He had been shot. He sat on the ground, leaning forward, elbows on his crossed knees. I panicked and tried to dart parallel over the tops of the dead and wounded. Men were dropping all around me. He waved me off, signaling that he was okay, wounded only in the leg.

"Keep on going," he shouted. I suppose it would have been suicidal for me to remain. I made a mental note of his location so I could return later. I glanced over my shoulder one final time and saw George, his mouth covered with black powder from biting open cartridge packets, sitting calmly in a torrent of iron and lead, puffing on his cigar and sipping fine southern bourbon from a small flask. The burnt powder from his ramrod was on his hands, and when he wiped perspiration from his face, he blackened himself from the roots of his red hair to his chin. He looked in my direction, raising the flask over his head he shouted in a robust voice, "Damn good brew."

In a half stooped-position, I turned away and struggled on. At the crest of the second hill I could see the dead and the wounded piled up in front of the stone wall. I continued forward. Over the crest I went and down the slope until I was directly below the wall. There I came upon a shallow gully. I was exhausted and breathless; I paused and knelt down for a moment to catch my breath before continuing.

General Garnett, straining his horse at a full gallop, crested the top of the hill. An explosive burst of musketry riddled his body and sliced a huge gash in his horse's shoulder. The horse wheeled around. Garnett's face looked bloodless, in intense pain, his lips pressed so hard against his teeth that his mouth was only a thread. The reins fell from his grasp. He reeled in the saddle and fell to the ground, seriously wounded within twenty feet of the wall.

Yet another of our color bearers was shot, but before our flag could hit the ground, Sergeant Garner rushed forward to retrieve it. Holding it aloft in the thickest of the raging battle, he waved it back and forth. The flag served as a rallying point. I heard him shout, "You may kill me, but I will never give up my colors." Within seconds, bullets pierced his body. With his right arm dangling at his side and his leg nearly severed, he crawled the last twenty or so yards on his knees, and with one final effort, gently laid our flag against the stone wall. A Yankee soldier tried desperately to retrieve the prize trophy, but Sergeant Garner had closed his hand in a death grip around the shaft to keep from surrendering it.

Volleys were being exchanged at such short range that men from both sides fell dead, almost in one another's arms. The overpowering numbers of the Yankees was not to be denied. I heard someone call out, "Follow me boys, over the wall."

I rose and, with a tremendous yell charged forward. A shell exploded next to me, ripping away my shirt, and damaging my hearing. I grabbed the wall, and tried to maintain my balance, but my knees buckled and my eyes no longer focused. I hesitated for a moment, then fell abruptly backwards. "Oh God no," I cried out. I sensed a burning sensation to my head. Through the haze, I saw Ossen racing toward me.

Although I knew what was happening I couldn't help myself. Ossen made sure he stood between the Yanks and me. As two men began dragging me to the rear I saw Ossen hit by mini balls that spun him around. He continued to stay on his feet, fighting off his attackers.

⊰∻

The ground felt soft beneath me. A soldier passing by took out his handkerchief and poured water on it from his canteen. He wiped the blood from my head and mouth and gently lifted my head to give me a sip of water.

"Can't make it any farther . . . I need to rest. Would you clasp my hand and stay with me a little while?

"I'll stay right here with you."

"Would you believe, just this morning, I was eating apples . . . from this very tree? . . . Seems so long ago. . . My name is Daniel Knight from Amherst County, Virginia . . . Could you get word to my family? . . . I know they'll worry when I don't write."

"I promise I'll let them know. I'm from Norwood in Nelson Country. It's right down the road from your home. My name is Elisha Smiley; I'm the wagon master."

"Elisha, tell papa . . . I was shot facing the enemy. I wasn't running away. Tell him I died with dignity."

Breathing became more difficult. "Tell Mama I will be closest to her whenever she prays. Return to my Sarah her letters; they're in my pocket. Tell her I will always be near her. Give Stephen my pocketknife . . . My sister Althea . . . tell her I didn't suffer. We were close, and she'll worry the most . . . I must close my eyes and rest for awhile . . . Papa . . . Papa, I can hear the angels singing, Nearer My God To Thee . . . I'm going home . . . .

∽৯৵

Elisha couldn't bring himself to leave the boy to die all alone on a battlefield. He didn't know what to do to ease his pain; he just held his hand. Daniel had lost a great deal of blood and drifted in and out of consciousness. His mind slipped deeper and deeper into darkness. His eyes opened once more. It seemed to comfort him, knowing someone was still there. In a barely audible voice, Daniel said "I am killed . . . Tell all good-bye for me."

A slight smile crossed his face and a glow appeared in his eyes. He seemed overcome by a sense of peace.

Elisha looked heavenward. The sun was ablaze and motionless. A lone bird soared above the smoke-covered battlefield. He asked God to receive this brave soldier.

❦

Daniel was killed during Pickett's Charge at the Battle of Gettysburg July 3, 1863.

He was nineteen years old.

Elisha received a sharp blow to his head from the butt of a rifle and was captured. At the end of the war, he was paroled and went directly to the Knight's home to tell them of Daniel's brave deeds.

There, Elisha met Daniel's sister Althea who took his heart away. He asked if he could call on her. With her fathers blessing she agreed.

∽ৡৡ৹

Six months later, on October 19, 1865 Althea and Elisha were married in the little white clapboard church that stands to this day in New Glasgow, Virginia.

Card 1

| | 19 | Va. |

Daniel C. Knight

Pvt., Co. K, 19 Reg't Virginia Infantry.

Appears on

Company Muster Roll

of the organization named above,

for July & Aug ..., 186/
dated Sept 1 ... 1861.

Enlisted:
When Aug 2-2 ..., 186/
Where Castle Hill Va.
By whom Jno. L. Elliot
Period 1 year

Last paid:
By whom
To what time ..., 186

Present or absent present
Remarks:

Book mark:

Qt. H. Bozarth
Copyist.

Card 2

| | 19 | Va. |

Daniel C. Knight

Pvt., Co. K, 19 Reg't Virginia Infantry.

Appears on

Company Muster Roll

of the organization named above,

for Sept & Oct ..., 186/
dated Oct 31 ... 1861.

Enlisted:
When Aug 22 ..., 186/
Where Apothecary to Va.
By whom Jno L. Elliot
Period 1 year

Last paid:
By whom Major Lewis
To what time Aug 11 ..., 186

Present or absent present
Remarks: Extra recd. no May-Nov Clothing

Book mark:

Qt. H. Bozarth
Copyist.

Card 3

| | 19 | Va. |

D. C. Knight

Pvt., Co. K, 19 Reg't Virginia Infantry.

Appears on

Company Muster Roll

of the organization named above,

for July & Aug ..., 1863.
dated Aug 31 1863

Enlisted:
When Apl 15 ..., 186/
Where Support to Hella
By whom J. L. Elliot
Period 1 year

Last paid:
By whom J. E. Blair
To what time Apl 30 ..., 1863

Present or absent absent
Remarks: Missing at the Batt of Gettysburg Pa July 3rd 1863

Book mark:

Qt. H. Bozarth
Copyist.

DANIEL'S PARTIAL SERVICE RECORD

Lynchburg, Virginia, April 14th 1865.

of Co. _____ Regt.

THE BEARER, _____

_____ ed Prisoner of the Army of the Confederate States, has per-

_____ main undisturbed, with arms &c.

_____ sion to go to his home.

E. A. Minnick
Capt. 11th Pa. Cav.

Pro. Mar.

PAROLED PRISONER'S PASS

COPY OF ELISHA SMILEY'S PAROLED PRISONER'S PASS

Virginia – County of Amherst to wit –

To any person licensed to Celebrate Marriages
You are hereby authorized to join together in the Holy State
of Matrimony according to the rules and Ceremonies of
your Church or religious denomination and the law of
the Commonwealth of Virginia Elisha Peter Smiley and
Althea Thomas Knight – Given under my hand as clerk
of the County Court of Said County. This 18" day of October
1865 –

      Jas Daniel Jr C

Time of Marriage 19" Octo 1865
Place of   " Amherst County Va
Full Names of parties Married – Elisha Peter Smiley & Althea Thomas Knight
Age of Husband – 25 years old
Age of Wife – 23 " "
Condition of Husband – Single
Condition of Wife   "
Place of Husbands Birth – Nelson County Va
Place of Wifes " Amherst " "
Place of Husbands residence – Amherst "
Place of Wifes " " "
Names of Husbands parents James W. & Jane J. Smiley
Names of Wifes " Wm. & Susan Knight
Occupation of Husband – Merchant –
   Given under my hand This 18" Octo 1865
       Jas Daniel Jr C

I certify that on the 19th day of October 1865 at the residence of
Wm Knight I united in marriage the above named and
described parties under authority of the annexed license –

     P Powell Garland &

MARRIAGE LICENSE FOR ELISHA AND ALTHEA

A Soldier Returns

JULY, 1888

My name is John Miller, a reporter for a local newspaper, assigned to cover the speeches and other activities planned for the twenty-fifth anniversary of The Battle of Gettysburg to be held at the site.

I noticed a distinguished looking gentleman standing next to a grove of trees, a few feet from the stone wall of Pickett's charge. He was dressed impeccably. By all demeanor, he appeared to be a businessman. His hat was in his hand and his head was bowed, as if he were saying a prayer. I didn't wish to disturb him, so I stood quietly and observed.

As he turned to leave, a small child cried out, "Grandpa, Grandpa, wait for me." He reached out, and in one sweeping motion, he lifted her up into his arms. He walked in my direction; as he drew nearer, I spoke to him.

"Excuse me, Sir, I don't mean to pry, but I couldn't help but notice, how long you visited that grave. Did you know any of those men?"

"Yes, I knew most of them."

"Could you tell me about them?"

The stranger removed his pocket watch and looked at the time. "I'm sorry, I have a train to catch, but I guess I can spare you a few minutes."

"Please tell me what you can."

"Coming back to Gettysburg today has brought back ten thousand memories of the past. How well I remember the day when Company H of the 19th Virginia Infantry, of which I was a member, left Amherst just as the painted daisies began to bloom. We boarded a train for Richmond. Many never returned. They fell facing the enemy in the thick of battle. Let me tell you about one boy in particular. His name was Daniel Knight; a braver, better soldier never wore the gray. He was my friend and I traveled here today to be with him, once more. He gave the supreme sacrifice, his life, for a cause he deeply believed in, defending states' rights for his beloved state of Virginia. Daniel was a good Christian, and I never heard him speak an unkind word to anyone. We will meet no more on this earth, but I look forward to having a grand reunion with him in heaven. He died during Pickett's charge and is buried in yonder grave, away from home and the people he loved. Here he has been sleeping for these many years and will continue to do so until the final roll is called. At that time he and I, along with the other heroes of our cause, will grasp hands and join in a reunion that will have no ending."

"Grandpa, why is Grandmother sitting so long on the ground beside that old stone wall? Can we go now? I'm tired."

The gentleman looked past me to the wall and called out, "Sarah, it's time to go. We don't want to miss our train."

I glanced over my shoulder. The woman he called Sarah was placing a single red rose against the wall. The flight of years had silvered her hair, but her soft gray-green eyes retained a youthful look. The old man quickly walked over to help her up. Holding his grandchild in one arm and his wife's hand with his other, they slowly walked down the path away from me. I called out, "Sir, what is your name, and where are you from?" He stopped, turned toward me, and with a slight cracking in his voice he simply said, "I'm The Reverend George Mays, this is my wife Sarah and our grandchild, Ida. We're from New Glasgow, in Amherst County, Virginia."

He turned and walked away, with his wife's left hand nestled in the crook of his right arm. I only wish I could have had more time to talk to him. I bet he could have told a lot of interesting stories.

Afterword

❦

Private: **PAUL MARSHALL KNIGHT**
2nd Virginia Cavalry, Jeb Stuart Division. Served
as courier for General Stuart.

Paul was shot in the knee, at the battle of
Seven Pines, May 31, 1862, and hospitalized for six
months. Wounded in action the second time on
May 8,1864 at Spotsylvania he remained in the
hospital at Richmond until March 25,1865.

The Knight family thought both Marcellus
and Paul had been killed because they had not
received any news from either of them. One day
while working in her garden, Paul's mother, Susan
and his sister Sue Paxton saw a man limping
toward their gate at the foot of the hill.

"I believe that's one of the boys," Sue said.
As he drew nearer, they both recognized it was
indeed Paul, the first to come home. Sue lifted her
skirt to the top of her shoes and rushed down from
the garden to hold her brother in her arms, crying
tears of joy. *

Paul died of natural causes at his farm in

Talcott, West Virginia, on Jan. 12, 1905. He and his wife Jane had seven children.
*(Ref. Family letter.)

⊷⊷

Private: MARCELLUS HARDY KNIGHT
2nd Virginia Cavalry Jeb Stuart Division
    Wounded at the battle of Seven Pines, May 31, 1862 Marcellus recovered and returned to active duty. He was wounded and captured the second time at Fort Kennon on May 24, 1864. He recovered and was paroled in Amherst on May 31, 1865. He died of natural causes May15, 1885.

⊷⊷

Private: OSSEN PERRY KNIGHT
28th Virginia Infantry Regiment
    Ossen was shot in the forearm at the battle of Gettysburg on July 3, 1863 and captured. He was exchanged from Chester Hospital on Aug.17, 1863. He returned to his unit Feb., 1864. Taken prisoner April 6, 1865 at Hatcher Run, he was held at Point Lookout Prison until released June 14, 1865. Upon discharge from the army, he purchased a farm at Coleman Falls in Bedford Country, Virginia. He died of natural causes, Feb. 5, 1908.

⊷⊷

AFTERWORD

Lieutenant: **SAMUEL HILL**
49th Infantry Regiment
Killed at the battle of Seven Pines May 31, 1862, Sam was 36 years old.

❧☙

Private: **ELISHA SMILEY**
8th Virginia Cavalry, Company B.
Wagon Master
Elisha received a skull fracture July 3, 1863 and was discharged due to disability. On Aug. 8, 1864, he re-enlisted and was subsequently captured in Richmond. He was paroled April 16, 1865.

Elisha and Althea were married in New Glasgow, Virginia, on October 19, 1865.

Born in Norwood Virginia on Aug. 8, 1840, he died in Lynchburg, Virginia, August 20, 1881.

Althea, born in New Glasgow, Virginia on Jan. 5, 1842, died at her home in Amherst, Virginia, January 29, 1916.

They had four children.

❧☙

Author: **BRAD SMILEY**

Born on April 13, 1934 Brad is the great grand nephew of Daniel, Paul, Marcellus, Ossen, and Sam. His Great grandparents are Elisha and Althea Knight Smiley.

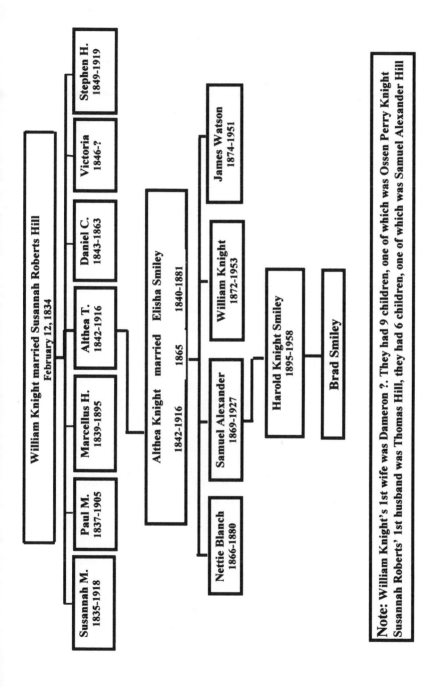

William Knight married Susannah Roberts Hill
February 12, 1834

Susannah M.
1835-1918

Paul M.
1837-1905

Marcellus H.
1839-1895

Althea T.
1842-1916

Daniel C.
1843-1863

Victoria
1846-?

Stephen H.
1849-1919

Althea Knight   married   Elisha Smiley

1842-1916   1865   1840-1881

Nettie Blanch
1866-1880

Samuel Alexander
1869-1927

William Knight
1872-1953

James Watson
1874-1951

Harold Knight Smiley
1895-1958

Brad Smiley

Note: William Knight's 1st wife was Dameron ?. They had 9 children, one of which was Ossen Perry Knight. Susannah Roberts' 1st husband was Thomas Hill, they had 6 children, one of which was Samuel Alexander Hill

BATTERY: The basic unit of artillery, consisting of four to six guns

BIVOUAC: A temporary camp for the night

BREASTWORK: A trench about chest high where a soldier could stand and fire his rifle

BRIGADE: Four regiments (approximately 4,000 men)

BUTTERNUTS: Confederate soldiers were some times referred to as butternuts. Grey uniforms were in short supply and home spun uniforms were dyed brown with walnut shells

CAISSON: A two-wheeled horse-drawn cart with a box attached for carrying artillery ammunition

CANISTER: A tin can containing lead or iron balls that are about the size of grapes, packed in sawdust. When fired the cylinder disintegrated, producing a giant shotgun blast that could literally shred a man to pieces

COMPANY: Approximately 100 men

CORPS: Four divisions (approximately 48,000 men)

DIVISION: Three brigades (approximately 12,000 men)

FLANK: Left or right side of a military formation. Used to attack or go around the enemy position

GRAPESHOT: Iron balls similar to those used in canisters. A heavy iron round top and bottom plate
held together by a long bolt and nut containing
nine balls that looked like a cluster of grapes.
On impact the balls broke apart and scattered

HARD TACK: Hard bread made of flour and water.
Pieces were usually three inches by three inches.
Frequently crumbled into coffee to soften

HAVERSACK: A one-strapped canvas bag carried
over the shoulder

KNAPSACK: A backpack used to carry small articles.
To lighten their load soldiers often discarded their
knapsack and carried small items in their haversack

LIMBER: A two-wheeled, horse drawn cart to which
a caisson or a gun was attached

MESS: A group of five to twelve men who worked,
ate, and fought together

MINI BALL: A soft lead slug that expanded
on impact and produced a devastating wound.
Spelled minié, minie, mini or minnie ball.

NAPOLEON: A twelve pound field artillery piece
(cannon) loaded from the front. The light
weapon could fire grape, canister shells, and
cannon balls. Because of its maneuverability
and effectiveness both long range and in close,

General Lee considered it the best gun for field service. Originally cast in bronze, it was later made totally from iron, when material became scarce in the South. Both the North and the South produced this weapon

PICKET: One or more soldiers on guard to protect against attacks

REBEL YELL: War cry of the Confederate soldiers.

REGIMENT: Ten companies (approximately 1,000 men)

SECESSION: The separation of Southern states from the Union

SKIRMISHER: Soldiers sent out in advance of the main body to scout out enemy positions. Also one who fights in a small fight.

YANKEE (YANK): Nickname for Union soldier.

SOURCES OF INFORMATION

The most informative source of information was letters written by Daniel Knight, never before published, which came from the Knight family Bible.

Other sources of information have been collected from the Archives and public libraries in Lynchburg, Amherst, Charlottesville, Nelson County, and Richmond, Virginia.

The library of Congress provided copies of Photos.

Philadelphia Weekly Times 1858-1877, newspaper clippings.

Jackson's ride (Farmers Field) as told by Captain Blackford, courier for General Jackson.

Albemarle county Historical Society in Charlottesville provided information on Albermarle county, history and the 19th Regiment's participation in the Civil War.

A vast amount of data regarding individual Confederate soldiers was obtained through the National Archives and Records Administration, General Reference Branch in Washington, D. C.

A large collection of letters is available for viewing through the military records division as well as colleges and universities. The Archives contains copies of letters gathered by the United Daughters of the Confederacy.

The Virginia State library, the Historical Society and the Confederate museum in Richmond provided diaries, letters, maps and individual soldiers records for review.

Newspapers were a source of information used to review current battle plans, weather, numbers of troops, and army conditions in general.

The "Lynchburg Virginian" newspaper provided a wealth of information, documenting times, and locations. It also described the moods and the feelings of the people and their support for the Confederacy at this time in history.

The United States War Department published histories of Regiments and Brigades, which contains official reports of battles a specific Regiment or Brigade participated in. However in some cases troop strength participating in a given battle must be viewed as estimates as commanding officers on both sides sometimes exaggerated numbers for a variety of reasons such as why they were requesting additional reinforcements or why they were forced to retreat.

Hollywood Cemetery, located in Richmond, is

the final resting site of many members of Pickets Division. Originally they were buried in a mass grave at Gettysburg, they have since been moved back to Virginia.

The tremendous amount of material available precludes the possibility of listing all sources consulted in the gathering of information for the writing of this book.

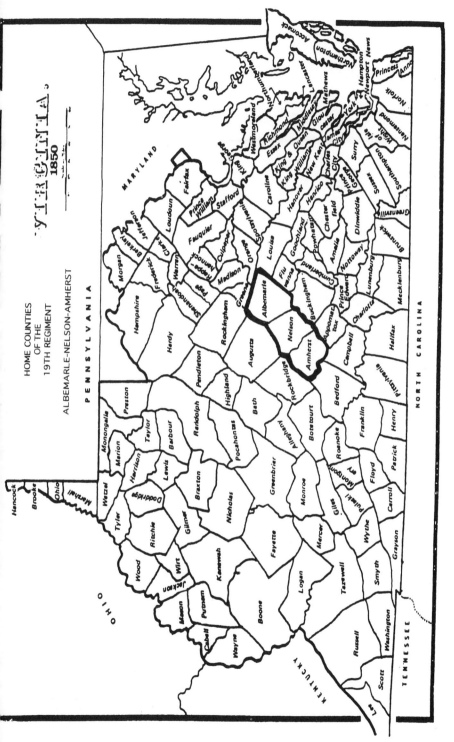

HOME COUNTIES
OF THE
19TH REGIMENT

ALBEMARLE-NELSON-AMHERST

VIRGINIA
1850

19TH VIRGINIA INFANTRY

19TH VIRGINIA VOLUNTEER INFANTRY REGIMENT

FROM ALBEMARLE COUNTY

TOWN	COMPANY	NAME
Charlottesville	A	Monticello Guards
Charlottesville	B	Albemarle Rifles
Scottsville	C	Scottsville Guard
Howardsville	D	Howardsville Grays
Hillsboro	E	Piedmont Guards
Stony Point	F	Montgomery Guard
Charlottesville	K	Blue Ridge Rifles

FROM NELSON COUNTY

Massie's Mill	G	Nelson Grays

FROM AMHERST COUNTY

Amherst	H	Southern Rights
Buffalo Springs	I	Amherst Rifles

Daniel Knight was a member of Company "H"

19th VIRGINIA REGIMENT BATTLES

MANASSAS   JULY 21, 1861

(Daniel joined the army in August of 1861)

YORKTOWN   APRIL - MAY, 1862
WILLIAMSBURG   MAY 5, 1862
SEVEN PINES   MAY 31 - JUNE 1, 1862
GAINES' MILL   JUNE 27, 1862
FRAYSER'S FARM   JUNE 30, 1862
2ND MANASSAS   AUGUST 28 - 31, 1862

(Daniel wounded August 30, 1862)

SOUTH MOUNTAIN   SEPTEMBER 14, 1862
ANTIETAM   SEPTEMBER 17, 1862
FREDRICKSBURG   DECEMBER 13, 1862
GETTYSBURG   JULY 1 - 3, 1863

(Daniel was killed July 3, 1863)

NORTH ANNA   MAY 22 - 26, 1864
COLD HARBOR   JUNE 1 - 3, 1864
FIVE FORKS   APRIL 1, 1865
2ND PETERSBURG   APRIL 1865
SAYLER'S CREEK   APRIL 6, 1865
APPOMATTOX   APRIL 9, 1865

The following pages are references to Gettysburg The history of the men of the 19th Virginia Regiment is full of stories both before and after Gettysburg. The wounded, captured, missing and killed are for this one battle alone.

※⟨∂≥

MUSTER ROLL FOR JUNE/AUGUST 1863
19TH REGIMENT
COMMANDED BY COLONEL HENRY GNATT
GETTYSBURG

COMPANY "A"

Bacon, William O.: Pvt., Joined in 1861 at age 18 (bricklayer)

Birkhead, James G.: Pvt., Joined in 1862 (farmer)

Birkhead, Joseph F.: Pvt., Joined in 1861 at age 27 (farmer)

Birkhead, Joseph R.: Pvt. (born 1830) no further information

Birkhead N. S.: Pvt., Joined in 1862 (farmer)

Bowen, John A.: Pvt., Joined in 1861 or 1862 **MIA**

Brooks, Andrew J.: Pvt., Joined in 1861

Browns, James J.: Pvt., Joined in 1861 at age 20 (laborer)

POW = prisoner of war WIA = wounded in action
MIA = missing in action

Brown, William H.: Pvt., Joined in 1861
Buck, James R. Jr.: 5th Sgt., Joined in 1861 at age 27
    POW
Clark, William D.: Pvt., Joined in 1861 at age 21
Cloar, William J.: Pvt., Joined in 1861 at age 22
    (shoemaker)
Culin, John Charles: Capt., Joined in 1861 at age 27
    WIA
Collier, John W.: Pvt., Joined in 1861 at age 21
Dennis, James M.: Pvt., Joined in 1862 at age 18
    (farmer)
Dewitt, John D.:   **WIA**
Dobbins, Robert L.: Color Cpl., Joined in 1861 age 22
Dodd, John B. Jr.: Pvt., Joined in 1861 at age 19
Dudley, James H.: Pvt., Joined in 1863   **POW**
Dudley, William M.: Pvt., Joined in 1863   **POW**
Durrett, John D.: Pvt., Joined in 1861 at age 28
    WIA / POW
Foster, William R.: Pvt., Joined in 1861 at age 19
Gulley, George A.: Sgt., Joined in 1861 at age 22
Harlowe, George N.: Pvt., Joined in 1861
    (shoemaker)
Harrison, Charles H.: Pvt., Joined in 1861
Hill, George Wesley: 2nd Lt., Joined in 1861
Houchens, John W.: Pvt., Joined in 1861 at age 21
    WIA / POW
Houchens, Thomas M.: Pvt., Joined in 1861 at age 20
Johnson, George Thomas: 1st Cpl ., Joined in 1861 at
    age 23 **POW**
Lane, Lorenzo: Pvt., Joined in 1862
Maure, William Wirt: 3rd Sgt., Joined 1861 at age 40
(bricklayer)

McMullen, Richard L.: Cpl., Joined in 1861 at age 19
Mooney, Thomas J.: Pvt., Joined in 1861 (farmer)
Perley, James: 2nd Sgt., Joined 1861 at age 27
Pierce, John N.: Pvt., Joined in 1861
Pointer, Joseph D.: Sgt., Joined in 1861 at age 20
Pointer, Polk: Cpl., Joined in 1861 at age 17
    WIA / POW
Rhodes, C. W.: Pvt., Joined in 1862 (farmer)
Thomas, John W.: Pvt., Joined in 1862
Vandegrift, Christian W.: Sgt., Joined in 1861 age 20
Vandegrift, Robert Carson: Pvt., Joined in 1861 at
    age 29
Webb, William C.: Pvt., Joined in 1861 at age 23
    (bugler)
Webb, William W.: Pvt., Joined in 1861 at age 22
Wingfield, Mathew Walker: Pvt., Joined in 1861 at
    age 30
Wingfield, Robert Ledbetter: Pvt. Joined in 1861 at
    age 31
Wood, William Nathaniel: 1st Lt., Joined in 1861 at
    age 21 **WIA**
Woodruff, David E.: Joined in 1862

⊷⊶

COMPANY "B"

Bellamy, John H.: Pvt., Joined in 1862
Bowyer, Leonidas R.: 3rd Sgt., Joined in 1861 at age
    18 (? killed with colors) **MIA**
Dolin, James W.: Pvt., Joined in 1862 at age of 31
    WIA

Dohn, James W.: Sgt., Joined in 1861 at age 32 (surveyor) **WIA**

Dunaway, William: Pvt., Joined in 1861 at age 30 (factory work)

Dunn, Albert S.: Pvt., Joined in 1862 at age 17

Dunn, Luther M.: Pvt., Joined in 1862

Garrison, Ira P.: Pvt., Joined in 1861 at age 18 (farmer) teamster

Garth, James C.: Cpl., Joined in 1861

Hammer, William P.: 2nd Lt., Joined in 1861 at age 19 **WIA**

Harris, Bernard B.: 2nd Cpl., Joined in 1861 at age 22 (farmer) **WIA**

Huckstep, Jacob E.: Pvt., Joined in 1862

Hughes, John: Pvt., Joined in 1861 at age 22 (laborer)

Humphreys, John H.: Pvt., Joined in 1862

Johnson Manoah D.: Pvt., Joined in 1861 at age 23 (workman)

Johnson, Robert Marcellus: Pvt., Joined in 1862 at age 20

Jones, William H.: Pvt., Joined in 1862

Jordan, John D.: 1st Cpl., Joined in 1861 at age 21 (workman)

Keblinger, Wilber J.: 3rd Cpl., Joined in 1862 **WIA**

Lumsden, Richard Washington: 4th Cpl. Joined in 1861 at age 23

Mooney, James M.: Pvt., Joined in 1861 at age 20

Morris, Abel: **WIA**

Morris, James E.: Pvt., Joined in 1861 at age 23 (workman) **WIA / MIA**

Noel, John G.: Pvt., Joined in 1862 at age 32

O'Brien, Timothy: 4th Sgt., Joined in 1861 at age 20 (workman)

O'Conner, Mike: Pvt., Joined in 1862

Pearson, Enoch J.: Pvt., Joined in 1861 at age 26 (workman)

Pearson, John T.: Pvt., Joined in 1861 at age 23 (workman)

Porter, Pulaski P.: 1st Lt., Joined in 1861 at age 19 (student)

Robinson, Rufus W.: 2nd Sgt., Joined in 1861 age 18

Rose, Rodgers: Joined in 1862

Smith, Thomas: Pvt., Joined in 1862

Sutler, John T.: Pvt., Joined in 1863   **WIA / POW**

Sutler, William M.: Pvt., Joined in 1861 at age 19

Taylor, Eugene Granville: 1st Sgt., Joined in 1861 at age 18   **WIA / POW**

Terrell, George W. P.: Pvt., Joined in 1861 at age 20 (workman)

True, John M.: Pvt., Joined in 1862   **WIA**

Walton, Richard T.: Pvt., Joined in 1861 (workman)

Watkins, Troyalous F.: Pvt., Joined in 1861 at age 25 (farmer)

Whitesel, John Wesley: 5th Sgt., Joined in 1861 at age 24   **WIA / POW**

Wirt, Richard West: Capt., Joined in 1861 at age 27 (merchant)

Wolfe, Luther T.: Sgt. Major, Joined in 1861 age 23

Wood, Richard B.: 2nd Lt., Joined in 1861 at age 19 **KILLED**

COMPANY "C"

Anderson, R.M.: Joined in 1862

Banton, Alexander: Pvt., Joined in 1861 at age 19

Blair, James Edwin: Capt., Joined in 1861 at age 24

Blair, John T.: 1st Lt., Joined in 1861 at age 26

Bowles, Robert S.: 2nd Sgt., Joined 1861 at age 19
WIA / POW

Burcher, James S.: Pvt., Joined in 1861 at age 20
(mechanic)

Campbell, Charles A.: Cpl., (orderly Col. Strange)
Joined 1861 at age 22

Clements, Benjamin F.: Pvt., Joined in 1861 at age 20

Clements, Joseph H.: 5th Sgt., Joined in 1861 at age
25 (boatman)

Clements, Robert L.: Pvt., Joined in 1862

Dameron, E. G.: Joined in 1861

Damron, William Thomas: Pvt., Joined in 1861 at
age 22 (farmer)

Dawson, William D.: Pvt., Joined in 1862 at age 33

Evans, Charles R. Jr.: 2nd Lt., Joined in 1861 at
age 24

Farish, Joseph: Pvt., Joined in 1863 at age 24

Ford, John P.: Joined in 1862

Freeman, Charles: Pvt., Joined in 1861 at age 24
(mechanic)

Goode, John D.: Pvt., Joined in 1861 at age 22
(farmer)

Goodman, John P.: Pvt., Joined in 1862

Goolsby, William F.: Pvt., Joined in 1861 at age 23
(clerk)

Hamner, Edward Bruce: Joined in 1861 at age 20

Harden, Hopkins: 2nd Lt., Joined in 1861 at age 22 (farmer) **WIA / POW**

Harris, John W.: Pvt., Joined in 1862

Harris, John Will: Pvt., Joined in 1861 at age 20 (mechanic)

Heffernon, John: Pvt., Joined in 1862

Irving, Charles Scott: Capt., Joined in 1861 at age 24 (farmer)

Irving, Robert R.: Joined in 1862

Kent, James W.: 1st Cpl., Joined in 1861 at age 26 (Merchant) **MIA**

Lewellyn, Charles M.: Pvt., Joined in 1861 at age 20

Lewellyn, John A.: 1st Lt./Adjutant, Joined in 1861 at age 21

Moon, Jacob N.: Pvt., Joined in 1862

Moon, Samuel W.: Pvt., Joined in 1862 **POW**

Morris, Nathaniel W.: Pvt., Joined in 1861 at age 20 (mechanic)

Morris, William L.: 2nd Cpl., Joined in 1861 age 18 (mechanic)

Napier, James M.: Pvt., Joined in 1862 (at home - wounded)

Napier, John R.: Pvt.

Omohundro, Robert L.: 4th Cpl., Joined in 1861 at age 23 (farmer) **POW**

Omohundro, Thomas W.: 3rd Sgt., Joined in 1861 at age 21 (farmer) **WIA**

Quinn, James F.: 4th Sgt., Joined in 1861 at age 21 (mechanic)

Robertson, Thomas D.: Pvt., Joined in 1862

Snead, Pleasant A.: Pvt., Joined in 1863 **MIA**

Spencer, Samuel T.: Pvt., Joined in 1861 at age 21

(mechanic)

Stone, William Beckwith: 1st Sgt., Joined in 1861 at age 21 **POW**

Thomas, Granville Smith: Pvt., Joined in 1862 at age of 14 **WIA**

Thomas, Marion L.: Pvt., Joined in 1861 at age 19 (farmer)

Thompson, Charles E.: Pvt., Joined in 1861 at age 38 (mechanic) **POW**

Vincent, John P.: Pvt., Joined in 1861 at age 32 (teacher) **POW**

White, Samuel H.: 1st Lt., Joined in 1861 at age 30 (druggist)

Woodward, William A.: 3rd Cpl., Joined in 1861 at age 30 (mechanic) **POW**

Wright, Robert Gilpin: Pvt., Joined in 1861 at age 20

❦

COMPANY "D"

Baker, Henry: 1st Lt., Joined in 1861 at age 20

Baker, John M.: 1st Cpl., Joined in 1861 at age 18

Brown, James A.: 4th Sgt., Joined in 1861 at age 25 (farmer) **POW**

Bugg, Samuel S. Jr.: Joined in 1861 at age 24

Curd, Albert H.: Pvt., Joined in 1861

Curd, Lafayette W.: Pvt., Joined 1861 at age 21 (carpenter)

Drumheller, Alexander: Pvt., Joined in 1861 (shoemaker)

Drumheller, Benjamin N.: Pvt. Joined in 1861 at age 22 **KILLED**

Duncan, William H.: Pvt., Joined in 1861 at age 18

Farrar, Charles S.: Pvt., Joined in 1861 at age 28 (farmer)

Ferguson,William H.: 2nd Sgt.,Joined in 1861 at age 26 (carpenter) **WIA / POW**

Fortune, Absalom M.: 3rd Cpl., Joined in 1861 at age 19 **KILLED**

Fortune, Joel M.: 3rd Lt., Joined in 1861 at age 21

Hall, James G.: Pvt., Joined in 1861

Harding, John B: Pvt., Joined in 1861 at age 28 (wheelwright)

Harlan, Richard J.: Capt., Joined in 1861 at age 23 (boatman) **WIA**

Harrison, C. C.: Pvt., Joined in 1863

Hughes, Henry H.: Pvt., . Joined in 1861 at age 24 (well digger) **WIA / MIA**

Johnson, James D.: Joined in 1862 **WIA** and (either) **POW or MIA**

Londeree, William Pendleton: 4th Cpl., Joined in 1861 at age 21

Maxwell, James M.: Pvt., Joined in 1861 **WIA**

Miles, Edward M.: 5th Sgt., Joined in 1861 at age 18

O'Neil, John: Pvt., Joined in 1862 **WIA**

Parker, Henderson: Pvt., Joined in 1863

Parrott, George W.: 1st Sgt., Joined in 1861 **WIA /DIED**

Patterson, George W.: 3rd Sgt., Joined in 1861 at age 21

Patterson, John M.: Pvt., Joined in 1861 at age 21 **WIA / MIA**

Patterson, Robert H.: Pvt., Joined in 1861 at age 23
Ponton, James E.: Pvt., Joined in 1862
Stinnett, William Thomas: Pvt., Joined in 1861 at age 26
Strange, Jacob: Pvt., Joined in 1862
    WIA / POW -DIED
Straughan, Stafford H.: Pvt. Joined in 1861
Taylor, Joel F.: Pvt., Joined in 1862   **WIA / MIA**
Tindall, John, Jr.: 1 Cpl., Joined in 1861 at age 26
    (farmer)   **WIA / POW**
Trevillian, Edeazar C.: Pvt., Joined in 1863
Walker, William J.: Cpl., Joined in 1861 at age 19
Wood, George W.: Pvt., Joined in 1861 at age 22
    POW
Wood, William H.: Pvt., Joined in 1861 at age 20
Woody Austin: Pvt., Joined in 1861 at age 35
    (carpenter) **POW**

◈◈

COMPANY "E"

Bowles, Robert S.: 5th Sgt., Joined in 1861 at age 19
    (teacher) **WIA**
Bragg, James Yates: 1st Lt., Joined in 1861 at age 21
    (farmer) **WIA / POW**
Brockman, James P.: Pvt., Joined in 1862
Cardin, William B.: Pvt., Joined in 1861 at age 20
    (miller) **MIA**
Carpenter, John F.: Pvt., Joined in 1862 at age 19
    MIA
Condry, Jerry: Pvt., Joined in 1862

Dowell, Major M.: Pvt., Joined in 1861 at age 25
(laborer) **MIA**

Durrett, Thomas D.: Pvt., Joined in 1861 at age 18
(laborer) **WIA / POW**

Eastman, David C.: 3rd Cpl., Joined in 1861 at age 23
(farmer)

Edwards, Samuel W.: 2nd Cpl., Joined in 1861 at
age 31 (farmer) **WIA / POW**

Ehart, Adam G.: Pvt., Joined in 1861 at age 32
(farmer) **WIA / POW**

Flynt, James T.: Pvt., Joined in 1861 at age 22
(farmer)

Flynt, William D.: Pvt., Joined in 1862 at age 24

Gilbert, Robert W.: 4th Sgt., Joined in 1861 at age 22
(farmer) **WIA**

Goss, William W.: Capt., Joined in 1861 at age 18
(student) **WIA / POW - DIED**

Hall, Henry J.: Pvt., Joined in 1861 **KILLED**

Hall, William S.: Pvt., Joined in 1861 at age 26
(mechanic)

Herring, Henry A.: Pvt., Joined in 1862

Herring, John Henry: Pvt., Joined in 1861 at age 22
(farmer)

Hill, William H.: Pvt., Joined in 1862

Joran, William Fleming: Pvt., Joined in 1861 at
age 25 (farmer) **MIA**

Leake, William James: Pvt., Joined in 1861 at age 22

LeTellier, Joseph Carter: Pvt., Joined in 1862 at
age 17 **WIA / POW**

LeTellier, William B.: 2nd Lt., Joined in 1861 at 21
WIA / POW - DIED

Madison, James A.: Pvt., Joined in 1861 at 18 (farmer)

MaHanes, Tavener O.: 4th Cpl., Joined in 1861 at age 22 (farmer) **WIA / POW**

Meeks, Henry M.: Pvt., Joined in 1861 at age 28 (farmer)

Minor, Peter H.: Pvt., Joined in 1861 at age 23 (farmer) **MIA**

Mooney, Madison: Pvt., Joined in 1862

Mundat, Jonathan B.: WIA

Mundy, Isaac L.: Pvt., Joined in 1861 at age 26 (farmer)

Mundy, Jonathan B.: Joined in 1861 at 24 (farmer)

Mundy, Thomas W.: 2nd Sgt., Joined in 1861 at age 22 (farmer) **MIA**

Nimmo, Hiram: Pvt., Joined in 1862 at age 34 **WIA**

Norvell, Joseph B.: Pvt., Joined in 1861 at age 29 (miller) **MIA**

Peyton, Charles Stephen: Lt. Col., Joined in 1861 at age 20 (farmer) **WIA**

Pritchett, Belfield: Pvt., Joined in 1861 at age 23 (farmer) **WIA**

Pritchett, James D.: Pvt., Joined in 1861 at age 30 (farmer)

Salmon, James: 2nd Lt., Joined in 1861 at age 24 (mechanic)

Sandridge, James J.: 2nd Cpl., Joined in 1861 at age 24 (farmer) **MIA**

Taylor, John R.: Pvt., Joined in 1861 at age 22 (farmer) **MIA**

Vaughan, Cornelius G.: Pvt., Joined in 1861 at age 21 (farmer)

Wood, Alfred Thomas: Pvt., Joined in 1861 at age 19 (farmer)

Wood, James F.: Pvt., Joined in 1861 at age 18 (farmer) **WIA**

Wood, Washington M.: Pvt., Joined in 1861 at age 21 (farmer)

৵১৵

COMPANY "F"

Barnett, Charles: Pvt. , Joined in 1862 absent (from wound)

Barnett, James A.: Pvt., Joined in 1861 at age 22 (laborer) **WIA**

Barnett, William: Pvt., Joined in 1861

Brown, Richard: Pvt., Joined in 1861 at age 23 (laborer)

Campbell, William B.: Pvt., Joined in 1861 at age 18 (laborer)

Clements, Thomas Madison: Joined in 1861 at age 25 (laborer)

Collins, James S.: Pvt., Joined in 1861 at age 21 (carpenter)

Comar, Michael: Pvt., Joined in 1862

Cranwell, Henry: Pvt., Joined in 1861 at age 40 (carpenter)

Criddle, Patrick H.: Pvt, . Joined in 1861 at age 20 (laborer)

Dayley, Jerry: Pvt., Joined in 1861 at age 26 (carpenter)

Die, John: Pvt., Joined in 1861 at age 25 (carpenter)

Grace, James: Pvt., Joined in 1861 at age 35 (carpenter)

Halley, J. O.: **WIA**

Hawley, James O.: Pvt., Joined in 1861 at age 26 (carpenter) **WIA**

Henderson, Ed: **KILLED**

Herndern, Edward J.: Pvt., Joined in 1861 at age 22 (carpenter) **WIA / POW - DIED**

Herndern, Nicholas W.: Pvt., Joined in 1861 at age 19 (carpenter) **POW**

Jones, Lucien S.: 1st Sgt., Joined in 1861 at age 19 **WIA - DIED**

Kennedy, Philip: Pvt., Joined in 1861 at age 31 (carpenter)

Langford, James: Pvt., Joined in 1861

Langford, William: Pvt., Joined in 1861 at age 21 (carpenter)

Madison, George D.: Pvt., Joined in 1861 at age 22 (laborer)

Madison, James: Pvt., Joined in 1861 **WIA**

McDonald, Charles: Pvt., Joined in 1861 at age 30 (carpenter)

McIntire, James D.: 2nd Lt., Joined in 1861 at age 20 (clerk) **WIA**

McLain, Abram S.: 3rd Sgt., Joined in 1861 at age 24 (carpenter)

Meeks, James H.: 3rd Cpl., Joined in 1861 at age 27 (teacher)

Meeks, John F.: Pvt., Joined in 1861 at age 18 (laborer)

Meeks, John N.: Cpl., Joined in 1861 age 44 (laborer)

Meeks, William Lewis: Pvt., Joined in 1861 at age 20 (laborer)

Melton, Cornelius J.: Sgt.: Joined in 1861 at age 23

(carpenter)
Melton, George S.: 5th Sgt., Joined in 1861 at age 21
(carpenter)
Melton, Henry: Pvt., Joined in 1861 at age 18
Murphy, Daniel: Cpl., Joined in 1861 at age 22
(laborer)
O'Toole, John: Pvt., Joined in 1861 at age 28
(carriage maker)
Philmore, Samuel P.: Pvt., Joined in 1862
Powell, Willard L.: 3rd Lt., Joined in 1861 at age 20
(harness maker)
Rhodes, Andrew: Pvt., Joined in 1861 at age 20
(laborer)
Rhodes, Robert P.: Pvt. , Joined in 1861 at age 18
(laborer) **WIA / POW**
Shiflett, James: Pvt., Joined in 1861 at age 19
(laborer)
Shope, John: Pvt., Joined in 1863 **WIA / POW**
Sprouse, Henry: Pvt., Joined in 1862 **WIA / POW**
Strange, James A.: Pvt., Joined in 1861 at age 22
(laborer) **WIA**
Taylor, Bennett: Capt., Joined in 1861 at age 24
(teacher) **WIA / POW**
Taylor, James: Pvt., Joined in 1861at age 33
(laborer) **WIA / POW - DIED**
Taylor, Joseph: Pvt., Joined in 1861 age 18 (laborer)
Walton, Charles P.: Pvt., Joined in 1862 **WIA /POW**
Willis, Rust: Pvt., Joined in 1863

∽∾

COMPANY "G"

Bolton, Thomas M.: Pvt., Joined in 1862

Booz, William G.: 1st Sgt., Joined in 1861 at age 18 (miller) **WIA / POW**

Bowles, William H.: Pvt., Joined in 1861 at age 22 (farmer) **WIA / POW**

Boyd, Waller M.: Capt., Joined in 1861 at age 18 (farmer) **WIA / POW**

Bryant, Charles P.: Pvt., Joined in 1861 at age 24 (farmer)

Campbell, Martin V.: Pvt., Joined in 1861 at age 20 (farmer) courier

Craig, James W.: Pvt., Joined in 1861 at age 25 (farmer) ambulance driver

Crist, Thomas J.: Pvt., Joined in 1861

Dillard, Oscar P.: Pvt., Joined in 1861 at age 20 (farmer) **POW**

Eubank, Elias D.: Pvt., Joined in 1861 age 20 (farmer)

Fitzgerald, Douglas: Pvt., Joined in 1861 at age 23 (carpenter)

Fortune, Meridith Winston: Pvt., Joined in 1861 at age 38 (distiller) **MIA**

Fulks, James M.: Pvt., Joined in 1861 at age 18 (farmer) **WIA / POW - DIED**

Gregory, Joseph F.: 3rd Lt. , Joined in 1861 at age 32 (cabinet maker)

Groves, William B.: Pvt., Joined in 1861

Hamilton, Jacob: 2nd Cpl., Joined in 1861 at age 21 (farmer) **POW**

Hamilton, James M.: Pvt., Joined in 1861 atage 19 (farmer)

Hamilton, Varland: Pvt., Joined in 1861 at age 24 (carpenter)

Harlow, William: Cpl., Joined in 1861 at age 25
   (farmer) **MIA**
Harvey, James: Pvt., Joined in 1861 at age 23
   (farmer) **POW**
Harvey, John: Color Cpl., Joined in 1861 at age 26
   (carpenter)
Hatter, Morgan A.: Pvt., Joined in 1861 at age 26
   (farmer)
Hatter, Powhatan B.: Pvt, Joined in 1861 at age 25
   (farmer)
Henderson, John Luke: Pvt., Joined in 1861
   WIA / POW
Henderson, William E.: Pvt., Joined in 1862 at
   age 17
Higginbotham, James L.: 4th Cpl., Joined in 1861 at
   age 21 (carpenter) **MIA**
Hughes, Moses P.: Pvt., Joined in 1861 at age 22
   (farmer) **MIA**
Hughes, Samuel P.: Pvt., Joined in 1861 at age 23
   (farmer) **POW**
Hundley, Joshua W.: Pvt., Joined in 1861 at age 19
   (farmer)
Johnson, Robert: Pvt., Joined in 1861
Johnson, William: Pvt., Joined in 1861 at age 20
   (farmer) **MIA**
Jones, William Lewis: Pvt., Joined in 1861 at age 18
   (farmer) absent
Jordan, Flemming: Joined in 1861 **KILLED**
Jordan, William F.: Pvt., Joined at age 25
   (farmer) **MIA**
Kidd, Alexander B.: Pvt., Joined in 1861 at age 22
   (farmer)

Kidd, Alexander R.: Pvt., Joined in 1861 at age 25 (farmer)

Kidd, Landon Rives: Pvt, . Joined in 1861 at age 30 (farmer)

Kidd, Lorenzo D.: Pvt., Joined in 1861 at age 23 (farmer)

Lorhorne, Joseph M.: Pvt., Joined in 1862

Loving, James E.: Pvt., Joined in 1861 at age 24 (carpenter) **POW**

Loving, John J.: 1st Cpl., Joined in 1861 at age 27 (farmer) **POW**

Loving, John J.W.: Pvt., Joined in 1861 at age 19 (farmer)

Loving, William H.: 4th Sgt., Joined in 1861 at age 21 (miller) **WIA**

May, George Preston: Pvt., Joined in 1861 at age 18 (blacksmith)

May, James Marion: Pvt., Joined in 1861 at age 21 (carpenter)

Mays, Robert D.: Joined in 1861 at age 20 (farmer) **WIA / POW**

McCrary, John H.: 2nd Lt., Joined in 1861 at age 19 (clerk)

Meeks, John S.: Pvt., Joined in 1862

Monroe, Charles: Pvt., Joined in 1861 at age 23 (farmer)

Monroe, Nelson: 3rd Sgt., Joined in 1861 at age 38 (farmer) **MIA**

Oliver, Samuel A.: Pvt., Joined in 1861 at age 18 (farmer) **POW**

Parsons, Dawson S.: Pvt., Joined in 1863

Plunket, John D.: Pvt., Joined in 1861 at age 25

Ponton, Henry E.: Pvt., Joined in 1861 at age 30 (carpenter) **WIA / POW**

Ponton, Napoleon B.: Pvt., Joined in 1862

Ponton, Richard Hartwell: Pvt., Joined in 1861 at age 20 (carpenter) **WIA**

Ponton William H.: Pvt., Joined in 1862 at age 18 **POW**

Powell, John Thurston: 1st Lt., Joined in 1861 at age 20 (student) **WIA**

Purvis, Albert A.: Pvt., Joined in 1861 at age 20

Purvis, Clifford Cabell: Pvt., Joined in 1861 at age 20 (farmer)

Purvis,Joseph Edward: 2nd Sgt., Joined in 1861 at age 20 (farmer) **POW**

Smith, Abraham: 4th Cpl., Joined in 1861 at age 26 (school master) **WIA**

Spencer, John James: Pvt., Joined in 1863 at age 23 (farmer)

Stevens, Albert L.: Pvt., Joined in 1861 at age 26 **POW**

Stevens, Richard P.: Pvt., Joined in 1861 at age 21 (farmer)

Stewart, John W.: Pvt., Joined in 1861 at age 18 (clerk) **WIA / POW**

Stratton, Henry F.: 2nd Cpl., Joined in 1861 at age 25 (farmer)

Thacker, Lafayette W.: Sgt., Joined in 1861 at age 18 (farmer)

Vaughan, William L.: Pvt., Joined in 1863

Whitehead, Kincaid: Pvt., Joined in 1861 at age 25 (dentist) **POW**

Wills, Willis C.: Pvt., Joined in 1861 at age 27
  (school master)
Wood, William D.: 5th Sgt., Joined in 1861 at age 18
  (farmer)

ఞఞ

COMPANY "H"

Barbour, John H.: Pvt., Joined in 1861 at age 22
  (farmer)   **POW**
Brown, Benjamin J., Jr.: Capt., Joined in 1861 at
  age 19 (farmer)   **WIA / POW**
Buck, John B.: Pvt., Joined in 1861
Burley, Thomas Dillworth: Pvt., Joined in 1861
Chiles, James M.: 1st Cpl., Joined in 1861 at age 22
  (farmer)   **WIA / POW**
Christian, Charles Asa: Pvt., Joined in 1861 at age 22
  (farmer)
Christian, Robert Wesley: Pvt., Joined in 1861 at
  age   23   (farmer)
Cox, Breckenridge F.: Pvt., Joined in 1861 at age 21
  (farmer)   **WIA / POW**
Daniel, James Madison: Pvt. , Joined in 1861 at
  age 18 (teacher)
Daniel, William S.: 3rd Sgt., Joined in 1861 at
  age 20 (gentleman)
Davidson, James: Pvt., Joined in 1863 (transfered
  from 2nd Cav)   **MIA**
Davidson, John: Pvt., Joined in 1861
Davies, John W.: Pvt., Joined in 1861 at age 23
  (farmer)

Delaine, W. P.: Joined in 1861

Drumheller, Abram: Pvt., Joined in 1861 at age 23 (farmer)   **MIA**

Ellis, John Thomas: Lt. Col., Joined in 1861 at age 34 (merchant)   **KILLED**

Garland, David S.: 2nd Lt., Joined in 1861 at age 19 (student)   **WIA**

Gilbert, Robert Norval: Pvt., Joined in 1861 at age 22 (grocer)

Going, George W.: 3rd Sgt., Joined in 1861 at age 21

Harvey, Marcellus B.: Pvt., Joined in 1861 at age 19 (farmer)

Haydeon, Alex W.:   Pvt.,   Joined in 1863

Henderson, James J.: Pvt., Joined in 1863 WIA/POW

Higginbotham, Clifton V.: Pvt., Joined in 1861 at age 18 (farmer)

Hite, Isaac W.: 2nd Cpl., Joined in 1861 at age 24 (farmer)

Jennings, Daniel R.: 4th Cpl., Joined in 1861 at age 20 (farmer)   **WIA**

Jennings, John T.: Pvt., Joined in 1861 at age 23 (farmer)

Joiner, Houston C.: Pvt., Joined in 1861 at age 20 (farmer)

Knight, Daniel C.: 3rd Cpl, Joined in 1861 at age 17 (farmer)   **KILLED**

Landrum, James E.: 3rd Lt., Joined in 1861 at age 19 (gentleman)   **MIA**

Mason, George B.: 4th Sgt., Joined in 1861 at age 21 (clerk)

Mason, Samuel Edloe: Pvt., Joined in 1861 at age 18 (farmer)

Mason, W. Archie: Q.M. Sgt., Joined in 1862

Mays, George W. Jr.: Pvt., Joined in 1861 at age 17 (farmer)

Mays, George W.: Pvt., Joined in 1861 at age 22 (farmer)

Mays, Marcellus H.: Pvt., Joined in 1861 at age 24 (farmer)

Mays, Nathaniel A.: 4th Sgt., Joined in 1861 at age 19 (farmer)

McGinnis, Edward B.: 1st Cpl., Joined in 1861 at age 21 (farmer)

McGinnis, Thomas W.: 1st Sgt., Joined in 1861 at age 19 (merchant)

Ogen, William Henry: Pvt., Joined in 1861 at age 18

Powell, James Jr.: Pvt., Joined in 1861 at age 34 (clerk)

Powell, James H.: Pvt., Joined in 1862

Proffit, Henry J.: Pvt., Joined in 1861 at age 22 (farmer)

Proffit, William N.: Pvt., Joined in 1861 at age 20 (farmer)

Richeson, Jesse V.: 1st Lt., Joined in 1861 at age 30 (farmer)

Rucker, William R.: Pvt., Joined in 1862 at age 22

Shroder, George L.: Pvt., Joined in 1861 at age 38 (grocer)

Stinnett, C. P.: Pvt., Joined in 1862   **MIA**

Stinnett, J. J.: Pvt., Joined in 1862

Stinnett, Paulus P.: Pvt., Joined in 1861 at age 19 (farmer) **WIA / POW**

Stinnett, Percival: Joined in 1863   **KILLED**

Stinnett, William Henry: Pvt., Joined in 1862

Tyree, Lucas P.: Pvt., Joined in 1861 at age 23

(farmer)

Ward, James: Pvt., Joined in 1861 at age of 23
(farmer)

Waller, William Macon: 2nd Lt., Joined in 1861 at
age 33

Webb, George S.: Pvt., Joined in 1861 at age 20

ക്ക

COMPANY "I"

Burley, Alexander: Pvt., Joined in 1861 at age 24
(farmer) **POW**

Campbell, Andrew: Pvt., Joined in 1861 at age 24
(farmer)

Campbell, Daniel Goode: Pvt. Joined in1861 at
age 20 (farmer) absent from wound

Campbell, James L.: Pvt., Joined in 1861 at age 24
(farmer)

Campbell, Josiah: Pvt., Joined in 1861 at age 24
(farmer)

Campbell, W. D.: Pvt., Joined in 1862 **WIA**

Campbell, William H.: Pvt., Joined in 1861 at age 31
(farmer) **WIA**

Campbell, William J.: Pvt., Joined in 1861 at age 29
(farmer)

Carpenter, Charles L.: Pvt., Joined in 1862 **POW**

Carter, Joseph C.: Pvt., Joined in 1861 at age 25
(farmer)

Cash, Otis: Pvt.. Joined in 1861 at age 30 (farmer)

Cash, Robert B.: Pvt., Joined in 1862 at age 22,
(farmer)

Cash, William H.: Pvt., Joined in 1861 at age 20 (farmer)

Cash, Zebulon: Pvt., Joined in 1862

Evans, John Taliaferro: Pvt., Joined in 1861 at age 25 (farmer)

Fonkhowitzer, John M.: Pvt., Joined in 1861 at age 41 (tailor)

Franklin, Abner M.: 2nd Cpl., Joined in 1861 at age 30 (farmer)

Franklin, Arthur W.: Pvt., Joined in 1861 at age 32 (farmer)

Fulsher, Paul C.: 4th Sgt., Joined in 1861 at age 19 (farmer) **WIA**

Gillespie, George Willard: 2nd Sgt., Joined in 1861 at age 19 (carpenter)

Hamilton, James P.: Pvt., Joined in 1861 at age 34 (farmer)

Hartless, Benjamin: Pvt., Joined in 1862 **POW**

Hawkins, Lucius P.: Pvt., Joined in 1861 at age 26 (farmer)

Henley, George W.: Capt., Joined in 1861 at age 32 (farmer)

Higginbotham, Aaron L.: Pvt., Joined in 1861 at age 33 (farmer)

Higginbotham, Joseph Absalom.: Joined in 1861 at age 33 (farmer)

Higginbotham, Paul M.: Pvt., Joined in 1861 at age 28 (farmer)

Hill, Charles T.: 3rd Lt., Joined in 1861 at age 22

Irvine, Robert H.: Pvt., Joined in 1861 at age 21 (student)

Jennings, Leroy P.: 3rd Cpl., Joined in 1861 at age 19 (farmer) **WIA / POW**

Lawhorne, Edward P.: Pvt., Joined in 1861 at age 20 (farmer)

Lawhorne, Isham: Joined in 1861 **KILLED**

Logan, David T.: Pvt., Joined in 1861 at age 19 (farmer)

Logan, Samuel P.: Pvt., Joined in 1861 at age 21 (farmer)

Massie, John W.: Pvt., Joined in 1861 **WIA / POW - DIED**

Mays, Anderson: Pvt., Joined in 1863 **MIA**

Myers, John W.: 1st Sgt., Joined in 1861 at age 30 (farmer) **POW**

Page, D.D.: Pvt., Joined in 1863

Page, Royal M.: Pvt., Joined in 1861

Powell, William H.: Pvt., Joined in 1861 at age 22 (farmer)

Quinn, Archibald S.: Pvt., Joined in 1861 **POW**

Seay, James C.: Pvt., Joined in 1861 at age 18 (farmer) **POW**

Smith, Horace: 2nd Lt., Joined in 1861 at age 31 (farmer) **WIA / POW**

Taliaferro, John N.: 1st Lt., Joined in 1861 at age 19 (student) **MIA**

Thompson, Thomas J.: Pvt, Joined in 1861 at age 20 (farmer)

Thompson, William H.: Pvt., Joined in 1861 at age 20 (farmer) **WIA**

Thompson, William H.: Pvt,. Joined in 1861 at age 23 (farmer)

Tucker, Charles J.: Pvt., Joined in 1861 at age 32 (farmer)

Tucker, James T.: Pvt., Joined in 1862

Tyree, J. S.: Pvt., Joined in 1863
Via, William: Pvt., Joined in 1862
Ware, Edwin Spotswood: 2nd Sgt., Joined in 1861
    WIA / POW
Ware, Paulus Massie: Pvt., Joined in 1861   **POW**
Ware, Robert A.: 1st Cpl., Joined in 1861 **WIA/DIED**
Wilsher, Charles T.: Pvt., Joined in 1861 at age 18
Wilsher, Stafford K.: 2nd Sgt., Joined in 1861 at
    age 22 (farmer) **WIA**
Wood, Tellman: Pvt., Joined in 1861 at age 21
    (farmer)
Wright, Charles H.: Pvt., Joined in 1861
Wright, Paul C.: Pvt., Joined in 1861 at age 27
    (farmer)
Wright, William: Pvt., Joined in 1862   **POW**

✥

COMPANY "K"

Bailes, John T.: Pvt., Joined in 1861 at age 31
Bailes, Merritt G.: Pvt., Joined in 1861 at age 22
Ball, Charles H.: Pvt., Joined in 1862
Black, Nicholas: 1st. Sgt., Joined in 1861 at age 20
    WIA / POW
Black, Nicholas M.: Pvt., Joined in 1861 at age 21
Black, Robert: 3rd Cpl., Joined in 1861 at age 23
Black, William: 5th Color Cpl., Joined in 1861 at
    age 23
Burton, Benjamin L.: Cpl., Joined in 1862
Cleveland, Benjamin F.: Pvt., Joined in 1861 at
    age 25

Davis, George D.: Pvt., Joined in 1861 at
    age 32
Fisher, William J.: Pvt., Joined in 1861 at
    age 19
Foster, George A.: Pvt., Joined in 1862   **POW**
Gillum, Thomas Mann: Pvt., Joined in 1863
Grinstead, James H.: 1st Lt., Joined in 1861 at age 26
    KILLED
Grinstead, Richard J.: 4th Sgt., Joined in 1861
Hawkins, Robert A.: Pvt., Joined in 1861 at age 29
Hawkins, Samuel Augustus: Pvt., Joined in 1862
    POW
Hays, Thomas T.: Pvt., Joined in 1862 **WIA/POW -**
    DIED
Johnson, James F.: Pvt., Joined in 1862 **MIA**
Kennon, James H.: 2nd Sgt., Joined in 1861 at age 22
Lane, James B.: Pvt., Joined in1862
Leathers, James A.: Pvt., Joined in 1863 at age 24
    WIA / POW
Leathers, William H.: 4th Cpl., Joined in 1861 at
    age 24
Lindsay, Asberry D.: 1st Cpl., Joined in 1861 at
    age 28
Martin, Henry H.: Pvt., Joined in 1862   **WIA**
Martin, John A.: Pvt., Joined in 1861 at age 22
Martin, Samuel H.: Pvt., Joined in 1861 at age 30
Martin, Sylvester G.: 3rd Lt., Joined in 1861 at
    age 28 **WIA / POW**
McCauley, Riland: Pvt., Joined in 1862
McMullen, William H.: Pvt., Joined in 1862
Moyer, Jacob: Pvt., Joined in 1862 at age 35 (farmer)
Powell, Thomas A.: Pvt., Joined in 1861 at age 28

Railey, William B.: Joined in 1861
Rea, William T.: 3rd Sgt., Joined in 1861 at age 18
WIA / POW
Reynolds, James R.: Pvt., Joined in 1862
Robinson, Aechelans J.: 1st Lt., Joined in 1861 at
age 34
Robinson, J. T.: Pvt., Joined in 1862
Thacker F.L.: Pvt., Joined in 1863   teamster
Wolfe, William C.: Pvt., Joined in 1861 at age 28
Wood, John M.: Pvt. Joined in 1861 at age 28   Wood,
William D.: Cpl., Joined in 1861 at age 28
Woods, John J.: 5th Sgt., Joined in 1861 at age 18
WIA / POW - DIED
Woods, Robert H.: Pvt., Joined in 1861 at age 23
Woodson, Daniel Perkins: Pvt., Joined in 1863 at
age 19 (farmer)
Woodson, James Garland: Capt., Joined in 1861 at
age 28   WIA
Woolfert, Henry: Pvt., Joined in 1861 at age 24
(laborer)
Wyant, James D.: Pvt., Joined in 1862
Yancey, John Farrar: 4th Cpl., Joined in 1861 at
age 19

❦❦

COMPANY UNKNOWN

Cardew,_____: KILLED
Dolin,_____: KILLED

19TH VIRGINIA INFANTRY

Regimental Chaplain

Slaughter, P.: Joined in 1861 at age 53

Regimintal Surgeons

Galt, James Dickie: Regiment Surgeon
Taylor, William H.: Asst. Regiment Surgeon age 26
   WIA

April 12, 1912

My dear Son—

Your letter desiring information as to who you are and from whence you came,--et cetera—came to us today and I feel in quite a mood to answer you just now. I wish you success in "climbing your ancestral rope", but, as one has said, "don't climb too far or you may find some one hanging there", for no family, if traced through many generations, can show a record without blot or mar. The proverbial "Black Sheep" will be in evidence somewhere to show the common origin of our race in one who failed to make good, and so left a proness to evil as a terrible heritage to all his descendants.

The above is an excerpt from a letter written by Henry Fiske Knight to his son. A descendent, Paul Knight of Alaska, generously gave permission to use this tidbit of wisdom.

BEGINNING YOUR SEARCH

<u>Rule to remember:</u> Write down your source - write down your source - WRITE DOWN YOUR SOURCE! You may think you will remember where you found or heard some bit of information, but you probably won't and may find yourself retracing steps. Even write down where you looked but found nothing.

First, write down what you already know. Look in old trunks, family bibles and photo albums. Talk to your relatives, begin your research by finding out as much as possible from family members who are still living.

- Names of ancestors, and their relatives
- Dates-birth, marriages, and deaths
- Places - towns, counties, states or provinces, and countries.
- School or religious affiliations
- Military service
- Any stories passed down from generation to generation

Remember in the last 150 years or so most people would have left a paper trail. Not like today but there is a trail. You just have to play detective, one clue leading to another.

Sometimes you will hit a brick wall but there is

usually a way around it if you just dig a little deeper. Also be sure to write down and check out different spellings of the surname. There were lots of changes and variations even in the same family. Include dates and spouses in your notes since families seemed to give the same name to descendants (sometimes even cousins had the same name. Organize your notes in a way that duplicate names will show up as obviously a different person.

Once you have exhausted your home and relative resources (or at least gotten the ball rolling) then you will need to look at Church and Government records. You will be looking for:

- Census records
- Marriage, Birth, and Death records
- Land ownership or sales records
- Wills and other court records
- Immigration and Naturalization records
- Military records
- Cemetery records

If you can go to the local Court House where your ancestor was born, did business, married and died you will find a real abundance of information. Also the local newspaper or library will have old newspaper announcements and articles on microfiche.

THE NATIONAL ARCHIVES AND RECORDS ADMINISTRATION (NARA) has many records that you will find useful in your research. Below are listed some resources they make available and the forms used to procure the information.

- Military service and pension records prior to World War 1, including Revolutionary War, War of 1812, **Civil War,** and Spanish-American War. Request and fill out Form 80
- Passenger Arrival lists 1820-1957 Form 81
- Federal population censuses, 1790-1920 Form 82
- Eastern Cherokee Applications Form 83
- Land Entry Files Form 84
- Military service records, World War 1 and later. Form 180

You can request a list of available records by contacting NARA. There are several ways in which to reach them:

- National Archives and Records Administration
  7th Street and Pennsylvania Avenue NW
  Washington, D C 20408-0001
- Public reference (202) 501-5400
- Genealogy Staff (202) 501-5410
- E-mail <inquire@arch2.nara.gov.>
- URL:http://www.nara.gov.

Many public libraries, historical societies, and other research facilities participate in a National

Archives Microfilm Rental Program.

≈∂≈

HOW AND WHERE TO FIND YOUR
CIVIL WAR ANCESTOR

Finding a soldier and following leads to his records, both official and personal can be accomplished in most instances. There are sources available that will identify the soldier and others that will provide information about his military service and personal life. The first and by far the most important step is to identify the military unit. All of the soldier's official records and many of his personal experiences will be tied to his unit or units.

To find his unit there are some books that are indispensable:

- **The Roster of The Confederate Soldier1861-1865** Broadfoot Publishing

- **Official Army Register** Published by Ron R. Van-Sickle Military Books

- **The Roster of The Union Soldiers 1861-1865** Broadfoot Publishing

- **The Roster of the Union Soldier - United States Colored Troops.**

These volumes are set up alphabetically by name. Here you will find the state and the outfit. Armed with this information you can contact the National Archives requesting the appropriate form.

◦⊱⊰◦

The most exhaustive collection of genealogy materials can be found at The Family History Centers operated by the Church of Jesus Christ Latter Day Saints. They provide access to a complete selection of census records. These include every state and federal census available.

People of any faith are welcome to use the vast collection of material collected by the church. The microfilm is housed primarily in the main library in Utah, but Family History Centers are in many churches all over the United States. The local libraries focus on the surrounding area but usually other parts of the country are also available. If the microfilm you need is not on the premises, it can be rented for a nominal fee from the library in Utah. Workers at the library will assist you. They are friendly and helpful.

For information write:
    The Church of Jesus Christ of Latter-Day
    Saints
    Family History Department
    P.O. Box 30700
    Salt Lake City, UT 84130-9802
To find a Family History Center in your area:

GENEALOGICAL RESEARCH

- Call 1-800-346-6044
- Visit one of the following web sites:
  www.kbyu.byu.edu/ancestors.html
  www.lds.org

The Family History Library in Salt Lake City has over two million rolls of microfilm containing copies of original records from more than a hundred countries. They include census, church, land, and probate records plus much more.

The 2nd largest genealogy collection in the United States is reported to be held in Fort Wayne, Indiana at the:

Allen County Public Library
900 Webster Street
Fort Wayne, IN
Phone: (219) 421-1200
URL:http://www.acpl.lib.in.us/

Other good sources are:

- Library of Congress
  Genealogy Reading Room
  James Madison Memorial Bldg.
  Washington, D.C. 20540

- National Genealogical Society Library
  4527 17th St. N.
  Arlington, VA 22207=2399
  Phone: (703) 525-0050
  URL:http://www.genealogy.org/~ngs/

If you have access to the Internet you will find many interesting genealogical sites. Some of my favorites are:

- www.rootsweb.com/rootsl/
- www.rand.org.personal/Genea/
- www.genhomepage.com/
- E-mail genhome@henhomepage.com
- www.firstct.com/fv/tmapmenu.html
- pbs.org/kbyu/ancestors/resourceguide/

LIBRARIES, HISTORICAL SOCIETIES AND ARCHIVES

～ALABAMA～

Alabama Public Library Service
6030 Monticello Drive
Montgomery, AL 36130
Phone: (334) 213-3900 or
In state 800-723-8459
Fax: (334) 213-3993

Alabama History on Line
Phone: (334) 242-4363
Fax: (334) 240-3433
URL: dependlet!dsmd.dsmd.state.al.us

Records Center
Phone: (334) 242-4306
Fax: (334) 240-3109
Reference (334) 242-4435
URL: nkerr@dsmd.dsmd.state.al.us

General information
Phone: (334) 242-4363

Research facility information
Phone: (334) 242-4435
URL: www.asc.edu/archives/intro/genfon.html

Alabama Archives and History
624 Washington Avenue
(mail address) P.O. Box 300100
Montgomery, AL 36130-0100
Phone: (334) 242-4441
URL: www.asc.edu/archives/intro/address.html

⚘⚘ALASKA⚘⚘

Alaska State Library
344 West 3rd Avenue, Suite 125
Anchorage AK 9950d1
Phone: Within Alaska 800-776-6566
Anchorage and out of state (907) 269-6570
E-mail: aslane@muskox.alaska.edu
URL: www.edu.state.ak.us/lam/library.html

⤚ARIZONA⤙

Arizona state Archives
State Capitol, Suite 442
1700 West Washington
Phoenix, AZ 85007
Phone: (602) 542-4159
Fax: (602) 542-4402
E-mail: archive@dlapr.lib.az.us
URL: http://www.dlapr.lib.az.us

⤚ARKANSAS⤙

Arkansas State Library
One Capitol Mall
Little Rock, AR 72201-1081
Phone: (501) 682-1527
URL: www.state.ar.us/html/statelibrary.html

⤚CALIFORNIA⤙

California State Library
Library & Courts Building I
914 Capitol Mall
Room 220
Sacramento, CA 95814
Phone: (916) 654-0174

State Information and reference Center
Room 301
Phone: (916) 654-0261
E-mail: cslsirc@library.ca.gov

California Research Bureau
Library & Courts Building II
900 N Street, Room 300
Sacramento, CA 95914
Phone: (916) 653-7843

◈◈COLORADO◈◈

Denver Public Library
10 W. Fourteenth Ave.
Denver, CO 80204
Phone: (303) 640-6200
TTY: (303) 640-6146
E-mail:
URL: www.denver.lib.co.us/

◈◈CONNECTICUT◈◈

Connecticut State Library
231 Capitol Avenue
Hartford, CT 06106
Phone: (860) 566-4301
Fax: (860) 566-8940
E-mail: rakeroyd@csl.ctstateu.edu
URL: http://www/cs;met/ctstateu/ed

⋖⋗DELAWARE⋖⋗

Delaware State Library
43 S. Dupont Hwy.
Dover, DE 19901
Phone: (302) 739-4748/Fax: (302) 739-6787
State Library Web Page
E-mail: webmaster@www.de.us
URL: http://www.lib.de.us/

⋖⋗FLORIDA⋖⋗

Leon County Public Library
200 West Park Avenue
Tallahassee, FL 32301
Phone: (805) 487-2665
TDD: (850) 922-0096
URL: www.co.leonfl.us/library/index.htm

⋖⋗GEORGIA⋖⋗

Atlanta-Fulton County Public Library
One Margaret Mitchell Square
Atlanta, GA 30303
Phone: (404) 730-1700
Fax: (404) 730-1990
E-mail: jhunter@cel.af.public.lib.ga.us
URL: http://www.co.fulton.ga.us/library.htm

⋘⋙IDAHO⋘⋙

Ada Community Library
10664 W. Victory Road
Boise, ID 83709
Phone: (208) 362-0181
Telnet: catalog.ada.lib.id.us Login as LIBRARY
URL: www.ada.lib.id.us

⋘⋙ILLINOIS⋘⋙

Illinois Gateway State Library
300 South Second Street
Springfield, IL 62701-1796
Phone: (217)785-5600
within state 800-665-5576
URL: http://www.sos.state.il.us/

⋘⋙INDIANA⋘⋙

Indianapolis Central Library
40 East St.Clair Street
Indianapolis, IN
Phone: (317) 219-1700
E-mail: webmaster@ai.org.
URL: http://www.ai.org/general.html

Indiana Historical Society
Library Division
Phone: (317) 232-1879
Fax: (317_ 233-3109
E-mail: bjohnson@statelib.lib.in.us

Allen County Public Library
900 Webster Street
Fort Wayne, IN 46802
Phone(219) 421-1200
URL: http://www.acpl.lib.in.us/

໙ໄ෧IOWA෧ໄ෧

State Library of Iowa
1112 East Grand
DesMoines, IA 50312
Phone: (515) 281-4105
E-mail: siloweb@www.silo.lib.ia.us
URL: http://www.silo.lib.ia.us

໙ໄ෧KANSAS෧ໄ෧

Kansas State Library
Third Floor Statehouse
Topeka, KS 66612
Phone: (785)296-3296/in Kansas - 800-432-3919
URL: http://www.kumc.edu/kansas/KSL/ksl.html

ᏬᏬKENTUCKYᏬᏬ

Kentucky Historical Society
The Library-Old Capitol Annex
P.O. Box 1792
Frankfort, KY 40602
Phone: (502) 564-3016

Department of Military Affairs
Military Records and Research
1121 Louisville Road
Frankfort, KY 40601
Phone: (502) 564-4873

Kentucky Department for Libraries and Archives,
Public Records Division, Archival Services Branch
URL:www.kdla.state.ky.us/arch/refaddrs,htm

ᏬᏬLOUISIANAᏬᏬ

State Library at Baton Rouge
760 North Third Street
P.O. Box 131
Baton Rouge, LA 70821-0131
Phone: (502) 342-4913
Fax (504 342-3547
TDD: (504) 342-2476
E-mail: staffae@pelican.state.lib.la.us
URL: http://smt.state.lib.la.usl/statelib.htm

State Library at Lafayette
301 West Congress Street
Lafayette, LA 70501
Phone: (318) 261-5793
URL: http://smt.state.lib.la.us/flibdlis.htm

⊷⊷MAINE⊷⊷

Maine State Library
64 State House Station
Augusta, ME 04333-0064
Phone: (207) 287-5600 Fax: (207) 287-5615
E-mail: gary.nichols@state.me.us
URL: http://www.state.me.us/msl

⊷⊷MARYLAND⊷⊷

Vital Records
Division of Vital Records
4201 Patterson Avenue
Baltimore, MD 21215
Phone: (410) 225-5988 or 800-832-3277

Maryland State Archives
350 Rowe Blvd.
Annapolis, MD 21401
Phone: (401) 974-3914
In state (800) 235-4045
Fax: (401) 974-3895
E-mail: archives @mdarchives.state.md.us

URL: http://www.mdarchives.state.md.us/

Maryland Genealogical Web Project
www.rootsweb.com/~mdgenweb/mdstate.html

⊷⊷MASSACHUSETTS⊷⊷

Boston Public Library
Main Library
700 Boylston Street
Copley Square
Boston, MA 02117
Phone: (617) 536-5400
URL: www.bpl.org/

⊷⊷MICHIGAN⊷⊷

Michigan Library and Historical Center
717 West Allegan Street
P.O. Box 30007
Lansing, MI 48909-7507
Phone: (517) 373-1580
Fax: (517) 373-5700
E-mail: mla@mlc.lib.mi.us
URL: http://www.libofmich.lib.mi.us/

⤷⤶MINNESOTA⤷⤶

Minnesota Historical Society
Research Center
345 Kellogg Blvd. W
St. Paul, MN 55102
Phone: (612) 296-2143
Fax: (612) 297-7436
E-mail: mmatters@library.leg.state.mn.us
St. Paul Public Library - Central
90 West 4th Street
St. Paul, MN 55102
Phone: (612) 292-6311
Fax: (612) 292-6141
URL: http://www.stpaul.lib.mn.us/

⤷⤶MISSISSIPPI⤷⤶

Mississippi Library Commission
1221 Ellis Ave.
P.O. Box 10700
Jackson, MS 39289-0700
Phone: (601) 359-1036
Fax: (601) 354-4181
URL: http://www.mlc.lib.ms.us/ref.htm

Itawamba Historical Society
P. O. Box 7
Mantachie, MS 38855
URL: http://www.network-one.com/~ithissoc

⋖⋗MISSOURI⋖⋗

Missouri State Library
Supreme Court Building
Jefferson City, MO 65102
Phone: (573) 634-2464
E-mail: SOSmain@mail.sos.state.mo.us
URL://mosl.sos.state.mo.us/lib-ser/libser.html

Missouri State Archives
Office of the Secretary of State
600 West Main Street
P.O. Box 778
Jefferson City, MO 65102-0778
Phone: (573) 751-3280
Fax: (573) 526-7333
E-mail: arcref@mail.sos.state.mo.us

**State Historical Society of
Missouri Libraries**
1020 Lowry Street
Columbia, MO 65201-7298
Phone: (573) 882-7083
Fax: (573) 884-4950
E-mail: shsofmo@ext.missouri.edu

⋖⋗MONTANA⋖⋗

Montana State Library
P.O. Box 201800
1515 East 6th Avenue
Helena, MT 59620-1800
Phone: (406) 444-3115
Fax: (406) 444-5612
Reference: (406) 444-3004
E-mail: mslref@msl.mt.gov
URL: http://msl.mt.gov/slr/slridex.html

❦❦NEBRASKA❦❦

Nebraska Historical society
15th and R Street
Omaha, NE 68102
Phone: 402 4471-4751

Lincoln City Public Library
136 South 14th Street
Lincoln, NE 68508
Phone: (402) 441-8500
Fax: 402441-8586
Reference Information: (402) 441-8530
Heritage Room: (402) 441-8516
E-mail: library@rand.lcl.lib.ne.
URL: http://
interlinc.ci.lincoln.ne.us/Interlinc/city/library

❦❦NEVADA❦❦

Nevada State Library and Archives
100 N. Stewart Street
Carson City, NV 89701
Phone: (702) 687-5160
E-mail: webmaster@clan.lib.nv.us
URL:www.clan.lib.nv.us.docs/NSLA/nsla.htm

◌◌NEW HAMPSHIRE◌◌

New Hampshire State Library
20 Park Street
Concord, NH 03301
Phone: (603) 271-2392
Fax: (603) 271-6826
Family Resource Connection: (735-2964
E-mail: nhsl@lilac.nhsl.lib.nh.us (Reference)
URL: http://www.state.nh.us/nhsl/contact.html

◌◌NEW JERSEY◌◌

New Jersey State Library
185 West State Street
P.O. Box 520
Trenton, NJ 08625-0520
Phone: (609) 292-6220
E-mail: lkay@njsl.tesc.edu
URL:
http://ww.state.nj.us/statelibrary/njlib.htm

New Jersey State Archives
185 West State Street (Level 2)
P. O. Box 307
Trenton, NJ 08625-0307
Phone: (609)292-6260
Genealogy Office (Level 4 State Street side)
Phone: (609) 292-6274
Fax: (609) 984-7901
E-mail: colesar@njsl.tesc.edu

↭NEW MEXICO↭

New Mexico State Library
325 Don Gaspar
Santa Fe, NM 87501-2777
Phone: (505) 827-3800
E-mail: webmaster@stlib.state.nm.us
URL: www.stlib.state.nm.us/

↭NEW YORK↭

New York state Library
Cultural Education Center Empire State Plaza
Albany, NY 12230
Phone: (518) 474-5355
Fax: (518)474-5786
E-mail: refserv@unix2.nysed.gov
URL: http://nysl.nysed.gov/
Genealogy URL: http://nysl.nysed.gov/gengen.htm

᭡᭡NORTH CAROLINA᭡᭡

State Library of North Carolina
Archives and History
State Library Building
109 E. Jones Street
Raleigh, NC 27601-2807
Reference Desk
Phone: (919) 733-3270
Fax: (919) 733-5679
Genealogical Services
Phone: (919) 733-7222

URLS:
Library:
www.dcr.state.nc.us/hoursall.htm
Archives:
www.ah.dcr.state.nc.us/archives/archcents.htm
North Carolina Genealogy Page:
www.usgenweb.com/index.htm
North Carolina Genealogy Society:
www.moobasi.com/genealogy/ncgs

᭡᭡NORTH DAKOTA᭡᭡

North Dakota State Library
604 East Boulevard Avenue
Bismark, ND 58505-0800
Phone: (701) 328-4622
URL: www.sendit.nodak.edu/ndsl/info.html

ଔ𝕒OHIO𝕒ଔ

State Library of Ohio
65 S. Front Street
Columbus, OH 43215-4163
Phone: (614) 644-7061
In State: (800)686-1531
Fax: (674) 466-3584
E-mail: webmaster@winslo.ohio.gov
URL: http//winslo.ohio.gov/about.html

ଔ𝕒OKLAHOMA𝕒ଔ

Oklahoma Department of Libraries
Main Library Collections and Reference
Allen Wright Memorial Library
200 Northeast 18th Street
Oklahoma City, OK 73105-3298
Phone: 405) 521-2502
Fax: (405) 525-7804
URL: www.state.ok.us/~odl/index.htm

ଔ𝕒OREGAN𝕒ଔ

Oregon State Library
250 Winter Street N.E.
Salem, OR 97310-0640
Phone: (503) 378-4243
URL: http://osl.state.or.us/oslhome.htm

Oregon State Archives
800 Summer Street N. E.
Salem OR 97310-1347
Phone: (503) 373-0701
Fax: (503) 373-0953
E-mail: reference.archives@state.or.us
URL: http://arcweb.sos.state.or.us

❧❧PENNSYLVANIA❧❧

The Library Company of Philadelphia
1314 Locust Street
Philadelphia, PA 19107-5698
Phone: (215)546-3181
Reading Room (215) 546-2456
Fax: (215) 546-5167
E-mail: refdept@worldlynx.net
URL: www.voicenet.com/~lcp3/

❧❧RHODE ISLAND❧❧

Providence Public Library
225 Washington Street
Providence, RI 02903
Phone: (401) 455-8000
Fax: (401) 455-8080

Rhode Island Libraries on line
www.dsls.state.ri.us/genref/rilibs.htm

Genealogy Web Site
www.rootsweb.com/~usgenweb/ri/rifiles.htm

∽SOUTH CAROLINA∽

South Carolina State Library
1500 Senate Street
P. O. Box 11469
Columbia, SC 29211
Phone: (803) 734-8666
Fax: (803) 734-8676
URL: www.state.sc.us./scls/lion.html

Genealogy Web Site
www.sciway.net/hist/genealogy/genrecords.html

∽SOUTH DAKOTA∽

South Dakota State Library
Mercedes Mackay Building
800 Governors Drive
Pierre SD 575501-2294
Phone: (605) 733-3131
In State: 800-423-6665
Fax: (605_ 733-4950

E-mail: refrequest@stlib.state.sd.us
URL: www.state.sd.us/state/executive/deca/st_lib/
st_lib.htm
Genealogy Web Site
www.state.sd.us/state/executive/deca/st_lib/st_lib/
Www.bkmks.htm#Genealogy Resources

❧TENNESSEE❧

Tennessee State Library & Archives
403 Seventh Avenue, N
Nashville, TN 37243-0312
Phone: (615) 741-2764
Fax: (615) 741-6471
E-mail: reference @mail.state.tn.us
URL: www.state.tn.us/sos/statelib

Genealogy Web Page
www.tngenweb.usit.com/

❧TEXAS❧

Texas State Library & Archives
1201 Brazos
P.O. Box 12927
Austin, TX 78711-2927
Phone: (512) 936-INFO
E-mail: pio@tsl.state.tx.us

Genealogy Web Site
www.rootsweb.com/~usgenweb/tx/tsfiles.htm

❧❧UTAH❧❧

Utah State Library
2150 South 300 West
Salt Lake City, UT 84114-2579
Phone: (801) 466-5888
URL: www.statelib.ut.us

Utah State Archives
P.O. Box 141021
Salt Lake City, UT 84114-1021
Phone: (901) 538-3013
Fax: (801) 538-3354
E-mail: research@state.ut.us

❧❧VERMONT❧❧

Kellogg Hubbard Library
Main Street
Montpelier VT 05609-0001
Phone: (802) 223-3338

Burlington Library
235 College Street
Burlington, VT 05401-8317
Phone: (802) 865-7217

GENEALOGICAL RESEARCH

⬥⬥VIRGINIA⬥⬥

Library of Virginia
800 East Broad Street
Richmond, VA 23219
Phone: (804) 692-3500
URL: http://leo.vsla.edu/descnew.html
 or http://leo.vsla.edu/lva/lva.html

Virginia Roots (Genealogy)
Phone: (804) 692-3725
E-mail: LISTSERVER@LEO.VSLA.EDU
Virginia Archives & Research Room
URL: http://leo.vsla.edu/resroom.html

Virginia Historical Society
Phone: (804) 358-4901
Fax: (804) 355-2399

⬥⬥WASHINGTON⬥⬥

Washington State Library
P. O. Box 42460
415 15th Avenue S. W.
Olympia, WA 98504-2460
• (On the state capitol campus at 16th & Water Streets)
Phone: (360) 753-5592
URL: www.wa.gov/wsl
Public Reference Desk
Phone: (360) 753-3087
Fax: (360) 586-1671

❧WEST VIRGINIA❧

Kanawha County Library
123 Capitol Street
Charleston, WV 25301-2686
Phone: (304) 343-4646
E-mail: tyrees@wvlc.wvnet.edu
URL: http://kanawha.lib.wv.us
Reference Services
Phone: (304) 558-2045
Fax: (304) 558-2044
URL: www.wvlc.wvnet.edu/

❧WISCONSIN❧

Madison Public Library
201 W. Mifflin Street
Madison WI 53703
Phone: (608) 266-6300
URL: www.scls.lib.wi.us/madison

❧WYOMING❧

Wyoming State Library
Supreme Court & State Library Building
2301 Capitol Avenue
Cheyenne, WY 82002-0060
Phone: (307) 777-7281
Fax: (307) 777-6289
URL: www.wsl.state.wy.us/

Brad Smiley (center, top row) surrounded by some descendents of the 19th VA.

Photo courtesy of Frank Hartman